SIGRID NUNEZ

SALVATION CITY

virago

VIRAGO

First published in the United States in 2010 by Riverhead Books
First published in Great Britain in 2020 by Virago Press

1 3 5 7 9 10 8 6 4 2

The author is grateful to the Ucross Foundation and
the Ledig House International Writers Residency for their generous support.

A CIP catalogue record for this book
is available from the British Library.

ISBN 978-0-349-01423-4

Book design by Gretchen Achilles
Printed and bound in Great Britain by Clays Ltd, Elcograf S.p.A.

Papers used by Virago are from well-managed forests
and other responsible sources.

Virago Press
An imprint of
Little, Brown Book Group
Carmelite House
50 Victoria Embankment
London EC4Y 0DZ

An Hachette UK Company
www.hachette.co.uk

www.virago.co.uk

Sigrid Nunez has published seven novels, including *A Feather on the Breath of God*, *The Last of Her Kind*, *Salvation City* and, most recently, *The Friend*, which won the National Book Award. She is also the author of *Sempre Susan: A Memoir of Susan Sontag*. Among the journals to which she has contributed are the *New York Times*, *Wall Street Journal*, *Paris Review*, *Threepenny Review*, *Harper's*, *McSweeney's*, *Tin House*, *The Believer* and newyorker.com. Her work has also appeared in several anthologies, including four Pushcart Prize volumes and four anthologies of Asian-American literature.

Sigrid's honours and awards include a Whiting Writer's Award, a Berlin Prize Fellowship and two awards from the American Academy of Arts and Letters: the Rosenthal Foundation Award and the Rome Prize in Literature. She has taught at Columbia, Princeton, Boston University and the New School, and has been a visiting writer or writer in residence at Amherst, Smith, Baruch, Vassar and the University of California, Irvine, among others. Sigrid has also been on the faculty of the Bread Loaf Writers' Conference and of several other writers' conferences across the country. She lives in New York City.

Also by Sigrid Nunez

PART ONE

PART ONE

The best way to remember people after they've passed is to remember the good about them.

The first time Cole hears Pastor Wyatt say this he remembers how his mother hated when people said passed, or passed away. He'd come home from school one day and repeated the teacher's announcement: Ruthie Lind was absent that day because her grandmother had passed.

"Died. Say died, pumpkin," his mother said. "Passed sounds so silly."

She had called him pumpkin and she did not seem to be angry with him, but he had felt obscurely ashamed. Later he was told that people were afraid to say died because they were afraid of dying. Passed was just a euphemism. The funny-sounding word was new to Cole and for a time it kept recurring, floating into his head for no apparent reason. But the first time he saw the word in a book he did not recognize it, he was so sure it began with a *u.* Followed by an *f,* of course.

Pastor Wyatt does not always say passed. More often he says went home. ("Had a great-aunt went home at a hundred and three.") It all depends on whether the person he is talking about was saved or unsaved.

When he is preaching, Pastor Wyatt never says passed.

Pastor Wyatt is not afraid of dying.

"That's my job in a nutshell. I've got to teach people not to be afraid. We're all going to die, that's for certain. And the

3

thing for folks to do is stop wasting their energy being all headless and fearful like a herd of spooked cattle."

At first, whenever Pastor Wyatt spoke directly to him, Cole would watch Pastor Wyatt's hands. He was not yet comfortable looking Pastor Wyatt in the face. Cole was keeping so much in—he had so many secrets—he did not like to look anyone in the face if he could help it. He knew this gave the impression he'd done something wrong, and that is just how he felt: as if he'd done something wrong and was trying to hide it.

He still feels this way much of the time. He thinks he will always feel this way.

Pastor Wyatt himself has a way of looking at people that Cole would call staring. His mother would have called it fucking rude. But from what he can tell, other people are not at all disturbed by the way Pastor Wyatt looks—or stares—at them.

Cole understands that Pastor Wyatt is thought to be handsome, though Cole himself has no opinion about this. But he has observed that people are delighted to have Pastor Wyatt's attention on them, especially if they are women.

Pastor Wyatt always looks right into the face of the person he is talking to, and his eyes are almost like hands that reach out and hold you so you can't turn away. Somewhere Cole has read about a person giving someone else a *searching* look. He thinks this is a good description of what Pastor Wyatt does, too. But with Pastor Wyatt it's not something that happens once, or once in a while, but more like every time, and in the beginning Cole hated it.

He has never known anyone who looks so hard at other people. (He's got Holy Spirit high beams, members of the congregation like to say.) Cole has never known anyone who smiles so much, either. He smiles even when he preaches and when he is preaching about bad things, like temptation and sin. He smiles so that people won't be afraid. He is a tall man with a wide neck and naturally padded shoulders, and around shorter people he tends to slouch, bending his knees if need be—he does not like the feeling of towering over anyone. (Cole always thinks of this when Pastor Wyatt tells him to stand up straight, or not to hunch at the table.) When he is among children, Pastor Wyatt will sometimes do a full knee bend, balancing on the balls of his feet. It would break his heart to know that any child was afraid of him.

Pastor Wyatt still shakes hands with people. He pays no attention to the warning to switch to the elbow bump. Cole remembers learning about this while he was still in regular school. Public health officials were trying to get people to switch because touching elbows did not spread infection the way touching hands did. Cole knows there are many people who have switched, but he sees the elbow bump only when he is around strangers. The people he sees every day make fun of the elbow bump. They shake hands and they hug one another, even though Pastor Wyatt says the disease that spared them all this time around is neither the last nor the worst of its kind. Other plagues are coming, he says, smiling. And he thinks they will be here soon.

Pastor Wyatt's hands are of a whiteness and a softness that make Cole think of milk, of goose down, of freshly washed and bleached flannel sheets. It is impossible to imagine flu germs, or germs of any kind, lurking on such clean hands. Pastor Wyatt has never been sick a day in his life. If anyone else made such a claim, Cole would surely doubt it. But if Pastor Wyatt says it, he thinks it must be true.

Most marvelous are the fingernails, each tipped with a perfect little white crescent moon. He knows these nails are the work of Tracy, Pastor Wyatt's wife. He has caught her giving Pastor Wyatt manicures. Not that they try to hide it. They do the manicures right at the kitchen table, usually while listening to the radio. There is a television in the house, but Pastor Wyatt disapproves of television—the idiot box, he calls it—and Cole isn't allowed to watch much. But the radio is often on, playing Christian twang (Tracy's thing; Cole and Pastor Wyatt prefer Christian rock), or tuned to some talk show or sermon. Pastor Wyatt himself is a regular guest on the local station, on a weekly program called *Heaven's A-Poppin'!*

When he sees Tracy doing Pastor Wyatt's nails, Cole is embarrassed, almost as if he'd caught them having sex. He has no idea if Pastor Wyatt and Tracy have sex; he chooses to think they do not. He is a hundred percent certain he will never catch them having sex. He will never see either of them naked. It simply must not be allowed to happen. If it happens, he will have to die.

He thinks of the time he saw his parents lying naked on top of their covers, in broad daylight—the shades were up, sun fell across the bed—and how it was one of the worst moments of his life. He would have given all his toys to undo it.

First his parents pretended it never happened. Then something—most likely his behavior—must have changed their minds, and they insisted on talking about it. Which Cole would not do. Worst of all was when they tried teasing him about it. He would have given all his toys a second time for them just to forget it. Secretly he had vowed that no one would ever see him naked.

About sex he knew then just enough to feel shame. Certain photos he'd seen—ripped from magazines and passed around at school—had left him with images of unhealthy-looking grayish-pink flesh, like meat that had turned, and hideous tufts of dark hair where hair shouldn't even be, images that soured his stomach. It would have taken a miracle to connect them with the time he stumbled on Jade Korsky during a game of hide-and-seek. In the dark closet their teeth had clicked together like magnets, and they had tongued her cherry cough drop back and forth till it was the size of a lentil.

The moment he heard what intercourse was, instinct told him it was true. The knowledge had brought an anxious and bewildering sorrow, a feeling that would return when he learned what his mother's box of tampons was for. He did not share the excitement about these matters other boys couldn't hide. From what he could tell, his responses weren't normal, and he would not dream of revealing them.

Sometime—he cannot say exactly how long, maybe a year—sometime after he'd walked in on his parents lying naked, he walked in on them fighting and heard his mother say, "We never fuck anymore anyway, what the fuck do you care?" When they saw him they tried to explain, but only half-heartedly. And it was this halfheartedness that had enraged him, moving him to perhaps his first real effort at sarcasm. "Sure. I know. You guys were just rehearsing for a play."

No one had tried to stop him as he turned on his heel. He

remembers his cold satisfaction, leaving them speechless behind him. He remembers thinking, *Now they'll know how much I've grown up.*

But he is not sure anymore if in fact it was his mother he heard that day. Maybe it was his father. This has become a familiar problem. Cole gets mixed up. He is never completely sure of anything he remembers anymore. He was told that after his fever broke he did not even remember his own name. It wasn't exactly amnesia, but the illness had damaged his brain. He was not the only one to whom this had happened. It happened to many other people as well. It happened to the president of the United States.

Even now there are important things Cole knows he should remember that he cannot remember at all. He has resigned himself to perhaps never remembering them again. He knows he is lucky to know his name, lucky not to have worse damage, lucky to be alive. Though he wishes ardently to learn not to be afraid to die, he cannot help being glad—even if it sometimes makes him feel base—that he survived.

It was his mother, he decides. Both his parents used swear words all the time, but it was more like his mother to swear twice in one sentence.

Pastor Wyatt uses a cream that makes his hands smell like cookie dough.

Cole has nightmares. Some contraption is crushing him, some ferocious animal is about to devour him, an object he cannot live without is lost or taken away. He cries out, doggy-paddling in the dark. Then there is light, impossibly bright, stabbing his eyes. It is always Pastor Wyatt who comes, never Tracy. Because Tracy never says anything about these nights,

Cole thinks maybe she sleeps right through his screams and Pastor Wyatt getting out of bed. He knows married people don't always tell each other everything.

Pastor Wyatt sits with him for a while, stroking his head, praying with him. Jesus is here, he croons. But it is the smell of those hands that soothes Cole most.

In the upstairs bathroom one day, he uncaps every bottle and jar till he finds it. The cookie-dough smell is vanilla. It is one of his secrets, how much he loves that smell, and how he sometimes goes into the bathroom just to take a deep whiff. He believes that if he tells anyone, the smell won't have the same effect anymore. It is a secret also because he thinks of it as a girly thing. He pictures Les Wilbur and Peter Druzzi jeering.

Les Wilbur. Peter Druzzi. Cole wonders about them, as he wonders about all the other kids from school. He thinks he remembers that Les was sick, but it could have been Pete. Or it could have been both of them. He wonders if they have passed.

Died. Say died.

Ruthie Lind has passed, that he knows for sure. It happened before Cole himself got sick. Ruthie was one of the first to pass. Jade Korsky? He doesn't know. He and Jade hadn't been in the same school anymore. The closet, the cherry cough drop—all that was back in the city. Ages ago. When was the last time he'd played hide-and-seek?

His mother and his father, both of whom were afraid of dying, have passed.

The best way to remember them is to remember the good about them.

He knows that Pastor Wyatt is right. He does not know why it is so hard.

❦

ONE OF HIS BIGGEST SECRETS IS THAT he does not like Tracy. It is a guilty secret, because Tracy has always been nice to him. She cleans his room and washes his clothes and asks him every day what he'd like for lunch. She gives him only light chores to do and praises him for the smallest things, like helping to load the dishwasher. ("What a peach!")

Once, when he accidentally breaks a ceramic bunny he knows she loves, she looks crestfallen. But before he can apologize, she says, "Jesus hates it when we care too much about some silly old *thang*."

Tracy is Pastor Wyatt's second wife. She calls him WyWy, which embarrasses Cole, though not as much as her calling him Daddy, or DaDa, as she also sometimes does.

Pastor Wyatt tells Cole to call him PW.

Cole knows that Tracy is younger than PW, but he does not know how much. She will not say her age. Certainly she is too old to be saying DaDa. But she often talks more like a child than like a grown-up. PW drops his watch and she says, "Did it get hurt?" To her an alarm clock is a "warum." Her favorite letter is *b*. She says "bamburger" and "bumbrella."

Cole finds it strange that PW laughs at Tracy's mistakes but never corrects them. "We were going full bottle." "The house was infected with termites."

Why doesn't he correct her?

Cole knows Tracy doesn't have children not because she

didn't want any ("It was my dream since I had my first doll"), but because of a kind of cancer she had before she was married. When he asks if the cancer treatments made her go bald, she looks startled, but she tells him. All her straight blond hair fell out and grew back the way it is now, chestnut and wavy. She tells him also that because she lost so much weight when she was sick, even some people who'd known her all her life would walk right past her without recognizing her.

Cole would have thought that having cancer—which he knows can always come back and kill you even if it didn't the first time—and not having the thing you most want in life would keep a person down. But though at times he sees PW with a faraway expression on his face that could be called at least partly sad, Tracy always looks as if everything is going her way.

Sometimes she accuses herself of being negative, or she apologizes for getting up "on the bad side of the bed." Cole never knows what she's talking about. Even when the subject is something she hates—abortion, unnatural marriage, the elbow bump—Tracy does not seem particularly angry or upset. She'll bunch her lips or shudder or shake her head—"If that isn't enough to make you spit"—but in the very next breath she'll say, "How about yegg salad on rye fer yer lunch?"

He thinks of his mother and the pills she took every day to make her less negative. There were other pills she took to make her less afraid, especially if she had to get on a plane, or to help her sleep. When she did not get enough sleep, almost anything could make her cry. A dead robin on the lawn . . .

His father didn't take any pills and Cole had never seen him cry, but he can't remember a time when he didn't have to

II

watch out for his father's moods. A bad mood often had something to do with work. His father and his mother were both overworked. One time he heard his mother tell someone on the phone, "I have to work as hard as she does and I've got a kid. Compared to mine, her life's a fucking piece of cake." Too much work. But also, as Cole understood it, fear of not having enough work. Or of losing the work that they had.

The people his parents disliked most were people who cared about money. But from the way his parents talked, money was the most important thing to them, too. He remembers the time their accountant made a mistake and they ended up owing a lot of taxes. When the accountant called to break the news, his father had started screaming at him, and when the accountant hung up on him, he threw his cell across the room. For days after, the house was like a tomb.

Cole knew the school he went to was expensive, as the schools his parents had gone to were expensive, so expensive that they'd had to keep paying the bills for years after they weren't in school anymore. He knew they were worried about paying for his own education for years to come, and he wished he could bring them around to his own view, which was that school was not worth it.

As Cole understands it, if things had been different—if his parents had not had to work so hard all the time, and if they had not had to worry so much about money—he would have been born sooner. But he has always wondered about this. If he had been born sooner, on a different day in a different year, would he be exactly the same? Would he still be himself?

And if they had never moved, if they had stayed in Chicago, would his parents still be alive? Cole thinks the answer is yes, even though he knows that many people got sick and died in Chicago, too. In the big cities, so many people died so fast that bodies kept piling up and there were corpses everywhere, even outdoors. It is another one of Cole's guilty secrets that he wishes he could have seen this with his own eyes. That, and the riots.

Cole has heard people call Tracy pretty, but again he has no opinion about this. Or rather his opinion is that although grown-ups can sometimes look good in photos or in movies or from far away, up close there is always something blotchy or hairy or saggy, and most grown-ups, even the ones who don't smoke, smell.

The big exception was his great-grandmother, Ginia, whom he'd met only once, when he was six. Ginia was old but her face was freakily beautiful, like something carved out of soap, with eyes like Blue Jay marbles. She was *teensy*. A grown-up no bigger than himself! He could not see how anyone could stand, let alone walk, on such matchstick legs. When he thinks of her now, he thinks of an egret.

But she, too, had a smell. And in general old people are the ugliest and smelliest people of all.

He has always been sensitive to smells, but since his illness he is more so. His memory may be worse, but his senses seem to have got better. He is sure he hears better than he used to. PW says it's because Cole has never lived so far out in the country, where it's so quiet, especially at night. But being in the country is not a whole new experience for Cole. He has been to the country on vacations, and he has been to summer camp.

From school he knows that Native Americans had much

sharper vision and hearing than the white settlers had, and he likes to pretend he is one of them, a *brave* (how he loves that word), able to hear a fly land on the windowsill.

Riding a horse, he has also imagined himself a brave, nothing between him and the horse's warm, broad back. He has never understood why white people invented the saddle.

Tracy and PW say the Indians were not the first people in America, there were white people here before them. Cole is surprised to hear this. He is sure that's not what he learned in school—unless it's one of the things he no longer remembers.

It was his mother who'd pointed out that it was only human smells that bothered him, which is true. But then it is also true that he likes animals more than he likes people. He does not mind the smell of horses or dogs; in fact, he thinks horses and dogs smell good. He has never been bothered by the smells in a zoo. He could stay in the monkey house all day long. But once when he was sitting on a park bench and a homeless man sat down beside him, he had jumped up and fled without even caring that the man's feelings might be hurt. He does not feel so guilty about this because he knows he's not the only one who'd find the man's smell worse than a monkey's. But he has always wondered: why was that?

Besides keeping house, Tracy does church work, of which there seems to be no end. She is good with her hands, and in every room of the house there are things—quilts, pillows, ceramics—that she has made. Though constantly busy, she is always looking for more to do. ("Devil ain't gonna catch *this* lady with idle hands.") Yet the word Cole is unable to separate from Tracy is *lazy*.

They don't read, and they can't write to save their lives. They've never heard of most of the presidents of the United States, they think America won the war in Vietnam, they think Prohibition was a law that made it illegal to own slaves.

That was Cole's father, fuming about his students. Cole suspects at least some of this could also be said about Tracy.

And it's not just what they don't know, it's what they don't want to know.

Tracy is what his father would call intellectually lazy.

Every time this thought occurs to Cole, he feels guilty.

Not that he would even care, if Tracy wasn't his teacher.

The hours he spends on lessons with her are torture. He cannot hide his feelings completely, but fortunately everyone thinks he's just a normal red-blooded boy who'd rather be off riding his bike, say.

Though he has shared some of his secrets with PW, about Tracy he knows he will never be honest.

HE REMEMBERS HIS LAST DAY OF SCHOOL as if it were yesterday, and at the same time as if it were very long ago. He was still the new boy then. He and his parents had moved from Chicago during Christmas vacation.

His father said, "I know how hard it is for you to leave all your friends and jump in with a whole bunch of new kids in the middle of the year. But try to think of it as an adventure."

His new homeroom teacher, who reminded him of his father but whose name Cole can no longer recall, made Cole stand in the front of the room and introduce himself. Cole had never felt so exposed. (That night he dreamed he was standing in front of a roomful of strangers again, this time *naked*.)

Hating the teacher, avoiding eye contact with the two kids he instantly picked out as bullies, he prayed his voice would not crack. One bully glared at him the whole time; the other kept his eyes mostly shut. A boy in the front row with a face practically buried under freckles listened to every word with his mouth open, as if Cole were explaining sex. Two girls farther back put their blond heads together and whispered about him (what else?). Everyone else looked as if they weren't listening, Mr. What's-his-name (staring out the window) included.

Cole kept it short. He was from Chicago, he didn't have any brothers or sisters, his father was a history professor, his mother was a lawyer. Or rather she used to be a lawyer, but not anymore.

A hand shot up. (The teacher had encouraged questions.) How come his mother stopped being a lawyer?

Cole shrugged. She didn't like it, he said. He did not say because it was a dull, heartless profession full of people who cared only about money, as his mother always said when people asked her.

His father used to say, "Serena, you should've been born rich. You're just not cut out to work." But in fact, except for right after Cole was born, his mother had always worked at one job or another. It was true she had hated most of those jobs. But about a year before they moved she'd started working as the manager of a small theater company, a job she had loved. "If only it paid more!" (Always, the problem was money.)

Cole didn't tell any of this to the class. He didn't say anything about the fights his parents had had about moving. His mother said it wasn't fair. Just when she'd finally found a job that was right for her! She blew up when his father said she could always find something similar where they were going.

"Don't patronize me, Miles."

Then it was his father's turn to blow up.

"Let me get this straight. I'm supposed to pass up a great opportunity just so you can keep working for a nonprofit company that pays shit, and that you'll probably end up leaving anyway as soon as the novelty wears off?"

"But you don't even *like* teaching. All you ever do is complain."

"It's a great fucking job!"

"It's in fucking Indiana!"

In the middle of fucking nowhere, was how she usually described it. Not even a major city. "Like there are really major cities in Indiana anyway," she told her sister as she wiped her eyes—tears not from crying but from laughing at the name of the town: Little Leap.

No major cities. And no such place as Big Leap, either.

Aunt Addy lived in Germany but had come to Chicago for Christmas.

"I mean, the people are all right-wing, the climate sucks, there's no music or theater. There are no museums, no decent restaurants." The pills his mother was taking to make her less negative were not working at all. "All anyone cares about is fucking basketball. At least, I think it's basketball." Cole rolled his eyes.

Aunt Addy was more than his mother's sister: she was her twin. He never saw much of her because she lived overseas.

She was good at languages and worked as a translator and an interpreter for an international bank. She hated America, even to visit, and came back as seldom as possible.

"There are some twins who always dress alike and do everything together," his mother told him. "But Addy and I were never like that. Even as kids we rebelled against matching outfits, and as soon as we were old enough we got different hairstyles." Nowadays their hair was pretty much the same, short and fluffy, partly dark and partly light. But of course they were rarely seen together.

Aunt Addy had Total Freedom, his mother always said. Meaning she wasn't married and she didn't have kids.

Cole's father was a runner, a racer, a winner of marathons. In college his nickname had been Miles-and-miles. Though he didn't compete anymore, he still ran every morning to stay in shape.

When she was in a good mood, Cole's mother called his father Miles-and-miles. Her own nickname was Serena-anything-but. But people only used it to tease her.

"You know it's not my fault I didn't get tenure," his father said.

Cole's mother's silence seemed to say that it was.

But it wasn't just herself she was thinking about. Did he really want their son to grow up in a cultural backwater? *She* had grown up in a cultural backwater and had escaped to the nearest big city the first chance she got.

Maybe because of the word *backwater* Cole has always had

an image of his mother *swimming* to Los Angeles. (The truth is just as hard to picture: his mother—a *girl*—*hitchhiking* to Los Angeles.)

Cole's father was from Seattle and always said Chicago was a town he could take or leave. Chicago wasn't his mother's favorite town, either; she would much rather have lived in New York. They'd ended up in Chicago only because of his father's job. The one he lost when he didn't get tenure.

Cole thinks of Chicago as his hometown, but he'd lived a third of his life in Amherst, Massachusetts. Amherst was where he'd been born and where his father had been teaching at the time. But it was in New York that his parents had first met. His father was in graduate school then, and Cole's mother happened to be in town visiting her best friend from college.

"Your mom was the best-looking girl at this party, see, but I married her because she was the only one who laughed at my jokes" was one of his jokes.

Cole wonders if he will end up living in as many different places as his parents had lived. Pastor Wyatt has told him about visiting African villages on missions for the church, and Cole wishes he could visit them, too. He likes looking at photos from PW's African days. PW had a good friend in Kenya whose name was Mwendwa, and there are photos of the two men together. Mwendwa has a very long, narrow, dark face and the only smile Cole has ever seen that really does stretch from ear to ear, reminding Cole of a banana. Though Cole knows the people in the photos are very poor and don't have enough food or clean water or medicine, everyone—from tiny bare-assed toddlers to an old man missing both legs—looks happy, as if it was as good as getting toys or money just having your picture taken. There are some photos of men sitting on mats in a hut and carving wood, and in PW's house there are some wood statues—a bird, a turtle, a woman carrying a child on her back—that the men gave him when he had to go back to America.

Cole hopes to go around the world one day. One of his favorite words is *explorer*. During the pandemic people weren't allowed to travel anywhere unless they absolutely had to, and even now it's not the way it was before. There aren't as many airplanes. There aren't as many buses or trains, and there aren't as many cars on the highways.

Cole remembers his father saying that when he was a kid every boy wanted to be a sports hero or a rock star but that he wanted to be an astronaut. To Cole this never sounded terribly exciting, sitting strapped in for all those miles just to arrive at a place like the moon, where everywhere you looked was exactly the same and nothing was happening, no people or animals. But *Africa* . . .

PW says he would love to take Cole to Kenya one day, but it would be a lie if he said it was likely to happen. They were living in a whole different world these days.

"Let's just say if I go, I'll do everything to make sure you get to go, too. Fair enough?"

It was fair, but it was disappointing. And so PW made a promise he knew he could keep. For Cole's next birthday he would bless him with a camping trip to the Kentucky mountains. Cole's heart was full, and when PW said there would be just the two of them ("no girls allowed"), he thought it would burst from joy.

———

Cole doesn't know what he'll be when he grows up. Certainly not a lawyer. Not a teacher. Not a preacher, either. He can't imagine getting up in front of people and talking to them the way Pastor Wyatt and the other preachers do. When he and Tracy listen to Pastor Wyatt on the radio, Tracy says, "Isn't it something, how he doesn't sound a bit nervous? I could never do that, knowing all those people out there were listening to my every word."

"Me, neither," says Cole. And he remembers that first day of school, standing up in front of his new classmates.

No, his mother was not working right now. Yes, he liked their new house. The house belonged to the college where his father was teaching, and it was much bigger than the apartment they'd had in Chicago, and now they could have a dog. A sheepdog was what he wanted.

The bully with closed eyes popped them open at this and exchanged a sneer with the other bully, and Cole figured a sheepdog must be a girly breed.

He has no idea why he lied. In fact, they'd had a dog in Chicago, an old basset hound named Sadie (full name: Sad-Eyed Lady of the Lowlands), who'd died in her sleep a few months before they moved. And though it was true Cole wanted a new dog, he hadn't decided on any particular breed. So what made him say sheepdog?

Cole didn't tell the class his parents were getting divorced. Though she'd quit her beloved job at the theater and put all her energy into moving and getting them settled in their new home, his mother was planning to leave.

It was her secret, but Cole had found out about it.

If he had shared this with the class the other kids probably wouldn't have cared, but the teacher might have been pissed. It would have been one of those times—and Cole has learned such times are not rare—when you got in trouble not for lying but for blurting out the whole truth.

It never even occurred to him to tell his father what he'd heard his mother tell Addy on the phone.

He didn't know if he'd be leaving Little Leap, too. If it was just divorce his mother was looking for or Total Freedom.

What if she was planning to go all the way to New York? Or Berlin, which Addy always made sound like the coolest place on the planet. (According to Addy, New York City was *finished*.)

He couldn't ask his mother about any of this. Not because he was afraid she'd be angry at him for eavesdropping but because he figured knowing he knew the truth would only make her more upset than she already was.

In any case, as far as he knew, the plan was for him to finish middle school and then go away to some boarding school, location not yet decided.

Sometimes he thought he could not wait for that day; other times he prayed it would never come.

When it was over, the teacher made him stand and squirm for a few seconds, just so he'd know his performance had been unsatisfactory. Finally allowed to return to his seat, which *had* to be directly in front of one of the bullies, Cole realized he had sweat through his shirt.

The teacher asked the class to tell Cole something about his new state. They shouted out things like Hoosiers and Indy 500, as if he'd come from some foreign country instead of right next door.

The crossroads of America.

He knew about Michael Jackson and Larry Bird and Indiana Jones (and that he had nothing to do with Indiana the state). His father had made him read Kurt Vonnegut. He had never heard of James Dean.

Try to think of it as an adventure.

The same desks and chairs. The same scuffed linoleum floors. The same smells (BO, new sneakers, mac and cheese).

The same bullies. The same whispering girls.

The new school was not really much of an adventure.

Until everyone started getting sick.

THE SCHOOL STANK OF LYSOL, and several times a day they all had to line up and wash their hands. *Clean hands save lives* was the message being hammered into them. When it came to spreading infection, they were informed, they themselves—school kids—were the biggest culprits. Even if you weren't sick yourself, you could shed germs and make other people sick. Cole was struck by the word *shed*. The idea that he could shed invisible germs the way Sadie shed dog hairs was awesome to him. He pictured the germs as strands of hair with legs like centipedes, invisible but crawling everywhere.

Minibottles of sanitizer were distributed for use when soap and water weren't available. Everyone was supposed to receive a new bottle each day, but the supply ran out quickly—not just at school but all over. Among teachers this actually brought relief, because the white, slightly sticky lotion was so like something else that some kids couldn't resist. Gobs started appearing on chairs, on the backs of girls' jeans, or even in their hair, and one boy caused an uproar by squirting it all over his face.

Never Sneeze into Your Hand, read signs posted everywhere. And: *Keep Your Hands to Yourself* (these had actually been there before but now had a double meaning).

If you had to sneeze, you should do it into a tissue. If you didn't have a tissue, you should use the crook of your arm.

"But that's *vomitous*," squealed Norris (one of the two whispering blondes).

These rules were like a lot of other school rules: nobody paid much attention to them.

Some school employees started wearing rubber gloves. Cafeteria servers, who already wore gloves, started wearing surgical masks as well.

Cole lost his appetite. He couldn't stop thinking about hospitals. Flesh being cut open, flesh being sewn up.

How could you tell if you had the flu? The symptoms were listed on the board in every room: Fever. Aches. Chills. Dry cough. *What must you do if you had these symptoms?* YOU MUST STAY HOME.

Just as the school nurse was explaining all this, a boy sitting near the window started to cough and couldn't stop. Then someone else started coughing, and then another person, and then another, and another, until half the room was coughing and the other half choking with laughter.

The nurse looked as if some pervert had just flashed her. She glared at the teacher, but he only shook his head. He was sleepy-looking that day, and paler than usual, and the next day he would be out.

Cole had just begun to adjust. The other kids weren't so bad. He'd figured out how to turn being an outsider to his advantage.

"Chicago's off the hook—totally different from a dinkburg like this. I can't wait till we move back. Then you can come visit." (This time, Cole knew perfectly well why he lied.)

It turned out that one of the bullies, Pete, was mostly a problem only when the other bully, Les, was around. And Pete was dying to visit Chicago.

Cole's new teachers didn't particularly like him, but that didn't bother him. He'd been in the opposite situation, when a teacher had liked him a whole lot. She might as well have painted a target on his butt.

He didn't hate school but he didn't love it the way some kids (mostly girls, of course) did, either. This hadn't changed.

Though no one knew (or must *ever* know), Cole had already developed a crush. On the other whispering blonde, Kaleigh.

Kaleigh and Norris were joined at the hip, and they were both *apocalyptic*.

BACK IN THE FALL, at the beginning of the first wave—the milder and less infectious flu that would kill mostly old people or babies or people already weak from other diseases—back when Cole was still living in Chicago, the assistant principal (the principal was out sick) stood on the stage of the school auditorium and introduced a man from the public health department.

The man was normal-looking, but he had the kind of speech defect that makes you talk like Elmer Fudd. The mike he was using made it worse. It was hard not to laugh, and some kids weren't exactly trying.

"What's the worst outbreak of disease in human history?" he asked. "Anyone?" And about half the audience roared back, "*AIDS!*"

"I *knew* you were going to say that." In fact, the man sounded pleased that they'd got it wrong.

"I'm talking about a plague that killed nearly three-quarters of a million Americans and something like fifty, seventy-five, maybe even a hundred million people worldwide. And all that in just two little years."

A few kids madly applauded this, for a mock, but the man ignored them.

"I'm talking about influenza, the Great Flu of 1918. There was a world war going on at the time, but in the end more people died from germs than from all the bombs and bullets put together. But get this. *Most* of the people who got the flu survived. So if all those millions of people died, how many people must've been infected? I can't tell you the exact figure because we don't know it. But try at least five hundred million. In those days that was, like, more than a third of the world's population."

In fact, there was a good chance everyone in the auditorium had at least one relation who'd been touched by the Great Flu, he said.

He showed them a video made by the World Health Organization. Cole joined in when some other kids started booing at scenes showing rabbits and monkeys being used as test animals. But there was applause again when men dressed in hazmat suits were shown slaughtering chickens.

Cole thought he hadn't heard right. Every single chicken in Hong Kong? More than a million chickens. Cole didn't believe the men could possibly have got every single chicken. Some chickens, surely, must have escaped. He could *see* them escaping. He could see people hiding their chickens. (Chickens? What chickens? Ain't nobody here but us humans.) He didn't like watching the chickens get killed, but the next scene—in which it was pigs that were being killed—bothered him a lot more. Cole liked pigs.

He looked away from the screen for a few moments, careful to make the act appear casual so he wouldn't seem wussy. When he looked back, the pigs had been succeeded by various people caught picking their noses in public. Squeals of laughter or disgust. Shrieks of "Vomitous! Vomitous!"

Nose picking was one of the main ways flu germs got spread.

Cole's attention soon wandered again, and when it returned, a woman with black hair pulled back in a large bun— like the head of a smaller, darker person hiding behind her—was speaking. She was one of those people, like the Bosnian woman who worked in the school library, who puzzled Cole by speaking English with a strong accent but without making any mistakes.

"People must learn that shaking another person's hand is not a friendly thing to do. It is not a friendly thing to put other people at risk for infectious diseases."

She and several other people were shown demonstrating the elbow bump, and the auditorium got raucous again.

"We must also consider limiting the use of coins and paper money. For this, too, may cause diseases to spread. We must use technology and human ingenuity to develop ways so that, in their daily public transactions, people touch one another as little as possible. Ideally, we also want to touch as few buttons and handles and knobs as possible."

When the video ended, the man talked about some new products on the market that were supposed to protect against germs. Probably none of them would stop a person from getting the flu, he said, but at least they were good for a laugh.

He held up a belt with a short pole sticking out of it and a small red flag attached to the pole. "The latest thing in New York." He buckled on the belt, then sashayed across the stage. The pole swung from side to side—the flag was supposed to smack anybody who got too close.

Back at the lectern, after everyone had calmed down, the man showed them the other products. There was an air purifier you could wear around your neck, and what looked like an oven mitt for when you had to hold on to a bus or subway pole or push a shopping cart. There was a device you could install on a door and set to spray disinfectant a few seconds after the doorknob had been touched.

One thing the man did not show but which everyone was used to seeing by now was a T-shirt with an image of a handshake in a red circle with a red diagonal slash.

28

Cole's father had a T-shirt that said "Human Race, Get Out of My Face." Every time he wore it he and Cole's mother would argue about it. ("It's a *joke*, Serena." "A *so* not funny one, Miles.")

Back in the classroom, everyone groaned when the teacher announced that for homework that weekend they had to write a research report on—what else?

It was just like Ms. Mark not to have told them this *before* so that maybe they could have paid more attention. Maybe even taken notes? It was also just like her to give such a lame assignment. As if influenza hadn't just been done to death. But that's what happens in school: you begin with something interesting—say, even mad interesting—something you're glad to know about, and then somehow it gets turned into something you never want to hear about again for the rest of your life. It was part of the mystery of teachers in general, as if they just couldn't get how kids' brains worked. As if every group of students were the first kids they'd ever met. As if boys in particular were a brand-new alien species, every class, every time.

Ms. Mark had a deep, throaty voice and a distinct bulge in her neck, which had inspired the rumor that she had been born (a hundred years ago) male. She had gone into full-frontal freak when she discovered (and she must have been the last person on earth) what it meant when kids—boys—called a girl a PB.

Beautiful, wicked-hot girls were apocalyptic. At the other end were the ones known as partial births.

"I know most of you probably don't even know what those words mean."

Was she *kidding?*

They were supposed to go to the library instead of just searching the Internet, but Cole knew this was plain dumb.

"W.H.O. Officials Call Pandemic 'Inevitable.'"

"Study Shows U.S. Ill-Equipped for Major Pandemic."

"Dysfunctional Health Care System Would Doom Millions, Doctors Say."

"A Catastrophe Worse Than Hurricane Katrina, Some Experts Fear."

Cole clicked and clicked. There were thousands of articles, more than anyone could ever read. Cole was surprised so many of them were from long ago, way back before 2000. Had his parents read any of them? He supposed they must have, but he couldn't remember them ever talking about a pandemic. It was not on the list of things they were always worried about, like identity theft or climate change or how they were going to pay for his education.

The diseases his parents worried about were cancer (his mother's big fear; both her parents had died of it) and Alzheimer's (his father's father had it).

"New Flu Strain Similar to Deadly 1918 Flu, Study Says."

"Mom! Dad!"

They stood on either side of his chair and stared at his laptop screen.

"Oh dear," said his father, though his tone was more like "ho-hum." "Not this again. I know it sounds bad, Cole, but I wouldn't get too excited. We go through one of these scares every couple of years. But remember, we're not living in 1918. We've got resources people didn't have back then."

"Yeah, and we've also got a lot more *crowding*, Dad. And

people traveling a lot more and coming in contact with each other all over the world. It says here an epidemic today would probably be a lot *worse* than it was back then."

Cole sensed, rather than saw, his parents exchange a look above his head.

"So maybe you'll be the one who grows up to be the Nobel Prize–winning scientist who develops the vaccine that saves us all," his mother said.

He hated when his mother said things like that. He *hated* science.

He felt a surge of anger, mostly at himself. He should never have called them.

"Anyway," his mother said, mussing his hair with one hand while covering a yawn with the other, "I'd rather die of the flu than some other ways I can think of."

"What's *that* supposed to mean?" Cole said, ducking away from her hand.

"Oh, I don't know. I guess just that I'd rather be killed by Nature than by some suicide bomber."

His father groaned, and his mother swatted his arm and said, "You know what I mean! And at least there'd be time to say good-bye."

"Okay, that's enough morbidity for me," said his father. "I'm going to bed. And that's what I think you should do, too, kiddo. And remember what we said about spending so much time online."

His parents were on a new kick: reforming their electronic habits. Rule number one: no more idle Web browsing. They were weaning themselves off YouTube and watching less TV, avoiding completely the 24/7 news channels. They had given up social networking, were down to dealing with e-mail just three times a day, and though a mobile phone was hard not to think of as a necessity, they were experimenting with leaving theirs off for longer and longer periods of time. They had also started carrying earplugs with them, popping them in for protection against public noise or ubiquitous indoor music. Sometimes they even wore earplugs at home so they could focus better on work or reading. And they had another new rule: no more multitasking. None of this was easy—there was a lot of backsliding—but they were convinced that their former ways had been damaging their intellects and powers of concentration. Many experts thought they were right. And wouldn't it be wonderful if Cole's generation could learn from their generation's mistakes? At the very least, they wanted him to limit his time online to two or three hours a day.

But Cole stayed up late that night, skimming more articles (including one called "Mother Nature Is the Worst Terrorist"), then lying in bed, listening to some music he'd downloaded before dinner. Though she wasn't worried about the flu, his mother was worried enough about Cole's hearing to nag him constantly about listening so much to his iPod. (His parents had given up their iPods as part of their new discipline but also out of anxiety about hearing loss.) Too bad it was Cole's favorite thing to do. His parents didn't believe him, but he actually studied better when he had music blasting in his ears. If he were allowed to take his tests like that, he was sure he'd get better grades. Anyway, he'd heard about surgeons blasting rock and roll in the OR, so obviously it couldn't *hurt* your concentration.

He'd had the flu so far twice in his life. He remembered the worst headache he'd ever had, and throwing up and throwing up, and being too tired even to sit up in bed. No denying, the sickest he'd ever been—he could get a little nauseated just remembering it—but nothing like what he'd read about tonight.

His father was always warning him not to trust everything he read online. The Net was a mine of misinformation, he said. And in fact Cole was skeptical about some of these flu stories. People screaming from the pain, people bleeding from their noses and ears and even their eyes, people completely losing their minds—it was like one of those horror movies so over the top that instead of being scared the audience ends up laughing.

He remembered what his mother had said about having time to say good-bye. But here were stories about people being way too sick to know what was happening to them and people dying so fast, some even dropping dead in their tracks as if they'd been shot. But his mother was wrong anyway. It would be better to die in a big explosion, or in a plane or car crash, or falling off a mountain like the principal's son last year, than to take *forever* like Cole's grandparents. His mother knew all about how bad cancer was, but obviously she didn't know the flu could be a pretty horrific way to die, too. And Cole wasn't going to tell her. He wasn't going to bring up the flu again with either of his parents.

But maybe his father was right. Maybe what had happened in 1918 could never happen again.

"U.S. Reveals Detailed Flu Disaster Plans."

Cole decided to make this the topic for his research report. Plans for manufacturing and distributing vaccines and other medications. Plans to quarantine the sick and to call up extra doctors and nurses and to replace absent workers with retired workers so that businesses wouldn't have to shut down. Plans to keep public transportation and electricity and telecommunications and other vital services operating and food and water and other necessities from running out. Plans to mobilize troops (for Cole this was the only exciting part) in the event of mass panic or violence.

One day he would ask Pastor Wyatt why, despite all these plans, everything had gone so wrong.

"Son, that is just the thing. That is what people did not—and still do not—get. There is no way you can count on the government, even if it's a very good government. The government isn't going to save you, it isn't going to save anyone. There's no way you can count on other people in a situation like we had. People afraid of losing their lives—or, Lord knows, even just their toys—they'll panic. Even fine, decent Christian folk—you can never know for sure what they'll do next. So I say, love your neighbor, help your fellow man all you can, but don't ever count on any other human being. Count on God."

What Cole didn't know was that most of the plans he read about that night would have been sufficient only for an emergency lasting a few weeks.

His report was really just a cut-and-paste job from the Internet, but he knew it would pass. Ms. Mark never paid much attention to their homework. He didn't bring up the subject with his parents again, but just before he went off to school Monday morning they brought it up. Was he still worried about an epidemic? And though he said no, they heard yes.

"We're not going to die, pumpkin," his mother said.

"You really shouldn't be wasting precious kid time worrying about that."

"Precious kid time" was something his mother said a lot. She was always complaining that kids today were being forced to grow up way too fast and were being robbed of more and more precious kid time. But to Cole, who could not wait to be sprung from the trap of adolescence, this was totally wack.

He had his iPod with him and was inserting the ear buds when she said, "You want something to worry about? Let me tell you, Dad and I are already paying for the kind of music we listened to growing up. You want articles? I can show you articles, I can show you studies—" The rest of her words were lost. He was out the door, his iPod turned up max.

BY THE TIME THEY MOVED TO INDIANA, the first wave of the flu had come and gone. None of them had caught it. ("See?" said his mother. "We Vinings are made of sturdy stuff.")

In Chicago there had been dozens of cases of infection but only one real horror story. In a nursing home on the South Side, all but two of the residents had died. But what did you expect? A filthy overcrowded place like that. Old people whose health had been so neglected for so long, they had no resistance to any germs.

Though the first wave had hit much of Illinois and other parts of the Midwest, in southern Indiana, where Little Leap was, there were only a few cases, all mild.

When the second wave hit, everyone hoped it, too, would be mild. A hope that died by the end of the first week.

Later many people would say that if the schools had been closed right away, lives might have been saved. But at the time people argued that you couldn't just close the schools, because so many parents worked. If they had to stay home to take care of their kids, a lot of them would lose income, maybe even their jobs. Not to mention that businesses were already shorthanded because of all the employees out sick. Closing the schools might just make things worse.

But even before schools were officially closed, many parents had started keeping their kids home. Because teachers were getting sick, too, and there weren't enough subs, classes had to be combined.

"How stupid can you get?" a teacher who'd been fired for refusing to go in to work told reporters. "Anywhere people are crowded together is bad, but with school kids we're talking about a perfect storm of contagion."

From Addy in Berlin came the news that all social gatherings had been banned except for weddings and funerals, where the number of people could not be higher than twelve. ("I wonder if that's counting the bride and groom," Cole's mother said, and his father joked: "How about the corpse?")

In city after city, all over the world, the number of people appearing in surgical masks kept multiplying. Those still capable of frivolity added illustrations: luscious lips, stuck-out tongues, piano-keyboard smiles, and—most popular—vampire fangs. In Indianapolis, after hundreds of people fell ill over one weekend, no one was permitted to go out without a mask. But—as happened almost everywhere—there weren't enough masks to go around. Some made do with scarves or other pieces of cloth, or they tried taping gauze or paper to their faces. A lot of people just ignored the rule—and got away with it, the police being out sick in droves.

But a homeless man caught spitting in the street was mobbed and beaten to death.

The day before Cole's school finally closed was spooky. The halls had never been so quiet. The sound of a ball being bounced in the school yard was like the sound of a heavy door slamming. And when the bell rang, everyone nearly jumped out of their skin.

Cole's last day of school turned out to be his father's last day of school, too.

When the first college students started getting sick, some health officials called for nationwide campus quarantines. They warned that letting all those active young people—many of whom were already infected, though they might not know it yet—travel around the country, using all means of public transportation, would spread a disease that seemed to be growing more contagious by the hour. Much safer for them to stay put. A drastic measure, to be sure. But the rate of infection among college students was turning out to be drastically high—higher than any other group except prison inmates. Cancel classes and all other school business, these officials urged, but please keep those kids in the dorms.

The outrage with which students reacted to this proposal was matched by the outrage of their parents, who wanted their sons and daughters home *now*. So, leaving only those already too sick to get out of bed, the campuses began emptying out.

Not that any dormitory anywhere would remain empty for

long. Most would be turned into makeshift clinics as hospitals started running out of beds.

Had his father killed another dog? No, it was just his expression.

Coming home that other time his father had explained how, out of nowhere, a dog had dashed in front of his car. "All I could do was run over the poor thing," he said. He had looked shocked and awed, and for a while after, whenever he caught sight of Sadie, he'd mirror her own sad-eyed long face.

This time, though, it was the flu that had his father looking shocked and awed. The flu, which was now officially the only thing anyone could think about, the only topic of conversation. In less than a week, it had knocked half the student body flat. The lives of kids in perfect health just days ago now hung in the balance. Two freshmen and one sophomore had died.

The dude flu, people called it, as more and more young adults were taken down.

"Not to scare anyone," his father said, "but I'm not feeling so hot myself." Cole noticed that his father's skin looked dirty, smudged in places, as if he'd rubbed himself down with a sheet of newspaper. "I don't have a fever but I feel like I've been hit over the head or something."

"Oh my god." Cole's mother looked as if she'd been hit over the head pretty hard herself. "Don't touch Cole. Go upstairs. I'll call the doctor. Go straight to bed."

Without a word—like a sleepwalker, or someone obeying a hypnotist—his father turned and left the room.

"Don't go near your father. Don't touch him."

Why were his parents behaving like bots? His mother held her arms stiffly at her sides. She held her eyes so wide open Cole thought it must hurt. He thought of the pod people in the famous old movie whose name he couldn't remember. The way his father had climbed the stairs. They were changing— everything was changing.

Later, people would always say how everything had happened so fast—*overnight*, they said. But Cole would remember the feeling of dragging a ball and chain, of days unfolding in excruciating slow motion.

"I'll go call the doctor. Keep away from your father. Stay down here. Keep away from our room."

"Okay, Mom, I heard you the first time."

Cole turned on the TV. Not that he expected to find anything besides news about the flu. As he touched the remote power button, he remembered that the movie was called *Invasion of the Body Snatchers* and how one of his teachers had said it proved you didn't need to show a lot of violence to make a great scary movie. But Cole thought only a Neanderthal would find a clunky old black-and-white movie like that seriously scary.

He wondered how long school would be closed. Not that he missed it. In fact, it had disgusted him that his parents had made him keep going. It had not escaped his notice that it was mostly the cooler kids whose parents had let them stay home, even if they weren't sick. Kaleigh, for example, had been one of the first to stop coming to school. Had this not been the case, of course, Cole would not have wanted to stay home himself.

Now he just wished there were some way to delete the last time they'd seen each other.

She had caught him staring (usually he was more careful). "Why don't you just take a picture?" *Loud,* on purpose, so that half the cafeteria would hear. And stupidly he had shot back: "Why would I want a picture of you?" Not fooling anyone, of course. And then Kaleigh whispered something to the other kids at her table, something that made them all go *"Ooooo."*

Every day since then he had relived it, trying, at least in fantasy, to fix it. But he could never think of what to say. As usual, he couldn't imagine what the cool response would have been. He just knew it existed: the response that instead of making her sneer would have made Kaleigh like him.

And now he wished he *had* had the nerve to sneak-take her picture, even though kids caught doing that got their cells confiscated. He couldn't remember what clothes she'd been wearing that last time, but he remembered her hands. Only a short time ago he would have found green nail polish ugly. He would have found the stud Kaleigh wore in her nose vomitous. There were days when for some reason she had dark circles under her eyes. He knew they were supposed to be ugly (his mother hated it whenever she had them), but now they, too, were somehow attractive—one of those things, like the silver nose stud and the metallic green nails, that he liked looking at when Kaleigh was there and thinking about when she wasn't.

Whenever he saw or thought about those circles under her eyes, he wanted to kiss her there—even after he heard Pete Druzzi say, "When a chick's got circles under her eyes it means she's wearing the red mouse."

But by now his secret hope had been crushed. He'd held

on to it for as long as he could, the hope that here, in this new town, among all new kids, things would be different from the way they'd been in Chicago. Where the apocalyptic girls had looked right through him.

"Oh, those damn girls," his mother fumed. "Every school has them. Cold, mean, narcissistic, and usually dumb. They should never be allowed to get away with their destructive behavior. But trust me, Cole, they're not worth suffering over."

His mother was so wrong. Kaleigh wasn't dumb. She was one of the best students in the class, and already focused on getting into a good college. She was going to be an obstetrician. She already knew that. And she wasn't mean. Cliquish, yes, but not mean. She just didn't like boys staring at her. He could understand that. And everyone knew she was kind. They knew it because of Mr. Henderson, the Spanish teacher. Middle-aged, married "Hairpiece" Henderson. He was in love with her and unable to hide it. His heart was breaking for her and he couldn't hide it. Scream! Everyone knew, and everyone wanted to make something of it. But just try. Just try making fun of Mr. Henderson in front of Kaleigh.

"Oh my god, Cole. How awful!"

He had slid down on the couch with his head back and had been staring at the ceiling instead of at the screen. He had never turned up the volume.

There they were again: the men in the hazmat suits. Not chickens or pigs this time but people. Corpses. Laid out in rows. Being swung onto a gigantic pyre.

"I can't watch this," his mother said, gasping as if someone had just knocked the wind out of her. Cole shrugged and turned the TV off.

41

He didn't want her to sit down on the sofa next to him, but she did. He didn't want her to put her arm around him, but she did. He wanted to be alone. He wanted to go up to his room. He didn't want to talk, but he knew she would. Why did she always do the wrong thing?

Now that his father was sick she was all upset. His father, whom she was secretly planning to dump. ("The truth is, Addy, I feel like I've done my duty. I don't owe this man the rest of my life.")

She hadn't been able to reach the doctor. He was just a name to her: Dr. Corbutt. The only primary-care doctor in the area still taking new patients enrolled in the college's insurance plan. She had reached a recording saying people who thought they had the flu should not come into the office or go to the hospital. They should stay home instead and call a certain number. But when she tried calling that number it was busy.

"Of course, we don't know for sure if it even is the flu," she said. "Anyway, I'll try again later. Let's talk about dinner. I'm afraid it's slim pickin's."

Very long ago, it seemed, he'd been sent home from school with a pamphlet about Emergency Home Preparedness. Every home should always have on hand at least a three-week supply of food, water, and medication for each member of the family.

"But there's frozen pizza. You like that. I could heat up some vegetable soup, and we could have that with the pizza. Would you like that, sweetie?"

Something was being shredded inside him.

He wasn't afraid of the flu anymore. He wasn't afraid of everyone dying. He believed his parents when they said they weren't going to die. *They* were made of sturdy stuff. None of them would die. They would all go on living, day after day, in the same dumb, totally fucked-up way.

"Cole! What is it, Cole?"

Why did it always sound more loving when she said his name than when she called him sweetie or pumpkin?

"Are you scared, Cole? No? Then what is it? Are you home-sick? Do you miss your old school? Are you afraid you won't make any friends here? Come on, Cole. *Words*, remember?"

He remembered. She used to say it all the time when he was small. "Words, Cole, words. I'm not a mind reader. But if you give me the words, I'll bet I can make the bad go away."

And it was true! It had worked—*then*.

Rather than cry, he swore he would gouge his own eyes out.

Imagine you swallowed an empty balloon and then some-how it started inflating.

He didn't want to bury his face in her neck and ball his fists and sob and sob till he got the hiccups like some fucking five-year-old. But once he had done that, he felt better.

He still didn't want to talk. But he sat in the kitchen and kept his mother company while she heated the soup and the pizza. And then they ate together in peace.

THE NEXT MORNING his father was able to sit up in bed for an hour or so and work on his laptop. He was able to eat breakfast but refused lunch, saying he didn't think he could keep it down. By afternoon all he could do was sleep.

His mother kept calling both the doctor's office and the special number she'd been given but without getting through to either.

Cole was forbidden to enter the sickroom. From time to time, if he saw the door open, he'd stop and linger awkwardly in the doorway.

"You okay, Dad?"

"I'll survive, kiddo. Don't forget to wash your hands."

His mother, on the other hand, spent much of the day in the room, and at night she slept there, not in the bed but on a yoga mat on the floor. She used a cotton scarf for a mask—a blue bandanna that she wore to keep her hair back when she did yoga—and washed her hands so often they were becoming raw. She worried about his father's fever but couldn't say how high it was, the thermometer being one of several items that had managed somehow to get lost in the move from Chicago. And there were no more thermometers to be found at the drugstore.

And once they'd used up the aspirin they had on hand, that was it. Like surgical masks and thermometers, cold and flu medication had run out everywhere. Rubbing alcohol, mouthwash, bleach—anything containing germ killer was also sold out. Except, of course, online. The Web was full of ads not only for ordinary meds like aspirin but for a million products promising to prevent or cure flu.

A mine of misinformation.

Bloggers around the world swore by the power of this or that herb: holy basil, astragalus, elderberry.

If you drank a certain tea, if you ate a certain root, if you practiced meditation every day, if you took mega doses of Vitamin D, you would not get sick.

Rub yourself down with onion or garlic. Take garlic pills, chew garlic, carry garlic cloves in your pockets. Try acupuncture.

A positive psychological outlook was essential, and the more good deeds a person performed, the less likely he or she was to get infected.

Because the second wave was so much more severe than the first, a lot of people refused to believe it could be the same disease. It had to be terrorism. They didn't care what medical experts kept telling them, about how it was the nature of influenza to occur in waves and that there was nothing about this pandemic, terrible though it was, that wasn't happening more or less as had long been predicted.

No, not bioterrorism, others said, but a virus that had escaped from a laboratory. These were the same people who believed that both Lyme disease and West Nile virus were caused by germs that had escaped many years ago from a government lab off the coast of Long Island. They scoffed at the assertion that it was impossible to say for sure where the flu had begun because cases had appeared in several different countries at exactly the same time. Cover-up! Everyone knew the government was involved in the development of bioweapons. And although the Americans were not the only ones who were working on such weapons, the belief that they were somehow to blame—that the monster germ had most likely been created in an American lab, for American military purposes—would outlive the pandemic itself.

In any case, according to a poll, eighty-two percent of

Americans believed the government knew more about the flu than it was saying. And the number of people who declared themselves dead set against any vaccine the government came up with was steadily growing.

Just before she fell sick, the president addressed the nation.

"We have reached the point where our hospitals, clinics, and other health centers are overwhelmed. Communities everywhere are struggling with a shortage of health care workers, not only because of the many who are out sick but because of those who are quitting their jobs or refusing to show up for work. While the fear these workers must feel is understandable, our survival depends on them, and so we command all those whose duty it is to care for the sick not to shirk that duty. Your country needs you. At the end of the day, when this peril is behind, you will be remembered as America's heroes. Your courage and sacrifice will never be forgotten. And those who abandon their posts today should bear in mind that neither will this be forgotten. A day of reckoning will come.

"At this time we also call on all able-bodied retired doctors, nurses, and others trained in health care to volunteer their services. Some have already done so, and we praise and thank these fine people. But the need for skilled hands grows more urgent every day, and their number remains far too few.

"Finally, we call on all ordinary citizens to do their part. Who will take care of the sick if not their own family, friends, and neighbors? We are hearing far too many stories of people running away, leaving deathly ill loved ones behind. There have been heartbreaking reports of flu victims who might have survived had there only been someone to fetch them water.

"My fellow Americans, I ask you not to turn your backs

on one another in this hour of need. Volunteer to help out in your communities in whatever way you can. Knock on your neighbor's door and see if there is someone trapped and helpless who needs you.

"In many areas of the country, flu victims have been instructed not to go to the hospital but to wait for a visiting doctor or nurse to come to their homes. And yet every day we hear of new instances of people besieging emergency rooms and, in some cases, resorting to violence. Police, whose own ranks have been stretched thin, and who might be providing other emergency aid, have had their hands full protecting our hospitals and pharmacies. National Guard troops who might be delivering food and other necessities to places where they are in short supply have been engaged instead in a constant battle against rioters and looters.

"Furthermore, we are seeing a proliferation of fraud, one scam after another hatched by criminals seeking to profit from others' misery. We warn all citizens to beware of those selling counterfeit drugs. While the majority of these substances appear to be harmless, some have sickened and even killed those who have ingested them. We are also seeing a record number of assaults on the Web. It seems hackers have been working overtime to create monster viruses with the sole purpose of unleashing more chaos upon the world. Many businesses, including government offices here in Washington, had planned in the event of a pandemic to have numbers of employees work from home. But now this has become nearly impossible, as major government and business websites have been hit and one branch of the network after another has been shut down.

"But there appears to be no act too shameful that some

will not stoop to it. Certain people, some working as individuals and others as part of organized gangs, are making a business of preying on the sick and dying. They are breaking into homes and stripping weak and defenseless victims of their possessions. Reports of people robbing the dead are also increasingly common. It seems that for these scoundrels the only thing capable of trumping fear of infection is greed."

Weeks later, when she reappeared, convalescent, the president would confess that she had no memory of having made this speech, or even of some of the things to which it referred. Much else that had taken place during the period right before her illness had also been wiped from her mind.

Among the faces appearing on the news, Cole recognized a woman with a dark hair bun like a small head peeking out from behind her: the same woman in the video about influenza that he'd watched in school assembly last fall.

"Unfortunately," she said, "the new A-strain influenza virus has turned out to be resistant to the antiviral drugs we have available. Also, as we had feared, we are seeing a rise in cases of flu victims developing bacterial co-infections that are resistant to antibiotics. A new vaccine is still perhaps a month or so away. Then we'll be faced with the tremendous challenge of manufacturing the large quantity of doses needed and organizing for mass vaccinations."

"How can she be so calm?" Cole's mother wanted to know. It was a calm that riled rather than soothed her.

Most of the other people they saw on the news could barely control their emotions.

"They say stay home, wait until a doctor comes. But then

48

no doctor ever shows up. Meanwhile, my wife is getting sicker and sicker."

"First they warn everyone to wear a mask. Then we find out unless it's a special kind of mask it's not going to protect you at all."

"It's not just a question of beds. There's not enough linen, not enough gloves, gowns, hypodermic needles, disinfectant, meds, you name it. Not enough ambulances, not enough ventilators or other equipment. Hospitals are even running out of food."

"It's not like every other bad thing stopped happening to make room for the flu. People are still getting cancer and having heart attacks and strokes and road accidents. The idea that we could handle any kind of surge on top of that—whoever's fantasy that was, it was never going to happen."

"The retired workers they were depending on to take over for the workers out sick? Very few of those people ever showed. The volunteer doctors and nurses and the other helping hands—they aren't showing up, either. It's not like 9/11. There aren't any heroes rushing toward the danger. The danger is everywhere, and everyone's running scared."

"Let's face it, this is America. Anything that's bad for business, people don't want to hear. When it comes to money or doing the right thing, most people are going to choose money. Close up shop for months till they can make a new vaccine? How many businesses would still be alive after that?"

"This disaster proves what some of us have being saying about America all along: everything is broken."

"The bottom line is, sports events provide a boost to the

local economy. No one wanted to take the heat for calling them off."

"How can anyone behold what is happening and not see it as a sign? Brothers and sisters, we have entered the final days."

"Cancel a fund-raiser expected to bring in millions? I don't think so."

"When people think of the flu, they think of seasonal flu. They don't understand that a panflu is a whole other disease. They see people's skin turn dark blue and they think it can't be the flu, it must be bubonic plague or something. They see people crying tears of blood, and they think it must be the end of the world."

"God's kingdom is come. Whoever takes Jesus into his heart at this time will not be left behind."

"Thus far the so-called Guinea Worm has been the most lethal, taking down computer systems around the globe."

"Well, if it ain't the end of the world, I don't know what else you'd call it."

"How the hell do you tell people they can't go to church on the eve of the rapture?"

NOT BEING ABLE TO GO ONLINE whenever he wanted—it was as if his right hand were gone.

Not being able to leave the house was weird, too. First his mother makes him go to school every day, right to the bitter end; now he can't go past the front porch.

Cole was not yet used to the new house: its smell, its noises, the brown (instead of apple-green) walls of his room.

Also, to make the move easier his parents had sold most of their furniture on eBay and taken a house that was already furnished. Cole didn't really care about furniture one way or the other, but there seemed to be too much of it, so that somehow the six-room house felt more cramped than their old five-room apartment.

He stepped out a couple of times a day, sometimes sneaking a smoke. Found treasure: someone had left a half-full pack of Marlboros on a table at Burger King. Cole could not believe his luck. Of course, his mother would freak if she caught him. But then she was in full-frontal freak these days anyway.

Though he couldn't stand more than three or four puffs at a time, he was satisfied that he was on his way to being a real smoker. (Two things he'd decided were definitely in his future: cigarettes and a motorcycle.)

Even in normal times their dead-end street was quiet. The Vinings hadn't been living there long enough to know their neighbors, and Cole didn't expect they'd ever know any of them all that well. His parents had strong ideas about not getting too close to neighbors. It was one more reason his mother disliked small towns. In places like Little Leap the neighbors tended to be *over*friendly, she said. (And this would be one more source of bafflement for Tracy. "Loving your neighbor's just another way of loving God. And there can't never be too much of that!")

The day after they'd moved in, Cole had taken a walk by himself to the end of the street, and as he was coming back a long-haired boy on a bike had suddenly appeared, whizzing past him from behind. *"Outta my way, fag-boy!"* But Cole had never seen that boy again.

Though pedestrians were a rare sight, Cole saw two animals from time to time: a calico cat that appeared to live under the porch of the house directly opposite, and a slightly lame chocolate Lab that wore tags but was allowed to roam free. Whenever he saw either of them, Cole couldn't help wondering. Cats and dogs were smart, and they were sensitive, too. Did they have any idea that their human friends were in such deep shit? Cole knew animals could get the flu, too. In fact, there were people out there who blamed birds for what was happening and were shooting or trapping and killing them. There were crazies who believed any animal might carry the infection and were destroying every one they could get their hands on, even their own pets—the same kind of thing that had happened during the 1918 flu.

Cole's father had told him how, when the United States was at war with Germany, there were people who'd walk up to dachshunds in the street and kick them. ("I bet they wouldn't dare do that to a German shepherd," Cole said.)

But imagine all the human beings on earth getting wiped out. A lot of animals would have to be happy about that, wouldn't they? All those animals on the verge of extinction— they'd be saved then, wouldn't they?

There were those who'd come right out and said it. The pandemic might be the worst thing ever to happen to mankind, but it might turn out to be the best thing to happen to Planet Earth.

This is not the end of the world. It's Nature's way of saving it. Self-hating scum! Whoever thinks that deserves to die!

His mother wasn't the only one in full-frontal freak.

To Cole, it was pretty exciting, albeit in a sick-making way, like watching an ultra-realistic slasher flick, or going on a roller coaster when he was still young and dumb enough to think it was a death-defying thing to do.

Men in riot gear with snarling dogs storming people storming pharmacies. It was like an extreme version of the madness of grown-ups in general.

It always gave him some satisfaction, seeing grown-ups lose control. He didn't know why. It had to do with hating them, of course, but that begged the question: When had *that* started anyway? Cole couldn't say. And though it could seem that the way he felt about his parents these days was the way he'd felt about them his whole life, he knew this wasn't so.

"This is new," his mother told her friends. "He used to be Cole the Cuddly. Now he's practically autistic."

It was true he didn't want his parents touching him. Not that he could remember the last time his father had tried. What he did remember, though, was climbing onto his father's lap and his father snapping his legs straight so that Cole slid to the floor. This had happened about four years ago. At first Cole had thought it was a game. He'd started giggling but stopped when he saw his father's face. "You're too old for that." Voice like ice.

Cole often recalled this humiliation and how he had cast about in his mind for some way to pay his father back. But now that his father was so sick, thinking about this made him want to smash something.

Hard to believe only four mornings ago he'd watched his father, dressed in his usual tan and orange running clothes, sprint toward the house just as Cole and his mother were getting into the car to drive to school. Now, inside the house (or even out on the porch), you could not escape the sound of his hacking. It tore your own throat to hear it. When his mother was there, Cole saw how every cough made her flinch, like a whip being cracked in her face.

His mother was the only one who went out anymore. When she went out she always wore the same bandanna tied over her nose and mouth. It was the only one she had and it was getting filthy, she complained. The first time Cole saw her leaving the house with the bandanna on he warned her not to walk into a bank, and they'd both laughed. Now what he noticed (but did not say) was how covering the lower part of her face made her eyes look even bigger with fright than usual.

He'd seen his mother frightened before, he'd seen her worried and upset more times than he could count, but he'd never seen her quite like this. There was another element in the mix, and it took Cole a while before he could name it: he'd never seen her trying to be brave.

"I still say we're going to be all right." She kept repeating this, each time with a sharp little thrust of her chin. "Dad's strong. Dad's going to make it. We're all going to make it. By the way, don't you have any homework?"

Completely forgetting there was no more school! They'd laughed together about that, too. And then she had started to cry.

Being brave didn't mean she could stop herself from breaking down at least once a day.

Each time she returned from having been out, she'd collapse on a chair as if she had run on her own steam to and from her destination and needed to catch her breath. Then she'd report on how much emptier the streets were, how many more places had closed, how much less there was to be found on the shelves of the stores that were still open.

After the mailman hadn't shown up two days in a row, she went to the post office and found it closed. "Imagine, not even a sign on the door. You'd think they'd at least let people know what the hell's going on."

When she finally got through to the health department hotline, all they could tell her was to keep the patient in bed and give him lots of fluids. "It took all my strength not to start screaming."

Though from time to time she did scream—about the lack of information and how inept the people in charge were—she was mostly mad at herself. For not having been prepared. For not having understood the amount of danger they were in. There was a certain forgiveness-begging air she took on when she knew she'd hurt or let someone down, an air that made her look like a punished child. No matter how angry Cole might be, whenever he saw his mother like this he'd go straight from feeling angry to feeling sorry for her, a feeling he found particularly unpleasant— far more unpleasant than anger. It could happen with his father, too, in which case the unpleasantness was even worse. Except that it was a very rare thing for Cole to feel sorry for his father.

Her last trip to the supermarket she was gone less time than usual and returned in tears.

"Now they're not even letting people inside. I had to shout through the door and tell this guy what I wanted. Then he went and collected it all in a bag and put the bag on the ground outside the door. He yelled at me not to approach the bag until he'd closed the door again. And there was this locked box to slip the money in, and if you didn't have the exact amount, tough shit, they weren't making change. And this guy was so nasty, too, shouting *Keep back! Keep back!* like I was some kind of rabid dog. Plus he had a shotgun."

Among the few things she'd brought home this time was a loaf of raisin bread, which she confessed she had found in the parking lot. "Someone must have dropped it," she said. "It seemed crazy not to take it, since we don't know when all this is going to end. My god, what a time to be stuck in the middle of fucking nowhere! As soon as Dad's feeling better, we are so out of here."

There *were* some people in town who appeared to be organized, who had managed to collect food and other necessities and had put out the word that they'd help anyone who needed them. Some of them had even started going door to door. But they were Jesus freaks, his mother said, and she didn't want to get involved with them.

"I mean, these people are actually *happy* about this catastrophe. They think any day now they're going to be sucked up to heaven."

Cole knew what his mother was talking about, but he didn't understand. If God wanted to end the world, why wouldn't he just *do* it? What was the point in giving a whole lot of people the flu first?

"Don't ask me, sweetie. These people believe all kinds of things. All I know is, they think Jews like me are going to hell just for not being Christian. Let's not talk about them anymore, it's too depressing. Why don't you toast some of that raisin bread? I'm going up to see Dad."

———————

Months later, wearing clothes that fit him but that weren't his, and with his hair cut different from the way he usually wore it, Cole would find himself sitting across from a woman he didn't know, answering questions.

So he'd never been to church before? Or any other kind of religious service? Was he sure? Religion had never been a part of family life?

They were in some kind of living room, though not in a house. Cole didn't know if the building they were in was a church. It didn't look like a church, but there was a painting of Jesus on one of the walls, and a banner in the foyer read *Heaven. Don't Miss It for the World.*

Though the room was quiet and they were not sitting far apart, the woman had to ask him twice to repeat what he'd said. Her own voice was soft but clear. A flame-haired woman with a face like a platter and a shape that brought back Tickle, his old stuffed bear. Before she started questioning him she took his picture. When she asked him to smile, he tried, but the thought of Tickle made the corners of his mouth twitch, and for all he tried he could not prevent them from turning down instead of up. It's all right, the woman said gently, and she snapped the picture anyway. She was young and kind.

Was he sure only his mother was Jewish? Then what was his father's religion?

Atheist.

Well, atheism wasn't a religion. It was the opposite of religion, the belief that there was no God.

He knew that.

So his dad was an atheist, but his mom was a Jew?

They were both atheists.

And would it be correct to say that's what he was raised to believe, too? That there was no God and that all religion was wrong?

He'd been raised to believe religion was for retards. He'd been raised to believe people who were religious did more harm than good. He'd been raised to believe that God was a myth, that religion screwed up everything, that a person didn't have to be religious in order to be a good person, that religious education of children was a kind of child abuse, and that if God did exist he'd have to be an atheist, too.

None of which he said.

And was it accurate to say that everyone else he and his family spent time with—friends, relatives—they were all un-believers, too?

Now that he thought about it, yes.

Did he understand that whatever family he'd be placed with would not be atheists but most likely people for whom church was a very big part of their lives? Who worshipped God and believed that Jesus was the son of God, and who had taken Jesus as their personal savior? How would he feel about that?

He didn't care. All he cared about was getting away from the orphanage.

❧

EVERY MINUTE THAT SHE WASN'T with his father Cole's mother wanted to be with him.

"We don't have to talk," she said. "I just want to be in the same room."

With the TV *off,* if he didn't mind. Then how would they know what was going on? The radio, she said. At least until the power went out again. It had already done so a few times, always during the day, thankfully, since they had no candles. They did have a flashlight—but where were the extra batteries?

A battery-operated radio was on the Emergency Home Preparedness must-have list, so of course they didn't have one of those, either. Nor could all the money in the world buy them one now.

"Let's face it," his mother said with her look of a punished child. "I just wasn't thinking. But with the move and all . . ."

Cole looked away from her. He was not going to feel sorry for her this time. He knew what had really been distracting her. And now what would happen when his father got well again? Would she stay or go?

It was fine with him if she didn't want the TV on, but it wasn't fine with him that she also didn't want him to listen to his iPod. If he was listening to his iPod or playing a video game or, when he was able to connect, browsing online, it was—to her—as if he wasn't really there. He wasn't *with* her the way she needed him to be. For her to be happy they had to be doing the same thing.

Meaning, if she was reading he had to be reading, too.

Why two people reading or watching TV together was okay, but one person reading and the other one listening to music was not okay—even she couldn't explain it.

Besides, he didn't want to read and she knew that. He wasn't into reading, and, *boy,* did she know *that.*

It was a major family drama, how Cole's life was going to be ruined because he didn't like to read. In fact, he'd never read a whole book all the way through, not even when he was supposed to for school. He would read only as much as he had to in order to do the assignment. Depending on the book, he might skim all the pages or he'd read a chapter or two from the beginning, middle, and end. Sometimes he'd just Google or SparkNote the book. He'd never once got into trouble for not reading a whole book—proof that reading every page could not be all that important.

He wasn't making any kind of statement. He was truly bored by most of the reading assigned at school—and he wasn't the only one. Besides, he thought his parents were wrong. The kind of reading they did was something almost no one did anymore. Lots of successful people didn't read books and the smartest kids at school weren't necessarily the biggest readers, either. Things had changed, and Cole knew you didn't have to feel bad anymore for not reading novels or poetry. Even his parents didn't read poetry. And no, he didn't feel proud that his parents had tried writing novels themselves (his mother had finished hers but couldn't get it published; his father had quit before finishing his but was planning to get back to it that summer); he felt embarrassed.

Whenever he tried to read a book recommended by one of his parents, it could keep his attention for only so long. He'd put it down one day and then never pick it up again. And just because so many other kids thought Harry Potter was dope didn't mean he had to think so, too.

All those hours Cole spent on the Internet apparently

didn't count. That wasn't reading, that was viewing, his father said.

To his parents, Cole's failing—weakness, whatever—was so bizarre, so unlikely ("It's in your *genes*!"), that they'd had him tested.

But: "I'm afraid there's no excuse, m' boy," said his father. Cole didn't have dyslexia or any other learning disability. He was just *intellectually lazy*.

And: "If you don't start reading more—if you don't develop a love of literature while you're young—you'll probably always be an underachiever." Which was what everyone seemed to agree he was now.

But there was one kind of literature he already had a love for, and that was comic books. He'd always loved comics, a love his father shared—it was his father who'd given him his first Marvel comics. But unlike his father Cole also liked sketching and doodling. He'd always wanted to create his own comic book, and once he'd even tried.

They didn't know it, but it was his parents who'd given him the idea. It began with his mother talking about how many women these days—even very young women—had thinning hair.

"At first I thought I was imagining it, but Shireen" (her friend who also happened to be a dermatologist) "confirmed it. There's an epidemic of hair loss among women of all ages. No one knows exactly why, but it must be something in the environment—they think maybe plastics."

Another time, his mother had brought up something else she'd noticed.

"When I started middle school, I remember there were just one or two really busty girls, and it was *such* a big deal. Now it's the flat-chested girl who's the exception. And look at Krystal" (the ten-year-old next door). "She's got more cleavage than I do."

In this case, too, the cause was thought to be contaminants in plastics.

Cole hadn't noticed women losing their hair until his mother had said something. As for early breasting, he had noticed a lot—you couldn't help noticing Krystal—but he hadn't realized this was something new. Some of the girls in his class were so big he had trouble believing they weren't in pain. And how could you not feel bad for them? Never to be able to sleep on your stomach—because of *growths* on your *chest*? It wasn't exactly vomitous—after all, ginormous breasts were a big part of what made a lot of apocalyptic girls apocalyptic—but it was close.

His father said, "When it's warm out and the girls come to class half naked, it looks like something out of a men's mag. I know it wasn't that good when I was in school." He roared with laughter when Cole's mother said, "I guess that's how women will look in the future: humongous boobs and no hair."

And instantly they sprang to mind: *a race of supergirls . . . bald, blimp-breasted, disc-eyed . . . with long muscular legs that they could turn into laser swords . . . supernaturally smart, although, because of some genetic defect, unable to read the alphabet . . . The Dyslexichicks, who communicated not with words but through a kind of music, like birds . . . engaged in never-ending battle with the evil Stubs, a race of short, bushy-*

haired bookworms (Cole envisioned something like troll dolls) *who wished to rid the world of all music, even the music of birds . . .*

His parents had stood by him, but still it was awful.

All he'd wanted was to show his friend Kendall, who could draw almost anything himself.

"What ya got there, boys?"

Mr. Gert. Short, bushy-haired, evil Mr. Gert.

"Mind if I have a look-see, too?" Like he was really giving them a choice.

Actually, the whole business had died pretty quickly. In confrontations like this his mother was a champ at getting the opposition to back down—not to mention expert at mimicking Gert's sibilant voice: "Sssorry, but I know pornography when I sssee it."

But in private his parents were less blasé. They were completely on his side, of course, and they thought Gert should be sssued. But they admitted that they also found Cole's drawings disturbing. The sexy girls, okay, that was a normal obsession for a boy his age. But *evil bookworms?* Here was something they needed to talk about.

They didn't say anything else about the comic book, and though Kendall had delivered his praise like a blessing—"You got the gift, dude. Use it wisely"—Cole tore up the panels he'd drawn so far. He refused to discuss the subject with his parents, until finally they dropped it. But of course every math class he still had to face Mr. Gert, who treated him like a budding perv.

Proving there really was no pleasure grown-ups couldn't spoil if they put their minds to it.

But what was *wrong* with him? With his dad so sick and his mom trying so hard to be brave—couldn't he at least have some nicer thoughts about them?

In fact, this sounded just like his mother, who not long before had complained: "It's like you get colder all the time."

That was him. He was like a glass slowly being filled with ice water.

His mother also accused him of being ashamed of his own emotions.

Back when they were still in Chicago, his class had started doing something called mindfulness training. Fifteen minutes, three times a week. It was supposed to help improve everyone's ADD. Dimmed lights, chimes, something called elevator breathing. Close your eyes, drain your head, focus on your breath rising and falling. Lame. Cole breathed normally and let his mind wander. Which was how he found himself back in the summer when he was nine and his parents had gone away for two weeks without him. A friend of theirs had been getting married somewhere in Ireland, and after the wedding they wanted to visit Aunt Addy in Germany. Meanwhile, Cole would go to sleepaway camp, where he'd been wanting to go anyway, having heard from other kids that camp was awesome.

A perfect plan, but they were all anxious about it. After all, they'd never spent more than a night apart before, and Europe was so far away . . . Cole would always remember their goodbyes, the three of them on the verge of tears and at the same time laughing and teasing one another for being such big sillies.

And it wasn't that he'd had a bad time. Camp *was* awesome. The counselors were much better than teachers at breaking up cliques and keeping bullies in line, and in two weeks he'd gone from being a spastic swimmer to an almost smooth one.

It wasn't exactly that he was homesick, either. But never having been away from his parents before, he was unprepared for what it would mean to miss them. Even before the end of the first week, he was spending at least part of each day in agony. He kept it secret, of course; he didn't want to look like a baby, and homesick kids were often teased or avoided.

It was worse at night, when, lying on his cot in the pitch dark with nothing to distract him, his longing bloomed into a kind of insanity. For the first time in his life he had trouble sleeping. He could not shake the fear that something would stop his parents from coming home. Things happened, didn't they? Planes got hijacked. Buildings caught fire . . .

He dreamed that they had returned and had brought a strange boy with them. An ordinary-looking innocent-seeming little boy who wanted to be Cole's friend. But in the dark world of the dream, Cole knew without a doubt that the boy's appearance spelled his own doom. But you *asked* for a brother, his parents kept saying. Perplexed; annoyed.

And then, at last, their ecstatic reunion, it, too, like something out of a dream—but how could something that makes you so happy also make you feel like you were being beat up?

This was love, but it was also terror, and Cole didn't know what to make of it.

And now, he did not like to remember that time. Because even though it was about something happy, something good, it had become only painful to remember. And that particular day in school it had been too much to bear. Had it happened in the middle of a lesson, he would have had some major explaining to do. But mindfulness training was known to make some kids emo, and Cole's excuse, that he absolutely had to get to the bathroom, no time to raise his hand, was accepted without comment.

And it wasn't the teacher but Cole himself who sternly warned: *Don't you ever let that happen again.*

His mother was right. He was ashamed. He was totally ashamed even to have such feelings, let alone have them found out.

Later, when he was in the hospital, a volunteer grief counselor would come to see him. She took him out to the courtyard, where roses the size of melons were in bloom.

"What I'd like you to do for me," she said, "is to think back to a time when you and your mom and dad were all very happy, and describe that time for me." The woman's name was Eden. She was not a comforting sight. She had hooded eyes and deep dark lines running down her cheeks as if she had wept acid. They sat on a bench near a small fountain whose gurgle sounded like birdsong. There was real birdsong, too, and it almost hurt his ears, it was so shrill and excited. The day was cloudy. He had not been outdoors in weeks and he was sharply aware of the light and the air, almost as if he were experiencing them for the first time. Though he was well covered up, he felt naked. The least breeze made him shiver. The smell of the roses was strong, almost sickening, like the perfume of old ladies.

He didn't want to talk about the happy time, and so he invented something, some story that he then forgot almost immediately. But he would remember later how he'd gone on and on, dragging the fake story out, and how Eden had listened, watching him curiously, not interrupting until he finally stopped talking. Then she made no comment except to thank him for sharing. He had no idea if she knew that he'd lied. But it seemed to him that as she listened her mouth had tensed and something like dislike had crept into her face.

❦

COUGH, COUGH, COUGH, COUGH, COUGH.

It followed you everywhere, like footsteps. But then came worse.

It was as if behind the bedroom door Cole's father had split into several different people who could be heard at different times chattering, arguing, laughing, and once even singing with one another. Cole listened, his blood running cold.

"Get out, get out, you spider cunt! I'll kill you, Serena!"

Cole nearly collided with his mother as they both ran out into the hall. There was no color in her face. "Dad doesn't know what he's saying." But he kept saying it, over and over.

Once, he found her slumped on the landing with her legs tucked under her and her hands over her ears. Behind the door his father was calling, "Mom! Mom!"

Fever dream, his mother explained. "He's back in his childhood."

Yes. But why did he sound so scared?

Middle of the night. Cole woke to hear his parents talking. To his surprise, the noise (why were they being so loud?) came not from their room down the hall but from downstairs.

So his father's fever must have broken. He was probably in the kitchen, getting something to eat. He'd be starving, of course; he'd eaten hardly anything this past week. Cole wanted to see him! He wanted to go down and join his parents—but not if they were fighting. Wait—how could they already be fighting? And where did his father get the strength to raise his voice? Had his mother picked now of all times to announce that she was leaving? This, Cole could not believe. The only explanation was that Cole was still asleep; he was dreaming . . .

Morning. He found his mother in the kitchen, alone. She was sitting at the table, her laptop open in front of her. Instead of her bathrobe she was wearing her winter coat. His father wasn't there. He wasn't upstairs in bed, either. The door to his room had been wide open when Cole passed on his way down.

Before he could form the question, his mother spoke. "I'm sorry," was all she said.

Cole's head started jerking helplessly from side to side, as if someone were taking swings at him. The pounding in his ears was so fierce it felt like a sudden loss of hearing.

"But I heard him last night—"

"Don't shout," she whispered. She stood up and embraced him. They staggered together, gripping each other for support, a macabre little waltz. She let go of him then and coaxed

68

him down onto a chair, saying, "Sit, sit, sit." They were both crying.

She went to the fridge and took out a bottle of water. She took a glass from the cupboard and filled it with water and carried it to the table and set it in front of him. Every movement careful and slow, as if even the least gave her pain.

Cole stared at the water as if he had no idea what it was.

She gripped the edge of the table with both hands. "I have to lie down before I pass out." Her voice was a croak; her eyes looked as if someone had tried to scratch them out. "I've been up all night."

He wanted to help her. He picked up the glass and tried to give it to her but she waved it away.

She didn't want to climb the stairs. Without taking off her coat she stretched out on the living room couch, resting her heels on one of the arms so that her feet were higher than her head. Cole knelt on the floor beside her. He sucked in his lips to stop them from trembling.

It wasn't his father he'd heard, she said. His father had been unconscious.

"He needed to get to a hospital, but I knew I'd never get an ambulance to come here." She had run out into the street and started knocking on doors. Two houses down lived a retired widower—the owner of the chocolate Lab that sometimes roamed the neighborhood—who'd agreed to come back with her.

"I wanted him to help me carry Dad to the car. He tried talking me out of it. He said the hospital wouldn't be able to do anything. But I wouldn't listen. I hung on to his arm, I begged him until he gave in."

"Why didn't you wake *me*, Mom?"

"Oh, sweetie, I don't know." She looked at him imploringly. "I wasn't sure, I didn't think it would help if you—yes, maybe I should have woken you. Can you understand why I didn't think so at the time?"

Cole nodded, but inside he was screaming. He remembered waking up to the noise and how he'd decided against going downstairs. Mistake! Mistake!

The man wouldn't go with her to the hospital, she said. Suddenly she began to sob. "Why did we come here? We never should have come!" She sat up and gazed around the room with a look of terror. "We never should have come!" She was sobbing so hard Cole could barely make out the words.

He said nothing. He felt utterly helpless, under a spell, without the power even to put his arms around her. How would they live? How would they live without his father?

His mother had let herself fall back. She was still sobbing, but quietly, and Cole let her be. Minutes passed—he had no idea how many—and he saw her fall asleep, or pass out. A river of fear ran through him. He didn't want to be alone.

"Mom!"

Her eyes flew open. For an instant she looked blind.

"I'm sorry," she said. "I can't stay awake anymore."

Cole thought again of that old movie, the one where falling asleep meant worse than death. The one whose hero had the same name as his father.

"Let me sleep just a little," she slurred, eyes closing again. He was alone.

He got up and drifted back into the kitchen. He took a sip of water from the glass sitting on the table and poured the rest down the sink. How clean the kitchen was, all neat and shiny. The whole house was like that. It was one of his mother's ways of dealing with stress. If my hands are busy I'm not wringing them, she said. At other times, the house was a mess.

He sat down at her laptop and tapped the touchpad.

Addy, the worst has happened. Miles had a heart attack and died last night. I've been trying to call you but can never get through. I'm writing now mostly just for something to do until Cole wakes up. I don't know how I'm going to tell him. I swore to him Miles was going to get over the flu, and technically he didn't die of the flu, though I was told the attack was probably triggered by inflammation caused by the virus. I had to ask a stranger to help me get Miles to the hospital. He kept telling me it wouldn't do any good and I knew he was right, but if Miles was past saving I was determined at least to get his body out of the house. I didn't want to be like all those poor people forced to live with their dead or secretly dump them somewhere. What will happen to his body now I don't know, I suppose it will be burned, or buried in some mass grave. My god, I can't believe I just wrote that. I feel like a big part of me still hasn't taken it in.

I'm not sure how much Miles understood what was happening, either. His last lucid moment was around noon two days ago, when for a little while he was able to breathe a bit more freely and he could talk. And he looked at me with tears in his eyes and said, We blew it, baby. I still don't know what he meant. I thought he might have been talking about us separating, but it's possible he was talking about the flu and how we'd blown our chance to get away. He may not have realized there was nowhere to go. But these were his last words to me, and I will never get over that. I can't bear to think of him dying under the weight of such a heavy regret. And it was the first time he called me baby in such a long time.

But I can't let myself think like this right now or I'll go mad. I've got to think about Cole. And now that I've been to the hospital and seen with my own eyes what it's like, I couldn't live with myself if I didn't try to do something. I've made up my mind to volunteer at the clinic they've set up at the college, at least for a few hours a day. It will mean leaving Cole home by himself but I think he'll understand. Besides, if I'm around him all the time it just gets on his nerves. Poor Cole. When I think of all the trouble we've been having with him, how badly he's doing in school and how cold and sullen he's gotten with me, and now he's even smoking on the sly—how small all these problems seem now. Can you imagine losing Mom or Dad when we were that age, and without even being able to say good-bye?

Cole stopped scrolling and went upstairs to get his cigarettes.

It was chilly outside but he didn't put on a jacket. He paced back and forth on the porch, shivering, as he smoked a Marlboro down to the butt—first time he'd ever smoked a whole cigarette all at once. *Cough, cough, cough.* It stung his lungs and made him so woozy he had to sit down. He was afraid he might throw up.

The sky was the solid blue of any fine Midwestern winter day. Across the street, on the graveled drive, the calico sat cleaning itself just as if the end of the world were not taking place.

She should have woken him. It was all wrong. *She was always wrong!* He felt the heat expanding in his chest, the heat of his rage, but at the same time he was ashamed, for to be so angry at his mother now was all wrong, too.

He stared up the street, toward the house of the man who'd been in their house last night, an old geezer Cole had only glimpsed once or twice. Lumber jacket, ear-flap hat. One of the last people to touch his father. Cole beamed his anger there. That man should have stayed with his mother. That man should have done more to help them!

Cole was freezing now, his teeth actually chattering so that he bit his tongue. He went back inside.

A whole Marlboro turned out to be way strong—almost strong enough to knock you out.

He weaved up the stairs, but instead of going to his own room he found himself walking into his parents' room and diving into their rumpled bed. Immediately, his father's smell engulfed him. He pulled the covers over his shivering body, he pulled them up over his head, he burrowed his face in the pillow, inhaling the smell of his father.

The bed went slowly round and round, borne on a lazy tornado.

His mother was lying. His father was gone—hadn't she

wanted to be rid of him?—but he wasn't dead. It was part of her plan. Maybe his father was in on it, too. They had plotted together to *pretend* he was dead . . .

Later Cole would call this the sickest and craziest thought he'd ever had.

His parents had talked to him about death. They had talked about it at length after his grandparents died. What had they said? That it was irrational for a person to be afraid of death because if you were dead you didn't know you were dead, and how could you be afraid of something you didn't know. But also that it was perfectly natural to be afraid. Even people who got to live a long time weren't happy to die, they said. Death was always tragic, they said. But the worst tragedy was to have your life cut short. To die young.

When he thought about it, though, Cole didn't believe it would be such a bad thing to die. Even before the pandemic began, he'd caught himself thinking this. It was another one of his secrets (he knew his life would become unbearable if his parents ever found out). He imagined the actual moment of dying as something like sinking into Lake Michigan: deeper and deeper, colder and colder, darker and darker. He imagined it was something like being frozen stiff. And then you'd be dead but you wouldn't know you were dead, so you couldn't feel bad. You couldn't feel anything. You'd be free. Never to have to worry again about how people were looking at you, or talking about you. Never to have to pretend how awesome it was to be alive, how lucky to be a kid, enjoying every minute of your precious kid time.

A few weeks earlier, someone in Chicago had called to tell them Cole's old classmate Ruthie Lind had died. It wasn't that

Cole hadn't felt sad for Ruthie; he'd felt very sad, even if he hadn't cried. But he'd felt something else as well. A funny, nagging, must-keep-secret feeling. And already many times since hearing the news he'd caught himself thinking, *She got out.*

But his parents believed life was too short no matter when you died. They hated growing older, and once, when they heard Cole tell someone his grandmother had died because she was old, they had rushed to correct him. Sixty wasn't old, they explained, it was middle-aged. And to *die* at sixty was to die *young.*

His father was forty-nine.

His father had wanted to live forever. That was why he ran every morning.

Cole wanted to know, though he knew no one could ever tell him, if somehow, at the moment you died, you understood what was happening to you. He tried to imagine then how his father might have felt, and he could not imagine this except as something extremely frightening and painful. He could not believe that, in his father's last seconds, there had been any thought of rest or quiet or sleep or peace. What he imagined his father seeing and smelling and hearing was a saber-toothed tiger pouncing to tear him apart.

The year before, his father had had some kind of symptom, some stomach pain, and he'd gone to the doctor, who ordered some tests, one of which came back "iffy." The doctor had ordered more tests, and it was while they were waiting for the results that Cole had seen what a hard time his father was having. Though his father had gone about his business as usual, it was clear in everything he did, including repeating the same joke—at which his mother always laughed dutifully, though each time with a little more strain: "Who has time to die?" The day the doctor called with good news his father said he felt ten years younger. "And you look it, too!" said his mother, dabbing at tears of relief.

From time to time Cole had sat in on a class that his father was teaching. In fact, the last time he'd done this had been just three weeks ago. He had sat in on one of his father's lectures. It was a happy memory. His father complained endlessly about teaching, but that day he was clearly enjoying himself, and Cole had been particularly impressed with how he held the attention of those fifty or so students, even getting a couple of good laughs out of them. Anyone would have thought he and Abe Lincoln were bros. Cole remembered how bitter his father had been about not getting tenure. "If it was up to the kids, it'd be a different story. Just read their evaluations." The students loved him, his father insisted, and whenever he said this Cole would wonder how those students would feel if they knew what awful things Professor Vining said about them and how much he made fun of them, sometimes reading from their papers to his mother, the two of them roaring with laughter.

When the lecture was over, several students crowded around his father while Cole waited, staring at one girl with multicolored hair and glossy red-black lips and jeans so low-slung he could actually see some hair. She waited till the others were gone before approaching his father, and Cole had watched as she flirted with his father and his father flirted back.

And later, at the restaurant they'd gone to for lunch, his father had flirted with the waitress. Usually it bothered Cole when his father paid attention to young women, which he did any time Cole's mother wasn't around. But that day for some reason Cole hadn't minded. His father was having a good day. He'd had a good run, taught a good class, and in the space of an hour two pretty young women had shown their attraction to him. Cole knew his father was proud of his fit body and his still-thick, mostly still-black hair, and how happy it made him when people thought he was much younger than he was. That day, he was wearing a turquoise shirt that made his blue eyes almost glow. People were always saying what beautiful eyes he had. The kind of eyes, his mother said, that flirt all by themselves.

There would be a time when the thought that he'd never see his father again would crush Cole with a weight he feared he could not survive. But what he felt mostly in those first hours of grief was overwhelming sadness for his father himself. He felt sorry for his father, who would never see or do anything in the world again—more sorry than he had ever felt for anybody in his life. He saw how terrible it must be to be afraid to die, to want to live and live, and to not have any power to change what was going to happen to you. He told himself he would have been willing to die in his father's place—he would have done anything to save his father! And maybe if he had gone downstairs last night instead of going back to sleep, maybe he could have done something.

Why was he trying so hard to stop crying when he knew there was nothing wrong with crying, when the wrong thing would have been for him *not* to cry, and anyway there was no one to see? What did it say about him that he had an overwhelming desire to masturbate and that he did not think he was going to be able to resist?

They were on a motorcycle, it was nighttime, and Cole

was very tired—too tired to hold on tight to his father's waist. He kept falling asleep. His father had to keep reaching back with one arm to catch him, and each time he did this the bike veered and wobbled and they nearly crashed, until they did crash, and Cole sat up with a splitting head and a shout loud enough to wake his mother.

It was completely up to him, she said. If he didn't want her to go, she'd stay home.

"I know it must seem weird to you that I'd want to be with a bunch of strangers right now, but my sitting around here crying isn't going to help anyone. And you know the best thing for me is to keep my hands busy. But you still come first, Cole. You just have to tell me if you don't want to be alone, even for a couple of hours."

She asked him if he was feeling okay and he lied and said yes, hoping she wouldn't feel his forehead. If she knew the truth, she'd never leave.

She made him promise to keep the door locked and not let anyone in. "Even if they tell you Jesus sent them."

"There's still some raisin bread and some peanut butter, I think, though unfortunately not much else. I'll try to bring some food back with me. My god." She shook her head rapidly back and forth, as if to throw off her own unbearable thoughts. "It's like we're in a movie, isn't it? Or some crazy survival show. Oh, Cole, do you absolutely swear to me you'll be okay?"

He nodded, and she went to hug him. He twisted awkwardly in her embrace, hating himself when she pulled away and he saw her eyes brim.

It was hard, but he said it. "Bye, Mom. Love you."

"I love you, too," she said with a look she might have given someone who'd just saved her from drowning.

He wanted to ask her something, but he couldn't. He wanted to ask if sleeping in his father's sheets could have given him the flu. He hadn't thought about it yesterday when he crawled into bed. It had struck him only after he woke up, and he'd left the room in a hurry so his mother wouldn't find him there. He thought of the story about the American pioneers who gave blankets infested with smallpox to the Indians in the hope of killing them all off. The idea that he might have caught the flu from his father and that he, too, might soon be dead was both thrilling and terrifying.

If it was true—if he really was infected—he wanted to keep it from his mother as long as possible. But now he saw that this could not be very long: his mother was hardly gone from the house when he started coughing.

PART TWO

PART TWO

He had missed so much school, he figured he was going to have to repeat seventh grade. But since this had to be true for so many other kids as well, it didn't really bother him. He was even feeling a little excited about being back in school again. Then Pastor Wyatt told him to get ready for something different.

"I know the idea of homeschooling probably scares you somewhat. I'll bet you've heard all kinds of nonsense on the subject, but you've just got to give it a chance. And anyhow, the nearest school still open round here is so far away you'd have to spend a couple hours just getting there and back each day. And I'm pretty sure you wouldn't like that, now, would you, son."

Back when he was still in school, in Little Leap—and before that, in Chicago—Cole had been aware of kids who were taught at home by their parents, even though their parents weren't real teachers. But he'd never actually known anyone who was being homeschooled. Now it was just the opposite. Cole didn't know any kid in Salvation City who wasn't being homeschooled. Most of their parents had been homeschooled when they were growing up, too.

From now on his teachers would be Tracy and Pastor Wyatt. But it turned out the only subject he studied with PW was the Bible.

"I know all this is new to you, so I have to explain some.

But if you aren't studying *the* Book, there isn't much point in studying any other book. When we're reading Scripture, that is one of the times—another is when we pray—when we're able to bring ourselves closer to God. It's when he sees we're paying attention to him and trying to get at his truth. In fact, when we're engaged in reading the Bible with our absolute undivided attention, it really amounts to the same thing as prayer. We're not saying that math and science and all the other subjects aren't important. We're saying the Bible is altogether something else. Those other subjects will teach you plenty of things that are good to know, but all of them put together can't teach you how you should live."

Among the many books in Cole's parents' library had been a Bible, but the only thing he remembered about it was that it was the most ridiculously long book he'd ever seen. He could not imagine anyone reading it.

"Uh-oh," said PW. "I see that look on your face, and you can just chill right there. Nobody's saying you've got to learn everything in a day. We're going to take things slow, and trust me, nobody's going to make you sit in a corner and read the whole Bible cover to cover like some kind of punishment. So wipe that frown off and come give me a hug."

It had taken some getting used to, PW's eagerness to hug and be hugged. At first Cole had dreaded these moments, when he never knew quite where to place his hands or which way to turn his head. His face would color and he would hold his breath and stare at the floor. After a while, though, he lost his excruciating shyness and awkwardness, and now there were times when he wished it weren't over so quickly, that PW would keep holding him longer.

————

They do not start with Genesis. The first thing Cole learns is the Lord's Prayer. Some of it sounds familiar to him, though he knows he has never learned it before, he has never learned any prayer before. PW shows him where in the Bible the Lord's Prayer is from.

"You see, it didn't make sense for people to go on praying in the same old ways as before. Because Jesus' coming changed everything. What he was bringing to the world was something completely new, so there had to be a new way of praying, too. And Jesus told his disciples not to pray like hypocrites, making a big deal out of it, making sure everyone sees them doing it and using a lot of show-offy words. Pray like this, he said, and he taught them these very words you're learning now, over two thousand years later. Short and simple, yet somehow encompassing all: thankfulness, forgiveness, a plea for help in avoiding sin, and praise of God."

Cole learns the prayer easily, and then PW teaches him another prayer, or psalm, rather, from another part of the Bible. Again, Cole recognizes some of the words. *The valley of the shadow of death. Fear no evil.* He has come across those words many times before, in movies and comics and video games, but without ever knowing where they were from.

Cole is amazed that anyone could do what PW does: open that ginormous book to exactly whatever passage he is looking for. And he is amazed that anyone would spend hours every day studying something he already knows so well.

"Ah," said PW. "Your mistake there is in thinking the Bible is just another—albeit ginormous—book. Even those of us who've read and reread every word, we don't ever put the Bible away. Why? Because God inspired Scripture precisely so he and us could always be in communication with each other. The Bible may be ancient, but it ain't 'history.' It's today's news, every day. And we call the story of Jesus the Gospel, or Evangel, because those words mean 'good news.'"

They do not have set hours for their Bible study—they have to work around PW's busy schedule—but often they sit down together for a half-hour or so after supper. Tracy never joins them, but she reads the Bible on her own every day, and every Wednesday night she meets with her women's Bible group.

Cole also has a Bible study group, which is only for boys and girls his age and meets on Saturday mornings. There is Bible study for children of every age, even those who haven't yet learned to read, and several different groups for adults. Besides one for only women, there is one for only men. There is one for couples and one for singles, and there are other groups, called workshops, for people in some particular kind of trouble, such as drinking too much or post-traumatic stress from the panflu. Most of the groups meet at the church, but some, like the women's group, meet at different persons' homes. Whenever it's Tracy's turn to host, she bakes a red velvet cake and, for the dieters, Weight Watchers' brownies.

When Cole hears about a workshop to help married people stay together, he thinks about his parents. He wonders, if they hadn't died . . .

But it is becoming harder and harder for Cole to remember his parents clearly. Partly because of his illness, which burned away or distorted so much of his memory. (He understands better now what his father meant when he explained what

Alzheimer's disease had done to Cole's grandfather.) Partly because his life today is so different from his life before. He has a new home, he lives in a new town—still in southern Indiana but east of Little Leap. Called Salvation City, though not a city, not like Chicago, and not even as big as Little Leap.

And, for the first time, Cole has a church. The Church of Salvation City, which Cole figured was named after the town, but in fact it was the other way around. As the story goes, the church had been founded in 1995. It was for the millennium five years later that the residents voted to change the town's name from whatever it was (Cole can never recall) to Salvation City, too. Not every Salvation Citian belongs to the church, though even some who do not might come hear Pastor Wyatt preach at one of the three worship services offered on Sunday. Some people go to the Baptist church in the next town, and some don't go to any church at all. Cole has little to do with those who don't go to church, but when he sees them, downtown, say, or at the mall, he can't tell any difference about them. Many greet Pastor Wyatt as warmly as any member of his flock. There are times when PW will approach a person in public, whether it's someone he knows or not, and say, "Are you ready?" or "Have you thought about the Ten Commandments today?" And if the answer is no and the person gives him a chance, he'll explain what horrible danger the person is in and how they can be saved. There are some who've been approached by PW so often already that when they see him they try to avoid him. Mr. Hix, who owns the hardware store, always grins broadly at PW but stops him before he can even open his mouth: "Not today, brother, I got work to do."

Most things Cole remembers about the near past seem to

have happened much longer ago—years and years ago—and to have less and less to do with him as the days go by. He does not always feel that he belongs in Salvation City—at least, not the way he thinks everyone else belongs—but he has no desire to leave, either. And anyway, where would he go? Back to the orphanage?

But there are moments when he is struck by a sense of loss so keen, it's like an ax splitting him down the middle. The agony of seeing his parents become more and more ghostly. He has dreamed of them, standing side by side and waving to him from across some kind of empty stadium. Their waves are strikingly different: his father's arm almost straight, making slow, sweeping arcs, as if he were guiding a kite; his mother's hand close to her body and moving rapidly back and forth, like someone trying to rub out a stain. Then, although it's indoors, there is smoke, or fog. Closing in, making it harder and harder to see, denser and denser until it's impossible to tell if his parents are still waving, or if they're even still there. A dream turned throat-clogging nightmare.

"It might help," the woman called Eden had told him, "if you talked to them. You know, imagine your mom or dad is right there with you and you're having a chat. A good time to do this might be at night, right before you go to sleep."

And that night he had tried, but it had felt too strange. He couldn't pretend like that—it was not his way. And then he dreamed that he was indeed trying to talk with his father. But his father was speaking the language of the dead. He kept getting madder and madder at Cole for not understanding him. Finally, he punched Cole in the face. In real life his father had never hit him, but the dream punch came as no surprise. To Cole it seemed woeful but natural, even inevitable. Deserved. He'd half woken up, and when he drifted off again he dreamed that his parents had shrunk to the size of gerbils. He carried them around with him in a Tupperware bowl. He fed them jelly beans and nuts.

At first glance anybody—not just the kids in Bible group—would have found the group leader scary. One of his eyes is dead and lies buried under a patch of purple scar tissue. He has some fierce tattoos—snakeheads, skulls—and his head is shaved like a skinhead's. A silver stud through his right earlobe reminds Cole of a bullet.

Everyone knows Mason Boyle's story because he has told it during the part of Sunday worship when members of the congregation are invited to testify. They know about the fight in the bar where he lost his eye to "this other punk" wielding a broken bottle, and how that was even worse luck than it sounded. As a child Mason had been afflicted with lazy eye, and the vision in that eye had always been blurred and weak. The eye he lost in the fight was his other eye, the one with 20/20 vision.

"I was cast down so low, I hoped to die. I was so mad at the world, if I could've seen 'em I'd have punched out everyone who dared cross my path."

But then Mason started noticing something.

"My left eye—my bad, lazy eye—seemed to be getting stronger."

It took about a year, Mason's hardworking eye making a little more progress each day, until it was as good as his dead eye used to be.

"And then, man, it just kept going! I mean, my left eye actually got *better*. Doctor said she never saw anything like it, but today this here eye is twenty-*ten*!"

Even if they'd already heard the story, people would roar when Mason got to this part. And they would hoot and stomp and clap as he told the rest so that he had to raise his voice louder and louder.

"It was like God had taken pity on me, and not just a little-bitty pity but enough to forgive the fact that I had only myself to blame. Because, don't you know, I *picked* the fight in the bar that night. And I started thinking it was a miracle, and that within that miracle was a message for me. A message about blindness and healing. A message about laziness and strength. A message about work—about doing double duty and being rewarded with brand-new vision.

"And I knew that God was calling on me to put aside all my lazy, shameful, devil-delighting habits and to receive what he was holding out: a chance to accept his love and forgiveness and make myself worthy of the vision with which he'd blessed me. Mason the sinner had a new life, and Mason had a mission. Mason was blind no more. Now he must help the blind."

Mason earns his worldly living fixing cars. But as part of his selfless service, he helps make Braille Bibles.

Cole likes Mason—all the kids do—and he feels foolish for ever having found him scary. But secretly he wishes he did not have to study Bible with him.

Whenever Pastor Wyatt talks about the Bible, whether he's

preaching a sermon or talking on *Heaven's A-Poppin'!* or studying at home alone with Cole, he always makes it sound as if it had all just happened yesterday and he himself had been there. When he tells the story of Jesus, it's as if he'd seen it all with his own eyes—the miracles, the Crucifixion—and Cole is captivated by his big voice and the way he moves his hands, floating them up and down like white birds.

"I'm too deaf to catch most of what he's saying," Cole has heard an old lady sitting behind him in church say. "But I feel blessed just watching him."

"You want to teach folks, you got to hold their attention," says PW. "Won't do if they're bored."

But in Bible group Cole is often bored. In fact, Bible group reminds him a lot of school and of the kind of assignment he never liked. *(Imagine that you, like the narrator, are drafted into the army to fight a war that you think is wrong. What would you do?)* There is always a topic with a peppy title ("The Beatitudes vs. Bad Attitudes"), and though Mason picks the topic he has a rule about not doing much of the talking. He has another rule, about everyone having to write something about every topic.

"Okay, dudes, listen up. Say a Martian lands on Earth and this Martian comes up to you and he goes, 'What's this thing you Earthlings call Gospel?' How would you define it for him? Say a secular kid tells you his mama told him Jesus' story is nothing but a myth. How would you prove to this kid—without dissing his mama!—that she's wrong? Cite verses but use your own words."

But the worst assignments are the ones that are supposed to be fun. *Rewrite the Beatitudes as hip-hop verses.* The kind of thing that used to make Cole hate school.

But the other kids *do* have fun writing the hip-hop verses. And even when they might not like an assignment, they never get sullen or sarcastic or make a big show of how bored they are. And in this way Bible study is totally different from school. The other kids are happy to be there, and most of them throw themselves into the work. They want to please Mason, and they want to please God. Doesn't Cole?

Mason sees all. Mason is not fooled. Mason teases Cole for not paying attention, for not really trying, and though he does it gently Cole is humiliated, he is ashamed, he knows it's his same old problem. He has always been a bad student. Lazy, like Mason's left eye. He will always be an underachiever. Everything has changed, but not this.

Mason sees all. "Never give up on yourself, little bruh. Moses was once a basket case."

And in fact, it isn't that Cole doesn't want to learn. He loves the Bible stories. He thinks Daniel and Samson and David are superheroes. Every day he looks forward to the half-hour after supper that he spends with PW in the den. Cole has his own Bible, of course, but at these times they share an illustrated coffee-table-book-sized edition laid open on PW's desk. They sit close together, and sometimes PW drapes his arm around Cole, and the weight and warmth of that thick arm on his narrow shoulders (like a friendly boa constrictor, Cole thinks) calm whatever jitters he might be having. When they are finished for the evening, PW kisses the side of Cole's head. Once, he kept his lips pressed to Cole's temple an extra beat and sniffed, saying, "You smell like a good boy to me," and though Cole was embarrassed he was also pleased.

At first, when the inspiration comes to him, he puts off telling PW, afraid he might disapprove. But PW could not be more enthusiastic, and though Tracy's response is not as important to him as PW's, Cole is thrilled to hear her gush.

"Such a fine likeness of a lion! Nothing cowardly 'bout *him*, is there? And if that ain't the darnedest scariest Goliath I've ever seen. Look, WyWy, he went and made Samson look like our Mason."

Soon everyone in Salvation City knows about Cole's gift, and besides his Bible-hero comics he is emboldened to try sketches—some cartoonish, some not—from life.

He is skillful beyond his years, and he knows it. The only good thing to come out of his days at Here Be Hope.

Two strokes of luck in that place where luck was essential to survive. First, he happened to be right there when a donation of art supplies arrived, and he'd managed to grab a supply of sketch pads and colored pens and pencils before they ran out (in that place where *everything* could be expected, almost instantly, to run out). Second, he had found a spot no one else seemed to know about (a cavity under some back stairs), where he could hide for hours without being disturbed.

In that hiding place he drew and drew. He hadn't drawn anything in a while—not since the awful business with Mr. Gert. Now, in a flash, he finished a whole book about gladiators and was working on another one about mutant girl samurai. Works he was extremely proud of. Lost!

Sadly, those drawings had not made it to Salvation City. But Cole had let himself cry over this only once. For a while he consoled himself with the fantasy that they would be found by someone who would immediately recognize Cole's talent. Then, no stone would be left unturned until the artist had been tracked down. And when they saw how young he was, he imagined people would shake their heads in disbelief. Probably this would all happen soon. Any day now, Cole Abrams Vining, boy wonder, would be discovered. From this, everything a boy could wish for would follow. But success would not spoil him. In fact, riches and fame would only increase his natural-born goodness. He would never forget the little people. And despite his own terrible childhood, how unfair life had been to him and all the suffering he'd had to endure, he would always be loving and generous, noble and kind.

THERE IS NO SUCH THING AS AN ORPHAN, says Pastor Wyatt. Everyone has a father in God. But Cole knows it's because he's an orphan that everyone is so nice to him. His whole life, people have never been so nice to him as they are in Salvation City. There are other children here who've lost parents. There is a girl named Michaela, who, like Cole, lost both. But unlike Cole, Michaela has family who survived the flu: a sister and a brother. Michaela's case is unique, though, because she never knew her birth parents. A janitor found her in a high school gym locker when she was just a day old. So in a way Michaela has been orphaned twice.

Cole has heard it said that Michaela might be a rapture child. He has heard Tracy say it to PW. "Sometimes I think I can see her aura."

The first time Cole ever heard of rapture children was at

the orphanage, where there were three: a boy and two girls. Rapture children had been around before, but since the pandemic there were lots more of them. Rapture children were children who'd been sent by God to be lights in the coming dark. They would be among the first of the living to be caught up to Jesus' side (right after the holy dead). God had endowed them with special spiritual powers so they could lead others in the countdown to the final battle. Though PW says there is nothing in the Bible to justify this, Tracy is among those who believe it.

Tracy has a niece named Starlyn who is a rapture child.

The rapture children at Here Be Hope got so much attention, naturally everyone wanted to be one. Some kids declared themselves raptures and would do almost anything—including lie through their teeth—to prove it. But only grown-ups could say who was or was not a rapture child.

Cole has heard about rapture children performing heroic deeds and even miracles—the boy at the orphanage was said to have run into a burning house to rescue a baby when he was hardly more than a baby himself—but Cole has never seen anything like that. The older of the two girls said that every night when she knelt to pray, Jesus came and stroked her hair. But Cole has learned that seeing Jesus, or at least conversing with him, is not such a rare event.

Some rapture children are unusually gifted. Michaela plays music without having been taught and sings like an angel (there are those who insist rapture children *are* angels). But though everyone says Cole is gifted, too, no one has ever said he might be a rapture child.

One thing all the rapture children Cole has met have in

common is that they are good-looking. Almost every one of them is blond. (Michaela's hair is so pale it's more white than yellow; from the back you might even mistake her for an old woman.)

The biggest difference Cole can tell between rapture children and other children is that raptures have a way of making adults happy without even trying. He has seen Starlyn walk into a room and people light up as they do when dessert is set in front of them. He has heard grown men and women pour out their hearts to twelve-year-old Michaela, asking for her advice about grown-up things—should they take this new job, should they have another baby—or for her blessing. The same kind of thing that had happened in the orphanage. Some of the other orphans were a little afraid of the rapture children because of this power they had with the adults. And Cole is a little afraid of Michaela. The way she always seems to be either laughing or crying. The way, in church, she is able to keep singing out strong even with tears streaming down her face. A girl with almost no meat on her bones and enormous hungry-looking eyes. There would not be enough hours in the day for her to fill all the requests she got from people to pray for them.

Cole is afraid of Starlyn, too. But that is love (and a secret).

Though there is no Bible story about them, Cole would like to do a comic book about rapture children.

"Did you used to be one?" Even before he asks PW this, Cole knows the answer is yes. But PW gives a loud whoop as if Cole had said something crazy.

"Me? Oh my, no, no, no. I was—my mama would tell you—I was more of a—of a *reptile* child." And when Cole looks confused, PW stops laughing and says, "It don't matter, Cole. It don't matter what kind of child a person is. Like the song goes, Jesus loves all the little children." And he opens the Bible to Mark 10:13, to show Cole where it is written.

"CHILDREN TELL TALE OF REAL-LIFE 'LORD OF THE FLIES.'"

Pastor Wyatt had saved a copy of the article that had set him on the path leading to Cole. But long before that story appeared, he'd been preaching against the new orphanages.

"First we had all these horror stories about our inefficient and overburdened foster-care system resulting in all these abused and neglected kids. Then we had people saying why not bring back the old institutions? Why not dump all those kids in a group home and have the government be in charge? Can't possibly be worse than what we got now. As if the solution to 'the system's broken' was 'break it some other how.' But Jesus tells us straight out how he felt about children: the kingdom of God is theirs. And whoever seeks to live in the kingdom must love the children as he loved them. Meaning it is our inescapable duty to find Christian families for each and every child. And if that means moving children from parts of the country where good Christian families are hard to find to parts of the country where they are the majority, then I say that's what we should do."

Most people avoided calling them orphanages. They called them children's homes instead. And in the beginning, most home children weren't orphans at all but kids who'd been taken away from their parents. And although the homes might not have been the happiest places in the world for a young child to be, at least in the beginning they were safe and clean, the children got three meals a day and decent clothes, and, like other children, they were sent to school.

Before the pandemic the homes were kept as small as possible, and there were people who were angry about the expense, who complained about their tax dollars going to buy home children things they couldn't afford to buy their own children—though, of course, this was worse than an exaggeration.

But most people would have been too ashamed to complain. These were just kids, after all, poor and unlucky but innocent of crime, and they touched the heart in a way that people rotting in nursing homes, or in prisons (as was the sad case with many home children's parents), never could. In fact, in the beginning Americans everywhere opened their wallets. It didn't take long for the new orphanages to become one of the nation's top charities. Besides money, there were donations of everything from toys and computers to musical instruments and gym equipment. (One home in New Jersey found itself blessed with a stable of retired racehorses.) It was not unusual for a home to have more volunteers than were actually needed, and celebrities of all types could always be counted on to help raise funds or pay visits, especially at holiday time.

"An unlikely success story," reported *Time* magazine. "What began as a bold and risky experiment soon turned into a trend. Now people are calling it a movement. At first, many Americans were appalled at the thought of bringing back state-run shelters for parentless children. Visions of Dickensian hellholes danced in their heads. But by involving community organizations and local school boards and insisting on rigorous oversight, child welfare authorities are reinventing the orphanage into something Dickens would not recognize."

Nothing is perfect. Not every children's home everywhere ran smoothly all of the time. A scandal here, a scandal there—no one was saying it didn't happen. But overall the new system was hailed as a great improvement over the old, offering a better deal for all America's cast-off and mistreated children.

But who would ever envy these children? A lot of people, it seemed. At school, home children—especially boys—were among the most popular, the ones who set the style. Young people all over the world had taken razors, bleach, and lit cigarettes to their brand-new clothing to create the "diddy rags" American home kids were the first to wear, and when *The New York Times Style Magazine* did a spread, it used real home kids as models.

It was a bleak but inescapable fact that most home children remained at the bottom of their class, with a growing number expected to leave school without having learned to read or write. But everyone knew this was because there was no way you could be mad chill and a good student, too—and how many kids anywhere nowadays were convinced that reading and writing were the most important things in life?

Of all this Cole has memories, including one of his parents discussing, over bagels and chai, whether bringing back orphanages had been a good idea or a bad one. Cole's father said it made sense that it would be easier to monitor children who were in public institutions rather than in private foster homes, and that the group homes were probably the least bad solution to a terrible social dilemma.

"Maybe. But I can't imagine any sensitive kid surviving in a place like that," said Cole's mother. And she had glanced at Cole, sitting across the table.

Once, in downtown Chicago, Cole had seen a giant poster with a picture of the handsomest man in the world. It was a sight that had made his heart beat faster, and he had thought how, with a face like that—with such a strong mouth and jaw and such smooth bronze skin—and with such perfectly square shoulders filling out a uniform, you could be anything you wanted to be. Cole wanted to be a superhero. And later that day, he had told his mother what he had decided. He would join the Marines. They were sitting at the same table and in the same chairs, and it was the same look Cole saw on his mother's face both times. As though a voice had shrieked from the sky, and only she heard.

AT FIRST, TRACY IS EXCITED about her new job. "But you've got to be patient with me. It's a long time since I was in school myself, and I can't say I was the sharpest knife in the drawer back then. Not that I'm saying I'm the sharpest knife in the drawer now. Oh, will you just listen to me! Anyhoo, I will pray for guidance."

And she does pray, of course—just as Cole prays, every morning before they begin, thanking God for whatever portion of his truth will be revealed in that day's lessons.

In what way Jesus answers Tracy's prayers about homeschooling Cole cannot tell. But there is ample help from other sources. Most families in Salvation City are following the Christian homeschooling curriculum, and other parents are happy to give advice or to pass on whatever materials they might have used when their own kids were in Cole's grade.

But the growing pile of books and study guides and worksheets and tests only makes poor Tracy's head spin.

For moral support she turns to Adele, one of the women in her Bible group, a grandmother who once taught kindergarten and has homeschooled four children herself.

"I don't know, Adele. They say it's best to do a little bit of each subject every day, but if we're supposed to do math and science and social studies and language arts—which at first I didn't even know what it was—a little of each still adds up to a heck of a lot."

The trick, says Adele, is to be creative. "That way Cole won't get bored. Like, take medieval times. You don't want to sit there teaching him a mess of dull facts that aren't going to stick in his head anyway. But he likes to draw, right? So have him draw a medieval castle, you know, with the moat and turrets and all."

"Oh, I think he'd like that."

"And when you're doing the Civil War you can have him watch an episode of the old Ken Burns documentary. Then, for a writing assignment, he can pretend he's a soldier writing a letter home to his family."

Tracy is most anxious about teaching her own worst subject in school: math. But Adele says just because a person is bad at math doesn't mean he or she can't teach it. "You can go on the Web and print out the worksheets for square roots, say, and you can print out a quiz with the answer key. I'm no math whiz myself, but how do you think I got my own kids all the way through calculus?"

"Calculus!" Tracy yelps, as if it were the name of a lion to which the Romans were about to throw her.

"Oh, come on, girl," Adele says, laughing. "You know you're never on your own in Salvation City. You need any help, all you got to do is ask. And remember, if the Lord wants you to be doing this—and you know that he does—then you know he'll light up a way."

And it's true that, although Tracy is his main teacher, at least some days during the week Cole finds himself in a group class taught by one of the other grown-ups. For these classes the children usually meet at the church, where there might be a video or a talk on a special topic. One of the first topics is "Evolution or Not," taught by a guest speaker from the Creation Museum in northern Kentucky. But by now Cole has studied Genesis with PW and he doesn't learn much of anything new. Another time Adele shows them a video about preborns. There are photos showing babies who, though still seven months from coming into the world, have tiny eyes and noses and ears and mouths, and stubby little arms and legs, and hearts that beat strong. They look to Cole like cute little dolphins, and when he remembers how he and the other boys used to call some girls PBs he is ashamed. As he is ashamed when he remembers Ms. Mark and how much he used to hate and make fun of her. He wonders if she has passed.

And when, like every other boy or girl in the room, he is called on to answer the question "Would you yourself be willing and able to murder one of these innocent babies?"—like every other boy or girl in the room, Cole answers no.

But something funny has occurred to him. If Jesus was a baby, does that mean he was once a fetus, too?

Absolutely, says PW. Jesus was a fetus. "When God sacrificed his son he made him live through all the stages: conception, birth, childhood, manhood, death. Otherwise Christ couldn't have been fully human *and* fully divine. And, of course, he was as much the Christ at the moment of conception as he was at the moment of birth. And it's the same for every human being."

Cole pictures the Bible that belonged to his parents, its place on a shelf with other big books: reference books. He remembers his father saying that a person couldn't understand the history of art without some knowledge of the Bible. He remembers his parents and some of their friends playing charades one night after a dinner party, his father having to act out "My God, my God, why hast thou forsaken me?"

He has no idea how much of the Bible either of his parents had read, but he knows that the things that are sacred in Salvation City were never important to them. What Jesus said on the cross, what happened to the preborn, these were not matters of concern to them.

His parents did not know the truth. They lacked the information. There was no one like Pastor Wyatt to explain the Good News to them. Cole does not understand why it had to be this way. Now that he knows the story of Jesus by heart, he loves Jesus, but he does not believe his parents were treated fairly. Whenever he thinks about it, it's as if some spiny, muscular creature begins thrashing around inside him. He would like to talk about it, about why God would have wanted to save him but not his mother and father. He would ask PW, he would even ask Tracy, except it's as if there was an agreement among them not to talk about his parents. Cole has the feeling that, if he himself didn't bring them up now and then, his parents would never be mentioned again. Whenever he starts talking about his life before Salvation City, everybody acts as if the room had suddenly turned too hot or too cold. Now he is learning to be silent. But the spiny, muscular creature goes on thrashing inside him.

Tracy says, "I love this great big beautiful world and I know my life has been blessed. But when I see what's happening out there, all the violence and greed and perversion, well, I understand why it's time for this chapter of the story to end. I want to go where evil can't get its filthy hoof in the door. I want to be with all the people I've ever loved and all the good folks that ever lived, all of us happy together forever with the angels and saints and the Lord."

Everyone in Salvation City talks about being rapture ready. They even *joke* about it. ("Don't cry. It's not like it's not the end of the world.") They talk about the Second Coming and the Resurrection and being reunited with loved ones who've already gone home.

Mason tries to comfort Cole. How did they know his mother and father hadn't seen the light? Who was to say that, at the very last minute, they hadn't taken Jesus into their hearts? How could anyone say for sure that wasn't the way it went down?

Cole could say. For sure, his parents had not done that. And Mason cannot tell a lie. Unless that miracle occurred, Cole's parents would never be with God. And he opens the Bible to John 14:6 to show him where it is written.

He cannot bring himself to believe that his parents are in hell. It is very different from believing that they are not in heaven. He can understand why those who had never accepted or worshipped God would not ever be permitted to meet him. But it maddens Cole that anyone would think his parents deserved to be punished for not knowing Christ. The Christians he has met are not better people than his mother and father. Some of them, like Mason, have done things worse than anything his parents had ever done. Cole does not understand how, after Judgment Day, the saved are going to be happy in heaven knowing that at every moment they are enjoying themselves billions of other people are being horribly tortured. Wouldn't that be incredibly mean and selfish of them? He wonders if God intends to wipe the knowledge of hell from the minds of the saved in the way that, before the Fall, he kept Adam and Eve from knowing about evil. But that is another puzzle. If Adam and Eve knew nothing of evil, how could they have known right from wrong? And if they didn't know right from wrong, how could they sin?

"You're overthinking," PW tells him. "Which is one very good way of keeping the Lord at a distance."

Instead of overthinking, Cole is supposed to pray. But prayer does not come easily to him. It's not just that his mind tends to wander, as it did during mindfulness training. It's that it always feels more as if he was talking to himself or to the air than to God. He certainly has a very hard time believing God is listening. Besides, he is never sure what to pray for.

"Well, what would make you happy?" says PW. "Part of your prayers should always be telling God what your hopes are." But what if his hopes are against God's rules? What if his hopes are that hell doesn't exist, and that if it does exist his parents are nowhere near there?

"Think of all the things that had to happen in order for you to end up here with us," says PW. "Then tell me you don't see God's work in that." Cole knows what PW is saying. He has felt it, too: some kind of force, some hand. His coming to Salvation City has never felt to him like an accident. But he is full of questions and doubts. And since he can tell the others do not feel what he is feeling, he thinks this must mean he is unsaved. At his worst moments he is afraid that he accepted Jesus not out of faith but to please Pastor Wyatt. He is not a true believer. He became a Christian because he did not see how he could stay in Salvation City if he didn't.

He fills the moat with crocodiles. He draws a little medieval child about to fall in. A guardian angel poised on a turret, ready to swoop down.

WHEN THE PLAGUE STRUCK Salvation City, Tracy had not been among those who were passed over. Like Cole, she'd had a brush with death. One morning, when they were supposed to be studying tectonic plates, she told him all about it.

"It was touch-and-go with me for about two weeks. The way I felt was worse than being sick with the cancer. What it was really like was chemo. I was weak and dizzy as a top and I kept throwing up. And I remember it was just like I was dreaming, even when I was awake. I knew I should be praying nonstop, but there were times when I was just too sick. And though I always put my trust in God, I tell you, I was scared. You know, it wasn't as bad here as it was in some other places, but there were plenty of folks who didn't make it through, and some of the ones that did make it have never been the same.

"I remember lying there in my sopping sheets and starting to panic because I was having so much trouble breathing. And this great shivering took ahold of me, really like some kind of fit, and I had room for only one big thought and it was that my time had come. I tried to call WyWy but all I got out was a squeak. It was daytime, but all of a sudden the room got way dark, like night. Next thing I felt myself being sucked through that darkness, like a train racing top speed through a tunnel. Then I burst out the other end into this flashing light, which I knew right off was a holy light. And standing right in the middle of that light I saw him."

Holding up his hand like a traffic cop.

"Like, not so fast, ma'am!"

It was the second time Christ had appeared to her. The first time, she was in the hospital and had just had surgery.

"Only that time it *was* night and I was lying there wide awake. It's not like the doctors were mean to me but they didn't hide the bad news, either. I remember I turned my face to the wall and started crying harder than I've ever cried in my life. And then someone turned on the light. Or at least that's what I thought at first. Then I rolled over and saw him."

He was sitting in the visitor's chair by the bed.

"That really got to me, how he was sitting there with his legs crossed like any ordinary dude, except for the awesome light. And even before he said a word, I stopped crying. My family always loved me, and from the time they knew I was sick they were right there, doing everything they could for me. But nothing they ever did brought me anything like the peace I felt then. It was just a whole 'nother scale. I still thought I was going to die, but now I was ready."

Except what Jesus had come to tell her was a different story.

"You know me, CoCo, I got a memory like a sieve. But even though I didn't write them down, I never forgot his words. 'Your name is written in the book of life, and the day is near when you will be with me forever. But that time has not yet come. Do not be afraid of the suffering you will have to endure.' He was talking about the pain and the horrible chemo and the fact that I'd never be able to have a baby.

"I was raised to believe in God, and I always went to church and said my prayers and tried to be a good person. But back then, I confess, whole days would go by without my giving much thought to Christ. But ever since then I have felt him right here, and I have always trusted him. That's how I beat the cancer. I put my faith in his love, and in the end I got my reward. God sent me the best husband a woman could ever have, and then he sent us you."

Cole wants to know what Jesus looked like. Tracy laughs and pinches his cheek. "Like himself, silly puppy. Who else?"

Later, when he is alone, Cole ponders Tracy's story. To him it is not a comforting story. It is a splinter in his heart. *I was raised to believe in God, and I always went to church and said my prayers.* Tracy had already accepted Jesus Christ. Her name was already written in the book of life. So why did Jesus choose to appear to her, and not just once but twice? Cole's parents had not been raised to believe in God. His parents were not redeemed. Hadn't they needed to see Jesus a thousand times more than Tracy did?

And if Jesus could cure Tracy of cancer *and* the flu, why couldn't he cure Cole's mother and father of just the flu? Why couldn't he cure even one of them?

Which one? A voice so silky and sly it had to be the devil's, and Cole was afraid. He knew he should have called on Jesus then, he should have started praying. But he could not. He was too angry, and Jesus was too far away.

Instead, he did something he had not done in a while. He went to the upstairs bathroom and took from a shelf the jar of cream that PW used on his hands. He felt sneaky and not a little disgusted with himself, noiselessly unscrewing the cap and taking deep whiffs, like some kind of junkie. Not for the first time, he wondered how many secrets a person could have and still be a good person.

But the magic worked. The familiar vanilla balm spread through him. The splinter was still in his heart, but for a moment, at least, he felt comforted.

Besides the group classes, there are other activities, like softball and swimming, that bring homeschooled children together each week. There are field trips: the Creation Museum, Old Settlers' Village, the House of Rocks and Minerals, the snake farm. In good weather they go hiking or spelunking, and now that the baseball and racetrack museums in Louisville are open again (they'd been closed during the flu), there are plans to visit them soon.

Cole doesn't usually enjoy these outings. (In the past he'd always tried to get out of class trips, and these days he'd rather stay home and draw.) But better to be with the others than alone with Tracy (herself only too glad not to be teaching on her own).

Cole gets along with the children he meets in Salvation City, though he has yet to make best friends with any of them. He has never been the kind of person who makes friends right away or has more than one or two close friends at a time. Once he'd started middle school his parents had worried that he was too shy. One day his father said, "You know, they have some great medications for shy people now, especially shy kids." The very suggestion had brought on revulsion and paranoia (pharma mind control? no thanks), and Cole was relieved that his mother had not been on his father's side in this. But it had always bothered him. He had always thought it was his father's way of saying he wished Cole was more popular.

There had been an even worse period of time, before Cole got to middle school, when it seemed that almost everything he did got on his father's nerves. It was during this time that

Cole began to suspect that when his father was a kid, he might have been a bully. His mother tried to explain. "Dad's one of those people who's never quite sure how to be around children, maybe partly because he was an only child himself." The good news was that as Cole grew older, things would be different. "You'll see. You and Dad are just going to get closer and closer." And Cole had believed her. He knew what she was saying, and that lots of men couldn't connect with their sons until the sons were almost men themselves. And now he felt bitterly cheated.

But—in his own eyes anyway—he had never actually been the pathetically shy loner his parents were worried about. If he hadn't been exactly popular, or even part of any crowd, that didn't mean he was a total reject, either. The hardest part had been knowing how disappointed his father was that Cole wasn't the kind of kid *he* had been: good at school (not a grind but a great tester), good at sports. Cool. He knew that both his parents would probably have been less worried if he'd cared more about being popular himself, but most of the time he did not. He saw himself as part of the large herd—one of those kids, in between the mad cool and the loser geeks, who might as well have put on magic invisible-making hats when they got up in the morning—and he accepted that.

In Salvation City, things were different. To be sure, not all kids were equal. There were apocalyptic girls, there were alpha boys, and there were rapture children. But that didn't make everyone else invisible. And the ones who would have been called rejects and dweebs and skanks and PBs—those kids weren't taunted. No one bullied or excluded them.

"You won't find any bullies or gangbangers here," PW had

promised. "And just in case I'm wrong—in case I might be missing something—all you got to do is let me know. Or better yet, go to Mason. You just point out any bully to Brother Mason, and I think it's safe to say you won't have anything more to worry about."

But there has been no reason to go to Mason. No bullies—and no stoners or goths or super-annoying emo types, either, except maybe Michaela's sister, Clover, who wasn't permitted to watch *The Passion of the Christ* with everyone else, not after what happened at the snake farm. It was the sight of the snakes being fed live mice that started it. At first they thought it was the gift of tongues. But that wasn't ecstasy Clover was feeling. She had raved all the way home on the bus, terrifying the other children.

The closest thing to a bully Cole has met in Salvation City is Tracy's niece, Starlyn. But Cole would never say anything bad about Starlyn. And besides, he can't point to anything specific Starlyn does that could definitely be labeled bullying. It's more of an attitude. Darlin' Starlyn, people call her. Apocalyptic *and* a rapture child: how could you not have attitude?

In the same way that PW never corrects the mistakes Tracy makes when she speaks, Tracy doesn't correct Cole's written assignments. Every one is handed back with *Eggsssellent!!!* written across the top. No other comments.

"He's plenty bright and he knows so much already. And he reads the Bible all the time, God bless him. But he isn't into the lessons, I can tell, and he does bad on some of the tests. Honestly, though, I don't see the point in his spending so much time and effort on most of this stuff. It would be different if we were living years ago."

Adele has to agree with her friend. "Back in the day, I always thought about how I was preparing my kids for a chance at a good job. But it's doubtful Cole's going to have to worry about that."

"Be that as it may, there are rules and Christians still have to play by them," says Pastor Wyatt. "I do believe we are living in the end times, but the way to prepare isn't by changing our daily lives. We should go on living right, treating others with respect and kindness, witnessing, and of course praying. But the rest should be left to God. And I don't believe he'd appreciate us trying to second-guess him. I'd also like to remind everyone that among the highest Christian values, along with faith and purity, are accountability and self-control. And for those out there who are thinking, Guess there ain't much point in fixing the roof, now, is there? or Hey, maybe I can stop paying my mortgage or credit card debts—well, I believe such folks are playing with hellfire."

But Cole figures PW must also believe school isn't important anymore, because he pays almost no attention to what Cole and Tracy are doing.

"I'm not the one to ask about academics. I was a lousy student myself."

Cole remembers his parents saying that they could never fall in love with anyone who wasn't smart; they couldn't even be friends with people who weren't smart. And though they insisted that Cole, though unfortunately lazy, was very smart, too, he used to worry that he wasn't as smart as either of them wished.

"I married Miles for his brains," his mother always said.

Cole doesn't think PW would bless a marriage like that.

"Think Jesus cares how many IQ points you got?" Pastor Wyatt asks his congregation. "Remember, in this world the sharpest knife in the drawer could well be Satan."

Cole has noticed that people in Salvation City don't talk much about college. And he has noticed that a lot of parents don't seem all that concerned about how much their children know about things like square roots or medieval times.

"I'm totally down with the idea that I'm not gonna grow up," says Clemson Harley, a boy who, though a whole year younger than Cole, has already been allowed to preach (causing Cole, who has no desire whatsoever to preach, to suffer attacks of envy).

Cole doesn't care if he never goes to college, but he finds it hard to accept never getting to be a grown man. He'd been in a hurry to grow up for as long as he could remember. Not that he is sure what he'd do with himself as an adult, besides create comics. PW says that between Cole's desire to explore the world and his devotion to the Word, he has the makings of a missionary. Cole knows this is something he will never be, but because he also knows that this is PW's highest compliment, it makes him happy.

Cole has been living in Salvation City for about four months when, one day, on their way downtown to get haircuts, he and PW stop for gas. The gas station is next to a convenience store. While PW is filling the tank Cole drops into the store for a Coke. When he comes back out he glances up the road and sees a man running in their direction. Cole stands still, waiting for the man to get closer, his heart inching its way up his throat.

The same height and weight, the same tan and orange running suit, the same powerful but easy stride. Cole cannot believe his eyes, nor can he stop the bolt of maniacal joy that knocks the soda can from his hand. And then the man is there, the man is running right by him.

"Let's go, son." Cole thinks PW hasn't noticed anything, but when they have driven about a mile he asks very quietly if Cole is all right. Cole says nothing; his throat is still blocked. "It's okay, you don't have to say." PW reaches for Cole's hand. "It's not just you, son," he tells him. "Everyone sees dead people."

BOOTS LUDWIG, owner of the local radio station and creator and host of *Heaven's A-Poppin'!*, wanted Cole to be on his show.

"I want folks out there to hear your story."

PW agreed that anything that brought attention to the plight of orphans was a good idea.

The flu had hit most children's homes hard, but for every empty bed there was a long waiting list of new orphans, and while they waited they slept on the floor. In most cases, there wasn't enough staff to care for half the number of children they already had. (With the flu, the large pool of volunteers had evaporated.) Food, blankets, and medicines were also in short supply, and for lack of these things, even once the flu had waned, children died.

At the height of the pandemic, thousands of young children began showing up, sometimes without so much as a slip of paper to say who they were. Identifying and reuniting them with surviving family would take time; in some cases it might not even be possible. Those who'd grown up in the homes, or who'd been there a while, often hated the newcomers. Very quickly some homes began to resemble those Dickensian hellholes of people's fears. The worst were almost perfect replicas of the vicious world of adults behind bars.

But real bars, at least, would have protected the children from the outside. In a real prison, a stranger would not have been able to walk in off the street, slip a baby girl into a pillowcase, and carry her off with him.

And a real prison would not have been so easy to escape. But, alone or by twos or in groups, children trooped out of orphanages every day. When they did, the best thing that could happen to them was to be caught and returned (in fact, many returned voluntarily). Usually such children went unpunished, but to help discourage others from taking the same risk, runaways were sometimes asked to tell their stories. And there were children who would have done so but found they could not; they could not find the words. (Some had lost the ability to speak at all.)

The pandemic had caused major interruptions in the production and distribution of goods, and that included the illegal ones. At the same time, it had created hordes of unprotected boys and girls. As a growing number of these children—many more girls than boys—began to disappear, it was clear that they were falling into the hands of human traffickers, whose own numbers kept growing now that other illegal trades, like drug dealing, had become much harder to ply. Evil, too, has to eat. The traffickers kept their eyes on the children's homes, and runaways were sometimes overtaken within yards of their own front door. Sometimes the foxes didn't wait for the chickens to fly the coop. In Boston, a man, his wife, and their teenaged daughter all volunteered to work in the same children's home with the purpose of procuring minors for a porn ring.

Long after the last case of pandemic influenza had been diagnosed, the bodies of young people would keep turning up, victims of hunger, exposure, various infections, murder, and (more and more) suicide. But the pandemic had inured people to the sight of young corpses. Far scarier to many Americans were the living: kids of all ages who'd banded together and were surviving by their (criminal) wits, often under the head of one or more nefarious adults. Fierce and sometimes murderous gangs that had come to menace every city and suburb and many small towns, where they often outnumbered police.

In the wake of the pandemic, there was no shortage of places to hide out or squat. Houses and buildings and sometimes entire streets stood abandoned. The flu had even turned some rural villages into ghost towns. There were plenty of ordinary citizens who'd survived the virus but whose lives had been ruined by the pandemic in one way or another and who now found themselves squatting side by side with criminals. Those who'd seen the slums and shantytowns and refugee camps in countries crushed by warfare or poverty compared the new settlements to such places.

Though their house, like their income, was small, Pastor Wyatt and Tracy would have liked to take in more than one child. But, as Tracy put it: "The authorities keep banging us into walls." In fact, they now considered it a miracle they had managed to get Cole. Even in his case, there'd been so many questions and hesitations that Pastor Wyatt had lost his temper—only to be shouted down by a child welfare official who informed him that, bad as things were, they weren't so bad yet that people could just drop in and pick out a kid like a puppy.

"And let's face it," he told Pastor Wyatt unapologetically. "It wouldn't exactly be the first time a man of God turned out to be a you-know-what."

Boots Ludwig, though he was past seventy and had eighteen grandchildren, wanted to adopt "a whole football team and all the cheerleaders." He spent a lot of broadcast time thundering against the system. "Let my children go!" It was a matter of urgency in more ways than one: many of the orphans were unsaved.

"If it weren't for those godless pigheaded fools, we could get those kids right with God before it's too late." In which case, they would be spared the great tribulation.

Boots Ludwig liked to say the reason he loved radio so much was that he was too ugly for television. In fact, it wasn't so much that he was ugly as that he looked as if he'd been slapped together in a rush: one of his shoulders was higher than the other and he had tiny dark eyes, like coffee beans, stuck unevenly on either side of a nose that had been broken in boyhood and had healed askew. He always dressed Western, from the boots that gave him his nickname to his hat, and he wore several chunky rings, like brass knuckles, on each hand. Of all the people Cole had drawn, drawing Boots was the most fun.

PW said Boots was only joking about the reason he preferred radio. The truth was, both men regarded it as the superior means of spreading the Word.

"The idiot box has a way of putting everything on the same superficial plane. Plus the remote encourages a short attention span."

Contempt for TV was one thing PW and Cole's parents had in common.

"Televangelism," said PW. "To most folks today it's a dirty word. I can't tell you how much I hate the word myself. Oh, I can see how it looked like a great idea at first, preacher's dream, beaming the Good News into millions of homes—where's the downside? But just look what happened. Greed, theft, false testimony, megalomania, cult of personality. I'm not saying Satan created TV, I'm just saying he really knows how to work it."

Also like Cole's parents, PW thought people would be better off with a lot less "e" and "i" in their lives.

"I'm all for Christians connecting online, sharing stories and music and videos and such. But remember, it's always better to be together, in church or some other safe place, worshipping or doing Bible study or community service—whatever—than to be sitting home alone clicking away."

Cole had always thought it was lame the way so many ordinary people wanted to post pages with photos of themselves and lists of all their favorite things and have everyone follow their every dumb move—like, who cared? He'd never kept a journal, but he was sure if he ever did he wouldn't want it to be where the whole world could read it! What would be the point? Still, it was way strange at first, living in a house where the only computer you were allowed to use was in the breakfast nook (he was still in the hospital when he learned that his laptop, along with his parents' laptops and everything else of value, had been looted from their house in Little Leap) and set up so that every site you browsed could be checked by someone else. His parents had never done that, but they would have approved of PW's preaching a gospel of a less noisy and distracted life. They would have given an amen to his call for the need to break the hold the Internet had on people's lives, especially young lives. Say what you would about the pandemic, at least it had helped slow down the rat race. It had also got people thinking more about the world to come. In communities like Salvation City, life had become simpler and more purpose-driven. People were sticking closer to home, spending more time with their families. And everywhere church attendance had soared.

According to Pastor Wyatt, what Christians had needed to figure out was that they'd had it right *before*. Dirtying their hands in politics, trying to influence the government and change the laws—all that he and many other Christians now declared a mistake. "We only made fools of ourselves. Everyone seemed to forget the saying that politics is the art of compromise, and that's just not where our church is at. What do we care how we look to the rest of the world? What matters is how we look to God. Why should we waste energy trying to win other folks' respect? Don't we got a more important job than that? I want my flock to care less about what secular folks are up to and more about their own spiritual lives."

It was said that when the Antichrist came he would make use of the Internet to lure people from the true path. Certain hidden codes were said to be already in place, waiting to be activated.

But why was it the Antichrist who got to use the Net? Cole wanted to know. Why wouldn't Christ use it, too?

When Cole asked about this in Bible study, Mason's one eye twinkled and he said, "Who's to say he won't use it, little bruh? Maybe he will. Maybe he'll decide to have his very own blog. Wouldn't that be dope?"

But PW said, "Jesus won't need the Net nor any other worldly tool. He'll be on his white charger, he'll be wearing his blood-red robes, he'll have his sword and his army of angels and saints. All the trumpets will be blowing. *Behold, he is coming with the clouds, and every eye will see him.* Revelation, my boy! The King of kings! Say now, why would my Lord need a blog?"

Boots Ludwig and Pastor Wyatt were good friends, but that didn't mean they always saw eye to eye. When Boots and his wife, Heidi, came to dinner, the two men often argued, as they often argued when they were on the air. They argued about more or less the same things all the time.

Boots accused PW of being too soft. He made it seem easy to be a Christian, Boots said, when being a Christian was never easy and was never meant to be. These days, too many preachers made the church sound like a warm, cozy nest where all you had to do was curl up and be loved. At heart everyone was a good little boy or girl, and however they might have strayed, the good Lord, like some soft-touch daddy, was happy to forgive them.

"Oh, I hear you, Boots, and I know what you want. You want me to put a little more fire and brimstone into it. Use scare tactics. Send folks home with their knees knocking and their teeth chattering in their heads. But you know, nowadays, the last thing I want to do is foment fear. I think we've already seen enough of the damage *that* can do. You know as well as I do, when folks get scared, that's when 'What would Jesus do?' tends to go right out the window."

"Well, I'm the kind of man, if there's something that doesn't sit right with me, then you know I got to speak out—"

"And I am listening, my friend. Aren't I listening?"

"—and I don't like coming out of worship service and seeing every kind of expression on people's faces but the appropriate one. Seems to me, leaving church, you ought to have some mighty sober thoughts inside your head. It shouldn't be the same as if you were leaving a ball game or a party. People shouldn't be yakking away about what's for dinner, and why hello there, Mrs. Ludwig, you do look fine today, is that a new dress, and so on."

Speaking of Mrs. Ludwig, Tracy often did just that after listening to one of Boots's tirades, and usually it was the same two words: *Poor Heidi.*

Heidi Ludwig was amazingly fat—globular—a circus fat lady. Even her scalp was fat. She hadn't taken a plane anywhere in years, but the last time she'd flown, Cole was awestruck to hear, the airline had made her pay for two seats. Cole would have loved to sketch Mrs. Ludwig, but he didn't think it was possible to draw her as she was without seeming mean. He'd had the same problem with Mason, but then Mason himself had insisted he wanted Cole to draw him. Cole had done his best, but he simply could not get the scarred part right, and Mason had come out looking like a pirate.

Boots said, "I can't help feeling sometimes when you talk about sin it goes in one ear and out the other. Maybe it's because you're always smiling."

"That's what happens when I get filled with the Spirit."

Another thing Boots couldn't stomach was the praise songs of the church's worship band. "What's wrong with the old hymns? 'Victory in Jesus,' 'His Eye Is on the Sparrow.' Those are songs you could sing with your head high! And don't give me the same old argument about changing times. Nothing sadder than a bunch of Christians trying to prove they're every bit as hip as the lost—unless it's a bunch of Christians coming up with an idea like Testamints. I tell you, when Christ Almighty comes, he's gonna go after those who dare to sell things like breath mints in his name like he went after the sheep traders and the money changers—with a scourge! *My father's house is not a place of business.*"

"Boots, you know I don't like Jesus junk any more than you do, but maybe you need to lighten up."

"Now Heidi tells me the gals are starting a Knitting for Jesus group. I got nothing against knitting, but you know well as I do it's just another coffee klatsch. They're not knitting for the Lord any more than those Testamints are 'Christian' candy. And you know it gets to me, hearing the way some people jabber on about the end times. I mean, we are talking about Armageddon, the mother of all battles, like every WMD on the planet going off at the same time, and these gals—just listen to them. It's like they're planning a big shopping expedition or some kind of holiday."

Had the flu been a plague sent by God as a pre-Apocalyptic punishment? Boots thought so. "We know from the Bible that when a society violates God's laws he will punish that society long before Judgment Day." And when listeners to *Heaven's A-Poppin'!* are invited to call in, most of them say they think Boots is right.

But PW said nobody could know for sure, just as no one could know for sure what would happen to children in the rapture. PW believed all children who were too young to have accepted Jesus would be saved, but Boots insisted this was contrary to Scripture.

"The children of the saved will surely be raptured with their parents. But the others, well, take a look at the Flood. Take a look at the destruction of Sodom and Gomorrah. God didn't spare the children then, not even babies in the womb."

"But we know that Jesus loved children above all," argued PW. "We know that he is coming to destroy evil and bring perfect justice forever, and I cannot see him casting babies into the bottomless pit because their parents turned their backs on his gift. I can't wrap my mind around our just and merciful savior doing this cruel and monstrous thing. I admit in this case there's no crystal-clear verse. But I believe that although everything in the Bible is true, that doesn't mean every truth is revealed there. We have to accept there's a lot we don't know. God may have some special plan for these children that we won't find out about till the end."

One evening, as the two men argued straight through dinner, Heidi fell asleep in her chair. With a sigh Tracy got up and started clearing the table. Starlyn, who lived with her divorced mother in Louisville, happened to be visiting for the weekend, as she did once or twice a month. She, too, left the table and followed her aunt into the kitchen. After a few minutes Cole picked up his plate and carried it into the kitchen, where he found Tracy clutching her middle, all flushed and teary from the effort to contain her laughter. Before her stood Starlyn, a metal colander clapped upside down on her head and a wooden spoon in her hand. Hitching one shoulder higher than the other, she flourished the spoon like a drum majorette, silently moving her lips as Boots's voice boomed from the dining room.

Even making faces, even with the silly colander on her head, she looked beautiful. She was almost sixteen, and a head taller than Cole. She had rapture-child blond hair and gray eyes with gold dust in them, and her cheeks had the kind of plump round freshness you don't see much except on babies. It had never occurred to Cole before that a nose could be beautiful, in the same way it hadn't occurred to him that ears or feet could be beautiful. Nor could he have said what it was about Starlyn's nose that made it beautiful, but he could have stared at her profile for hours. It confused him, this attraction to, of all things, a girl's nose, and it shamed him, as did the bizarre desire that seemed to have come from the same confusing place, a place he hadn't known existed in him before: the desire to suck her earlobes.

Darlin' Starlyn. Cole did not have the courage to call her that, even if everyone else did. Mason had other names for her as well: Peaches 'n' Cream (those cheeks). Sweet Little Sixteen. Her birthday was just a few weeks away, and a surprise party was planned.

In the kitchen Starlyn glanced in his direction and, as usual, appeared not to see him. Tracy wiped the tears from her eyes and smiled in a way Cole knew was meant to make him feel he wasn't intruding. But his feeling of intruding was in fact too much for him; he dropped his plate clatteringly into the sink and immediately left the room again.

Anyway, as he thought later, he would have felt guilty joining them in making fun of Boots. Cole knew that a lot of people besides Tracy had problems with Boots, and that he tried even PW's patience. But of all the people in Salvation City who'd been kind to Cole, Boots Ludwig may have been the kindest. He was a little deaf, Boots, and like many people who don't hear well he sometimes forgot that others hear just fine. In the beginning, when Cole first arrived, he got used to hearing Boots murmur "tragic, tragic" whenever Cole happened to be around.

He's my nineteenth grandchild, Boots told everyone. Whenever he came to the house he blessed Cole with something, and it was always something good, like a new video game, something he'd made sure Cole really wanted. And he called Cole "my dear," as if Cole were a girl. Except that Boots didn't like girls. Girls and women were not his dears; girls and women chafed him. He didn't appear to like Tracy much, he was the only person in Salvation City not smitten with Starlyn, and he seemed angry with his wife most of the time.

"Poor Heidi," Tracy said. "If it wasn't for her, I'm not sure I could go on being nice to that man. All this nonsense about

126

some innocent little candy! And frankly, if bad breath isn't from the devil I don't know what is."

Cole agreed to be on the radio even though he didn't want to do it, and even though he'd been told several times he didn't have to do it. He agreed because he wanted to please Boots, and he wanted to please PW. But no sooner had he agreed than he began to regret it, afraid that he was going to let them down. But then he couldn't bring himself to say he'd changed his mind, afraid it would make him look like a coward.

He knew all about how this could happen, how your intentions could be not just good but noble, and still somehow you end up disgracing yourself and disappointing others. People you loved, people you wanted to make happy, people you wanted so badly to think well of you.

And now he would be forced to remember a time he had been trying to forget. He'd be forced to talk about things he didn't want, or even know how, to talk about.

His father used to accuse his mother of not being able to let anything go. She needed to learn to put the past behind her, instead of dwelling on what couldn't be changed. "Don't be like your mother," he warned Cole, "unless you want to be depressed."

And wasn't PW forever saying that letting go of the past was an important part of being a Christian?

"You take Paul. He had to learn to forget the bad things that had happened to him, forget the bad things he himself had done as Saul. 'Forgetting what lies behind and straining forward to what lies ahead, I press on toward the goal to win the heavenly prize to which God in Christ Jesus is calling us upward.' That's how he tells it in Philippians. Forget and press on. That's what we've all got to do."

But now they were asking Cole to *remember*.

He remembered being allowed to stay in bed for days after he arrived, even though he wasn't sick anymore. So many cots were packed into the room, you had to walk sideways. All through the night you'd be wakened by noise: a boy shouting in his sleep, a boy sobbing, two boys having a fight.

All day long boys came and went, some approaching Cole's bed to stare but rarely addressing him, and he'd watched one of them steal another one's sneakers, shaking a silencing fist at Cole before making off with them.

He wasn't sick anymore, but it still hurt sometimes just to think. He still zoned out, momentarily forgetting what he was doing or where he was; he still had memory gaps. He felt like a man in a spy movie he'd seen, whose enemy injects him with drugs to skew his mind. But Cole knew his own mind was actually getting better.

In the hospital, after his first bout of fever, he'd had to be told all over again that his father was dead. Pause. His mother was dead, too.

Passed, they said. *Your mother passed a week ago.*

Immediately, his temperature had shot up again.

He knew, of course, that it was a lie, for when he was alone she came to him. She was working on a plan to get him out. His job for now was to go along with his captors, to play dumb. He must understand, they were in serious danger: these aliens were capable of anything. He must be vigilant. One slip on his part could doom them both.

But he did slip. He panicked one day and bit one of them, the one he saw most often, a woman, tall and green, like a spear of asparagus. Always frowning. She and her evil syringe. After he bit her he was put in restraints. He cursed and cursed. To punish him they loosed stinging insects between his sheets. Because of the restraints he was at their mercy. He screamed and howled. He didn't care anymore what the aliens knew, or what they would do to him, he kept calling for his mother. She came one last time. It was no good, no good, she said, twisting her hands; she couldn't attempt a rescue now, it was too risky. She had to go meet his father. Not a word about coming back.

He had never been so frightened, he had never known that kind of pain. And when it was over, when the fever and the delirium had left him for good, it was as if part of his identity had vanished, too. As if half his life had never happened.

He was told that, after his relapse, he had not been expected to recover. "But you put up such a fight!" said the doctor, pumping his fist. Dr. Hassan was unmistakably proud of him, though Cole didn't see how a sick person deserved credit for getting better. Dr. Hassan and other members of the hospital staff were gathered around Cole's bed. Except for Dr. Hassan, they were all in green. They all beamed down at him, they were all proud, and after Dr. Hassan spoke, everyone clapped and the nurse Cole had bitten cuffed his cheek playfully with her bandaged hand.

Cole hadn't been able to look any of them in the face. He hadn't been able to say anything, either. He would never have said what he was thinking, and he was angry with Dr. Hassan, he was angry with all of them. How could they not know how he felt?

Eden knew. "Sometimes when things turn out this way, survival can feel like betrayal."

She told him that his parents were together now, they were together in heaven, from where they were able at all times to look down and see him. He knew the story, knew that this was all it was, a story: his parents themselves had told him so. He knew that they were not able to see him, and that he would never see them again. This was what their being dead meant. And yet his mind could not take it in, that they had been here on earth—never a time in his life when they had not been here—but now they were *nowhere*. They had become *nothing*.

But you can't be angry at nothing, can you? And he was most definitely angry at them.

None of it had had to happen, he believed. His parents had not had to die. He had not had to get sick himself. He refused to accept that nothing could have been done. His parents had been stupid, careless. His father was right: they had blown it. *The whole world had blown it.* He remembered all those warning articles he'd read. Why hadn't they been prepared? Someone was responsible. Someone had to be to blame. And indeed, now that the virus had passed, this was what *everyone* was saying.

"Now is not the time for accusations and finger pointing. We would do better to join hands and look not back but ahead. Let us take up the vast work before us, let us pull together, as one nation, bound in sorrow by this terrible tragedy but full of hope for our future."

When the president appeared for the first time after her illness, thin, hollow-eyed, and still so frail that she had to support herself on two canes, even among those who hadn't voted for her—even among those who hated her—there was an outpouring of emotion. America's mother had been brought to the brink of death, but she had survived. And America would survive, too.

In memory, it was as if he'd never left Chicago. The move to Little Leap and the house he lived in briefly there and the school he so briefly attended—all this he remembered hardly at all. Ironically, some of his most distinct memories turned out to be false. His father had brought home a new dog, a stray he'd almost hit with his car. A feisty young sheepdog that chased a cat under the porch of the house across the street and got into a fight with another dog, an old Labrador.

Zeppo, he'd named the new dog.

Only there was no Zeppo.

Dr. Hassan promised that, in time, his mind would return to normal. "Maybe you won't be able to remember everything you want to remember *when* you want to remember it, but for all practical purposes your memory should function just fine."

No one said anything, though, about what recovering certain memories might do to him.

For the first time in his life, he had migraines. He had ringing in his ears. He had constant nightmares and episodes of sleepwalking.

Occasionally, when he spoke to someone, the person would

look at him blankly. Rather than what Cole had intended to (and heard himself) say, out came gibberish.

Once when he tried to stand up from a chair, his legs would not obey.

If people hadn't kept telling him such things were also happening to other flu victims, he might have gone out of his mind for good.

Nurse Asparagus told him about a famous writer who'd been a child math prodigy until he came down with a case of common flu and mysteriously lost his gift. "We can't explain it, but we know a fever high enough to cause delirium can scorch things right out of the brain."

The boy in the bed next to Cole's had spoken both Spanish and English before he got sick but now could speak only Spanish. Another nurse translated: "Where are my parents?" "I see cockroaches!" "No more needles, they hurt!"

And Cole would hear many other stories like this, including stories of people who'd come through the flu blind or paralyzed or mentally retarded, or who'd go on to develop symptoms of parkinsonism. And the more he heard, the more he understood that he had been lucky.

It was Tracy who said putting Cole on a live radio show might not be such a good idea.

"Why not?" demanded Boots, bean eyes jumping with irritation, and when Tracy replied that she wasn't quite sure: "In other words, no reason at all? Just women's intuition or some like nonsense?"

Tracy knew better than to argue with Boots. And since she

believed firmly in a wife's biblical duty to submit to her husband's authority in all things, she did not challenge PW's view that she was just being an anxious mother hen.

But as late as the day of the broadcast—that morning—she reminded Cole that no one was forcing him; he could still change his mind.

"Maybe it's just me, Cole-cakes, but I don't think I've ever seen you look so pale. And I know you haven't been sleeping so good."

But Cole couldn't imagine surviving the shame if he backed out now.

It was true he'd been sleeping poorly all week, but it was not just at night that his mind was unrestful. The thought of the upcoming show—"We'll keep it real easy and relaxed. Just you and me for about fifteen minutes, then we open up the phones to questions"—had naturally got Cole wondering what he might be asked and how he was going to answer. And it was as if a fissure had opened in him out of which more and more of his past life seeped through.

Now that his memory was so much better, he was able to see how the false had got mixed in with the true. No dog named Zeppo, but his father *had* hit a dog with his car one time. And Cole remembered lying to his new classmates about wanting a sheepdog, and then wondering why he'd lied. He remembered the first day of school and the last day of school and all the chaos in between. Dogs: the chocolate Lab that belonged to the man who lived on their street, the old man who'd helped his mother carry Cole's father to the car but refused to go with her to the hospital—he remembered all that. He remembered wanting to hurt that man.

Cough, cough, cough, cough, cough. That sound lived so deep in him he didn't see how he could ever have forgotten it, even for a while. But then, forgetting your own name—how unlikely was that?—and he had done that, too.

His mother at the kitchen table, buttoned up in her winter coat—had she ever finished writing that message to Addy?

I'm sorry for your loss. A man—not a doctor or a nurse—a man dressed in street clothes. Visitor's badge, hair-choked nostrils, crooked brown teeth. A man with a laptop. *We need to talk about next of kin.*

Cole was still feverish, his head was like a noisy machine churning mud. He tried to churn up answers. Somewhere in Florida were his grandparents: his father's father who had Alzheimer's, and his father's mother, paralyzed from a stroke. In a home for old people but—and this had always puzzled Cole—not the same home. He could not remember the name of the town or the last time he'd seen them.

No brothers or sisters on his father's side; on his mother's side only Addy. When the man asked him where Addy lived, Cole slipped and said Chicago. Sometime after his second, more severe, bout of illness, he was told his aunt had not yet been found. He was confused; he had no memory of telling anyone about Addy.

He would be living at Here Be Hope for weeks before the mistake about Addy's whereabouts was discovered. But Cole thought if Addy had been trying to reach him she'd have done so by now, and he was not surprised when one day, not long after he'd moved to Salvation City, PW gave him the news that she had passed. PW didn't say anything about Addy's being Jewish, or about her being unsaved and therefore

134

condemned to hell. He only repeated what he'd told Cole before: the best way to remember people after they've passed is to remember the good about them. And then they had prayed together.

That loss did not touch his core. He'd never been close to Addy, or even had a chance to get to know her. He'd never been quite sure what to make of her, especially after hearing his mother say Addy was the kind of woman for whom having kids would've ruined her life. It wasn't that he took it personally (Addy had always been perfectly nice to him), but it had made him a little wary.

His father used to say that part of his mother's dissatisfaction in life had to do with the fact that growing up a twin, she'd never felt she was unique or special enough. Which perplexed Cole, not just because he would have given anything to have had a twin brother but because he thought being a twin meant that you *were* special.

Once he'd absorbed the fact that Addy, too, had vanished from the earth, his strongest feeling was not loss but gratitude that his mother had been spared this. Because even though they had lived far apart, and even if his mother had not been happy about being a twin, he knew that she had loved Addy. He remembered that Addy was the first person she had turned to after his father died.

Remember not the former things (Isaiah). *Forget and press on.*

But in the days leading up to the broadcast, Cole found himself living more and more in the past. As if his memory were like an empty stomach now, needing to fill itself up.

Lying in his parents' bed, in his father's flu germs—this he remembered so well it could have happened that morning. Cole had never spoken out loud his wish to die. (The secrets piling up, one after the other; he carried them with him, stones in a sack.) That feeling had passed; he'd stopped wanting to die.

He did not have the strength for such a powerful wish.

The pills he was given in the hospital, the ones he was promised would make him feel better, he'd cheeked them and later flushed them away. *Feel better for what?*

And when he was well enough to be moved to the orphanage (actually a converted warehouse for an electronics supply company that had gone out of business), it had helped not to care. It made the transition easier, as things are easier when you don't care what happens to you.

He did not feel better, he did not feel worse. He was a stranger inside his own skin. He did not eat much, some days not at all. Either he had trouble falling asleep or he slept around the clock.

He did not make friends. He avoided people—and not just the ones you had to avoid if you didn't want trouble. He avoided everyone, other kids and grown-ups alike. But in fact, unless you were a gangbanger or a rapture child or injured or very sick, you were not likely to attract much grown-up attention.

"Sounds to me like it wasn't much better than a kennel. Is that right, my dear? You got food, water, and shelter, but not much else?"

"Yes," Cole said—truthfully, yet his face reddened as if he'd

136

lied. He knew he was expected to say more, and he could have said more. About the way kids fought over food. About how some kids would take food away from other kids, partly out of hunger, but mostly to be mean. They'd throw the food around (Here Be Hope food fights were epic), or do something to it so that even the hungriest kid wouldn't eat it. (Though there was the time a boy had a coughing fit, and when a chunk of meat flew out of his mouth another boy caught it midair and stuffed it into his own mouth.) It had happened a few times to Cole, having his food snatched (usually by Da Phist), but since he was never very hungry it hadn't affected him too badly.

They had names like Pharocious II and Grime-Boy and Niggahrootz and Da Phist. The black kids.

The white kids called themselves Methastofeles and Skull Mother and Kid Hammer and Dude Snake.

The grown-ups did whatever they could to keep them apart, and when they failed there was mayhem.

He knew this was what he was supposed to be talking about, what he had already talked about with PW, who in turn had told all to Boots. But in the sound booth, Cole had gone all but mute. He knew what he was supposed to say, but the words wouldn't come, and Boots was being forced to do most of the talking.

"We've all heard people call these places Dickensian. Would you say that's a fair and accurate description?"

"Yes."

At first, before he'd heard it so many times, he hadn't been completely sure what "Dickensian" meant. He'd always assumed it had something to do with Christmas. He thought of the dreadlocked giantess who told everyone to call her Mama Jo, but whom everyone called by another name instead, forever fuming about the "Dickensian" or "barbaric" state of things, and how funny it was the way she shook her fist at God at the same time she was begging him to help her.

Mama Ho. In a quiet moment alone with her (haircut, delousing), Cole once heard her say the pandemic had set life back a hundred years. She was crying then, and he'd worried she would nick him, the way her shoulders were jerking. But those were the days when, rather than stop whatever they were doing, people would just go about their business in tears. Everyone was used to the sight. His mother—

"Why don't you share more about it with us? You know, just—in your own words." Boots was smiling and his voice was calm, but Cole knew Boots couldn't be very happy with him at this moment.

Come on, Cole. Words. Remember? But now was not a good time to be thinking about his mother.

"It was like life was set back a hundred years?"

"Ah. Well said. Can you elaborate?"

"Like, we didn't have any computers or cells, and that was weird. There were a couple TVs, but they all got smashed or stolen. We didn't have lots of books. We had some paper and some pens and pencils. But we didn't have real school." These few lines had exhausted him, but he labored on. "We had classes. Sometimes. Only not real classes. I mean, they'd put us in groups and make us talk about something, and maybe they'd give us homework. But it wasn't like, you know—it wasn't like school school."

None of the kids could get over it. Days and weeks passing

without any school, and no one able to say for sure when they'd be going back again. The rumors that, in fact, there were schools reopening out there. Just none ready to take orphans.

"What about religion?"

"I didn't go to church."

"You don't have to 'go' to church, son. Church happens wherever and whenever folks come together to pray and ask forgiveness for sins and worship the one true God. No special edifice required. Did that ever happen? Did people ever read the Bible together? Did anyone lead you boys and girls in prayer?"

Cole shook his head. Boots frowned, but without losing his smile, and pointed to Cole's microphone.

The great thing about radio, PW had told him, is that people can't see you and you can't see them, so you don't have to be all that nervous.

But from the moment he entered the sound booth Cole had seen them: sitting in their kitchens or in their cars or offices or shops, listening to him the way he and Tracy listened when PW was on the air, listening to every word.

He had also seen himself, through their eyes, larger than life, the world's biggest retard.

And besides, what about the people—Mason, for one—who Cole happened to know were tuned in right now, and who knew exactly who this retard talking (or not talking) was? How was he ever going to show his face to those people again?

Through the window he could see Tracy and PW, sitting outside the booth but able to hear everything through the speakers. Whenever he glanced their way, PW would bob his head enthusiastically while Tracy flashed her widest smile, probably without realizing she was wringing her hands at the same time. Cole was aware of Beanie Gill, a young man he knew from church, sitting in a smaller booth built into the opposite wall. Like Cole and Boots, he had headphones on, and he was constantly monitoring some controls. From what seemed like another room Cole heard Boots repeating his last question, and there was a quaver in Cole's voice as he replied that he didn't know, he couldn't remember.

Yet as soon as he said it he did remember. There'd been plenty of religion at Here Be Hope, he just hadn't taken part in any of it, hadn't been forced to. It was there that he'd first learned what a rapture child was, and he remembered how everyone—grown-ups even more than kids—trailed after those children, pestering them about the Second Coming. It was then that he'd first started to understand what the Second Coming meant. He remembered how, at night, in the crowded room, boys could be heard saying their prayers before going to sleep, just as he himself did now. Mama Ho carried a Bible with her and read from it, sometimes to herself, sometimes out loud to others. In fact, he didn't think he'd ever forget the sound of her voice as she read, a little-girl voice that sounded cartoonish coming from such a large woman, and the way she punctuated each passage with a brief snort, like a horse or a bull. He remembered all this in the instant after he'd spoken, but he was too shy to open his mouth again. It was too late to change his answer; it would only make him look dumber. He kept quiet, avoiding Boots's eyes. He would not look at PW, either. Shame was like a sticky substance he could feel on his scalp and under his T-shirt. Later, listeners would tell him how they'd been able to hear him breathing.

The agony went on and on (in reality, just another few minutes) as Boots tried to draw him out. He asked questions about the gangs and about the fights that had ended with somebody knifed or knocked senseless. He asked about the boy who'd hanged himself with the same belt one of the guardians, in a drunken fury, had used to beat him. He asked about the runaways and about girls who got pregnant. Using the word *violated* (a word he'd prepared Cole for beforehand), he asked about rape.

Cole was good at keeping secrets, but not at faking. One thing he knew he could never be was an actor. And so it was hard for him, knowing that Boots already knew the answer to every question he asked. Cole understood that by pretending not to know, Boots was just trying to make the program more interesting. But to Cole it felt not only dishonest but silly. Mostly he just answered yes or no.

"Sounds to me like a living, breathing hell," Boots said solemnly. Cole said nothing. His throat was constricting. He felt a surge of emotion as it struck him that, in fact, it had not been hell. Though he'd longed to escape it, the orphanage had not been so bad at all. The thought brought a sizable shock— never would he have believed while he was there that he could think such a thing. But looking back now, he realized that, again, he had been lucky. And he hoped people listening to the radio wouldn't think he wanted them to feel sorry for him. He worried that maybe he'd exaggerated when he told PW stories about the orphanage. If he could find his tongue now, he'd explain how it was mostly about hiding from the bullies, who had a way of picking on the same kids all the time anyway. You were lucky not to be one of those kids, but to stay lucky you also had to avoid them. You had to be ruthless, you had to refuse to have anything to do with them. You had to refuse to help them. Today, the memory of this shamed Cole. But it had all been so complicated. The most dangerous and despicable thing you could do was to snitch, and nine times out of ten helping someone was going to mean snitching. Still, he liked to think that if he ever had to go back, or if he was ever in that kind of situation again, he would do the right thing. It was a hard truth for him to acknowledge, how far away he was from being a hero. He liked to think if he had another chance he would act differently. He would not abandon the weak. He would battle against injustice. He would protect and defend the unlucky ones.

And there was another reason the orphanage meant more to Cole than just brutal memories, and this had everything to do with his secret life in that cavity under the stairs. And then it had turned into a blessing, not having any friends, because it meant he could disappear and no one would notice; he could hide out for hours without being missed and no one would come looking for him.

It was at Here Be Hope that Cole discovered he could sit and sketch for longer and longer stretches without getting bored or distracted, as he used to do. And for the first time he understood that he carried this in him: the ability to shut everything out—not just the unhappiness of the moment but the past with all its pain and loss and the future with all its question marks—by concentrating on this one thing, which happened also to be the thing that made him happier than anything else he knew how to do.

He imagined this was the way someone like PW or Tracy must have felt when they prayed. He himself had not yet experienced such a feeling while praying. And not that he was saying prayer and drawing were the same, he knew that wasn't right; but in his mind they lay so close they touched.

"I have here a newspaper article."

Cole had known Boots was going to bring up the dog.

He never knew exactly where they'd found it. There were the runaways, many of whom you never saw again, and there were the kids who sneaked in and out whenever they felt like it and who sometimes stayed out overnight or even longer— and what were you going to do about it, kick them out for good? They came back with loot like cigarettes and vodka and weed, and bursting with stories about what they'd been up to—usually, if true, even worse than what they did at "home."

They could have found the dog anywhere. The pandemic had orphaned pets, too, and you couldn't go far in any direction without seeing strays. Stray dogs formed packs, some harmless but others a danger to anyone they happened to scent. Dogs didn't get the flu, but neglect or violence had been killing them and other animals off by the score, their unburied remains yet another danger.

Kid Hammer and Dude Snake, brothers two years apart— with Dude Snake, though the younger, being the bigger and meaner—claimed to have hunted and killed the dog, but Cole didn't believe them. Not that he didn't think they were capable of this, but the way the muzzle was pinched said the dog had been dead a while.

The dog was dead, but they tortured it anyway.

"Then they cut off its head."

A female. From the look of her—the thick skull and boxy jaw—Cole thought at least part pit bull. He'd been surprised there wasn't more blood.

"They stuck the head on a broomstick."

"Like with the pig in *Lord of the Flies*?"

"Yeah."

He had never read *Lord of the Flies*, though his father had kept pushing it on him. When it was assigned in class, he had SparkNoted it, even though this was against the honor code (which, of course, no one took a molecule seriously), so he knew the story. His father kept saying it was the kind of book boys Cole's age really liked, and Cole did know kids who said it was off the hook, but the notes made it sound boring. In any case, why would he want to read a whole book about bullies?

"Then what?"

"I don't know. They kinda marched around with it. They took turns holding the broomstick and chasing other kids with it."

After a day or so the lips had shrunk away from the teeth, giving the head a vicious mad-dog grin, like it was going to bite you and laugh about it at the same time. Another day or so and it didn't even look like a dog anymore but more like some kind of wild beast or mutant.

"They propped it up in this closet, and they played this game where they'd catch kids and lock them up alone in the dark with it."

Little kids. They would scream and pound on the inside of the door. Some of them pissed or shit themselves, or threw up. A boy named Arnie, who'd lost most of his hearing after having the flu, did all three before passing out.

"I understand one time it was you who got locked in with the monster?"

However fond he was of Boots, at that moment Cole wanted to punch him. *Monster!* If only he'd never told anyone that stupid story.

"Yeah, but it was nothing. It's not like I was scared." (Like he really thought a dead dog could hurt him.) "They were just trying to show me because of something I said. They said I dissed them."

"Why? What did you say?"

"That I didn't believe they killed the dog."

It still bothered him. The only person to whom he could remember saying he didn't believe Kid Hammer and Dude Snake had killed the dog was Mama Ho. But she wouldn't have gone and repeated it, would she? He couldn't believe she'd be that clueless. On the other hand, he could think of plenty of instances of an adult getting a kid in trouble just by being uncool. Like the girl in his class who wrote a poem about touching her girlfriend between the legs (well, more than just touching), and whose teacher showed it to both girls' parents. Even Cole's mother said that was wrong.

It was possible someone else had overheard him. He remembered a kid named Kelvin hanging around that day, weak little nerd, no shoulders, no chin, chief bully target and one of the first to be locked in with Jaw Head. Possibly really pissed at Cole for not lifting a finger to help him.

They treated Cole the same as they treated Kelvin or Arnie or any other little kid, shoving and bitch-slapping him as they pushed him inside, barking and snarling like dogs themselves as they trapped him by sitting with their backs against the door. They knew he wasn't scared, but they weren't trying to scare him; they were trying to do to him what they did to other kids when they stripped them and forced them to march around naked.

You would have sworn Jaw Head was singing to itself, but it was the flies. A black velvet mask of flies. Maggots frothing in the eye sockets. Every inhale torture. Cole breathed through his mouth, cupping his hand over it so he wouldn't inhale a fly. That was the worst of it, the flies landing on him, the same flies that had touched the putrid head settling on his skin, his face, even on his lips before he covered them. He'd been in a rage then, a rage that had stayed with him for days, maybe longer, but that rage was gone now. He was less angry at what those boys had done to him than at being reminded again how far he was from being a hero.

By the time the reporter came, Jaw Head had long since been seized and tossed into the trash like a worm-eaten cabbage, but no one had forgotten it. Not the worst Here Be Hope story by far, but one a lot of kids would rather tell than any other. The reporter heard it many times, and though it wasn't the only story she wrote about in her article, it was the one that got into the headline.

Not that Cole was going to go into all this on the radio. According to a large clock on a wall outside the booth, fifteen minutes were almost over. Which would have been a vast relief if it hadn't meant that now Boots was going to invite people to call in. Always when Pastor Wyatt was on the show there were plenty of callers. Cole was thinking he'd never make it to the end when he saw Boots lean sharply toward him, a worried look further warping his crooked features.

Boots was dressed as usual: Western shirt, bolo tie, Wrangler jeans, rodeo belt buckle, ostrich boots. Cole had often seen him dressed like this, had seen him in this very outfit before. But at this particular moment he looked different. He looked very strange. Cole knew, of course, it was Boots, "Grandpa" Boots, sitting there. But somehow at the same time sitting there was a person Cole didn't know at all, and suddenly he was afraid. Who was this weird old dude? What did he want? What were they doing there in that tiny room, into which some kind of gas was now being released?

Cole's heart bulged as if he were trying to lift something too heavy for him. Then a dark, smothering cloud pressed down on him. The headphones hurt like a vise. Tiny bright lights flashed at the corners of his eyes, and a force like an undertow dragged him by the ankles off his chair.

When he opened his eyes again he was outside the booth. He was on his back on the cold floor. Someone was singing. A chorus; a hymn. *I sing because I'm happy, I sing because I'm free.* Cole smelled vomit, but fought the idea that it could be his.

PW and Tracy were there. They knelt on either side of him. Their faces were all tender care, but they might as well have been holding daggers at his throat. For an instant Cole saw nothing except a pulsing black rectangle with a fiery border.

"Let me go, get the fuck away from me!" Swinging fists, thrashing feet. Grazing PW's chin, accidentally kneeing Tracy's chest. He watched her face turn white before crumpling. Then she was gone, though not far—he could hear her trying to catch her breath as Boots took her place, helping PW to restrain him.

"Where's my mother? What did you do to my parents? I want to see them. You can't keep me here!"

Moments later, he lay still. He lay curled on his side, his face hidden in the crook of his arm. His hair and his shirt were wet with perspiration. He felt like a rag someone had wrung out and flung down. His stomach felt wrung out, too. He had no idea what could have happened to him. He knew only that he had disgraced himself.

Tracy was there, gently massaging his back. He might as well have kicked her on purpose for all the guilt he was feeling. And he doubted anyone had ever said fuck to her face before. But when he turned he saw no trace of anger in her expression, and later, when he tried to apologize, she hugged him and said, "It'd take a lot more than that to rattle this lady's cage." But as PW and Beanie were helping him to the car, Cole caught the parting look she shot Boots, a look that hissed *I told you so!*

Warm bed, warm milk, the doctor's deep warm voice. No, Cole wasn't losing his mind again. Overexcitement. Nerves. Stress caused by traumatic memories. All that—a lot!—but nothing a day's rest wouldn't cure. And, of course, prayer. "Still the best medicine."

(Instantly Cole's thoughts flew to pretty, cat-faced Dr. Ming, his pediatrician in Chicago, who finished every exam by tickling his ribs and reminding him that *laughter* was the best medicine.)

Left alone, Cole lay in bed feeling very tired but not at all sleepy. It was the middle of the afternoon, and though the blinds were closed, bright sunlight leaked around them. He felt stifled under his covers, but as soon as he threw them off he was freezing. He turned round and round, like a rotisserie chicken, unable to get comfortable. His mind was racing. He thought back to a day when Pastor Wyatt had come to see him at the orphanage. Not the first time—not the rainy gray Saturday on which they had first met—but a later visit. They were sitting and talking in one of the common areas when PW dropped the word *adoption*—and even though Cole was already fond of PW and felt perfectly safe with him, a rush of fear had made him jump up and run away. It was the same kind of fear he had experienced years earlier, when he was around five or six and obsessed with the idea that if his mother let go of his hand when they were out in public, someone might try to snatch him.

Afterward he had been embarrassed, and he had felt bad for PW, whose feelings Cole was sure he'd hurt and whom he guessed he'd never see again. But in fact PW came again the very next day, and the first thing he said to Cole was, "We've got to get one thing straight. There can't ever be any adoption without your consent."

"What a place," said PW, shaking his head.

It was three weeks later, and this time PW had come to Here Be Hope to take Cole away with him.

"Looks like they can't find your stuff."

He was referring to Cole's few clothes and other belongings, which had been packed into a large cardboard box by one of the staff. That morning at Here Be Hope had been particularly chaotic; several children besides Cole were leaving for new homes the same day. PW thought maybe Cole's box had been taken by someone else by mistake.

"In which case, they should return it. Anyway, we're not going to sit around all day while they try to find it."

There were some papers in the box, including Cole's birth certificate and his medical records, but Cole barely gave those a thought. He was far too upset about his drawings, and about another item, one he never mentioned to PW or to anyone else and which he tried to forget once it appeared that the box was probably missing for good. Something he'd managed to bring with him from the house in Little Leap and hold on to throughout his long illness. It had gone with him, washed and folded and tucked into a pocket, when it was time for him to leave the hospital and move to Here Be Hope. He had promised himself he would never lose it, but now it was gone: his mother's blue bandanna.

COLE WAS EMBARRASSED by all the get-well calls and messages. He was embarrassed by all the prayers. He became flustered when Mason dropped by the house and greeted him with a high five. "You did good, bruh."

Mason shrugged off Cole's fear of having ruined the program. "What? We heard a little commotion, then silence for a bit, then 'His Eye Is on the Sparrow.' No biggie! Nothing for you to feel bad about. Besides, dude, it was yesterday."

An echo of what both Boots and PW had already assured Cole, who nevertheless remained doubtful. You make a public spectacle of yourself, life can't just go on like before, can it? True, no one laughed openly at him. But he didn't think he was imagining it when, the next time he was at church, a few people avoided looking him in the eye.

Fortunately, there was something new for everyone to focus on: Starlyn's birthday party. Actually, there were going to be two parties. One was the Saturday afternoon surprise party her aunt would be throwing in Salvation City. The other would take place in Louisville the Friday evening of the week before, a much bigger and more grown-up affair in the banquet room of a hotel: a dance party. Cole wished he could be at that party, too, mostly because he wanted to see Starlyn in the fancy new dress he'd heard her tell Tracy all about—specifically, to see how any dress that was both strapless and backless could stay on. And he was curious to see her date, her boyfriend, about whom there'd been talk as well.

It took his mind off his fresh humiliation to be working on Starlyn's gift: a charcoal portrait based on one of Tracy's many photographs of her niece. Tracy had also helped him pick out a frame for the drawing, one with real pressed flowers under the Plexiglas, which made Cole happy every time he looked at it.

Cole was fairly satisfied with how his drawing finally came out, but when he imagined Starlyn unwrapping it in front of everyone else he felt almost sick, and so he was more relieved than disappointed that there were so many presents for her to open, she couldn't spend time fussing over any one of them. He could tell she liked the drawing from the way her eyes lit up when she peeled the paper away. In the photo she was smiling, but Cole had drawn her with her lips closed and slightly pursed. Tracy said it made her look like she was praying, but that wasn't what Cole had been thinking about.

Starlyn scanned the crowded living room to find him, half hiding in a corner, and blew him a kiss. It was enough.

No, it was not enough. Not if he was honest. Maybe it was all those hours he'd spent poring over her photos, making sketches, working so hard to get her features right (and the nose, he'd despaired, would never ever be right). Now, from the safety of his corner, he could not take his eyes off her. Once, he happened to catch PW watching him watch her, and there was something in his look—not disapproval, exactly, but something that made Cole feel chastened nevertheless.

Maybe it was the lacy white slip she was wearing. Not that he hadn't seen her and plenty of other girls dressed like that before. It was one more thing Boots could get worked up about: *Gals coming to church half naked.* But Starlyn, who was thin, and whose breasts were smaller than most girls' her age, didn't look as exposed as some other girls—or as Tracy—did. Cole had been surprised to learn that girls and women in the Church of Salvation City didn't have to cover up, and that they were allowed to wear makeup. He was surprised, too, that smoking wasn't forbidden and that although heavy drinking was considered a major sin, alcohol wasn't strictly forbidden, either.

"We ain't the Taliban," PW had told him, grinning. "We love music and laughter and a pretty dress, and we know that sometimes a man needs a drink and sometimes he's just got to cuss."

Starlyn had long arms and legs but tiny bones. She was perfectly healthy, had survived the pandemic without becoming infected, but she looked delicate.

"I always feel like a big oafess next to her," said Tracy, who, except for her breasts, which were about the size of roast chickens, was quite small herself.

But Cole didn't see how Starlyn could be warm enough dressed like that. The urge to cover her kept rising in him—and not with, say, the flannel shirt he was wearing over his T-shirt today, but with his whole body. And with this urge each time he grew too warm himself and dreamed of cooling his face in the marble curve of her neck.

Her cooling him, him warming her—Cole had to wonder sometimes where ideas like that came from. This one would not leave him alone. All day he would veer between guilt and excitement.

It was like having a fever again. All that great food, including meat loaf and three kinds of birthday cake, and no appetite. A houseful of people, including Mason and Clem from Bible class and a few other kids Cole was normally glad to see, but he kept ending up in some corner, alone, too listless to do more than look on. Starlyn herself kept getting swallowed up by one gaggle of guests or another—Cole seemed to be the only one lacking the nerve to go up and chat with the birthday girl. When her mother came up to tell him she thought his was the most special of all the gifts Starlyn had received, he froze with self-consciousness, unable to move his lips to say thanks.

As usual at such gatherings, PW, too, was always surrounded. There were times (and today was one of them) when

Cole couldn't help being annoyed at how people—how women, especially—demanded PW's attention. Even Tracy had had enough, complaining that some women used the excuse that he was their pastor to ignore the fact that he was also her husband. But anyone could see that PW was enjoying himself, all smiles and big hugs—the same way he always was when he mingled with parishoners after a service.

Cole was feeling more and more restless and downcast. The memory of the radio broadcast returned to gnaw at him. He thought of slipping away, going on a long bike ride, something that always managed to soothe him, but he knew it would be rude for him to leave in the middle of the party, and his disappearance would probably only make people worry about him.

He was relieved when Clem found him collecting dirty paper plates and cups on the back porch and asked if he wanted to play a video game. It gave him something to do without having to talk much, and when the game was over they played a few more, and then Clem's mother appeared, saying it was time to go home.

Women were putting away leftovers, men were carrying presents out to Starlyn's mother's car. PW had retreated to his home office in the den. Cole looked for Starlyn, and when he didn't see her he decided to go up to his room.

The party was over, but no one had turned down the music that had played all afternoon (and had driven some of the older guests home early), and so they didn't hear him. They didn't see him, either, because instead of continuing down the hall to his room, Cole turned and hurried back downstairs.

But if Mason's face hadn't been buried in her hair, his 20/10 eye could not have missed Cole.

He was standing with his back to the wall, leaning against it as she leaned into him. Her arms around his neck, his face in her hair, and his hands—looking almost black against the bright white fabric—kneading her flesh so hard that her short skirt was scrunched up, uncovering the backs of her thighs and a smile of white underpants.

"You okay, Cole?" said Tracy. "You look mad or something."

Tracy and Starlyn's mother, Taffy, were drinking coffee at the kitchen counter.

"Just thirsty," said Cole. (Half true, at least.) He took a can of root beer from the fridge and slid into a chair at the table.

Taffy, who was older than Tracy and looked like an overfed, overtired version of her, swiveled in Cole's direction. "I was just saying how much I can't wait to get home and hang your picture." And as the two women launched into a duet of his praises, agreeing how lucky Starlyn was to have such a great artist for a friend, Cole felt a prickly sensation behind his nose that was only partly from drinking soda.

What sounded like some kind of dance step made them all turn their heads in time to see Starlyn lollop into the room.

"There she is!" said Tracy, flinging her arms wide. But Starlyn twirled past her and across the floor to flop down at the table with Cole.

"You look like you just run a race," Tracy said, and Starlyn began to laugh. She had a brash toot of a laugh, one thing about her that was not delicate at all.

"Oh, she's in a race, all right," Taffy drawled. "The race to be all grown up." This made Starlyn laugh so hard she lost her breath, and her mother said, "Uh-oh. Looks like Birthday Girl's had enough excitement for one day. We better hit the road."

Cole was studying Starlyn as closely as he dared. Her mouth looked fuller than usual—awesomely close to what he'd had in mind when he was drawing it—and there were pink marks on her upper arms where the flesh had been pressed, which made him think of other marks that he couldn't see but that he knew must be there.

Tracy said, "It's Cole's turn next"—causing him to slosh root beer up his nose before he realized she was talking about his own birthday coming up. "Did I say? The boys are taking a little trip."

Just then, Cole noticed PW standing in the kitchen doorway. He was staring at Cole with the same meaningful look on his face as before. How long had he been there?

Suddenly it was too crowded for Cole. As PW crossed the room to get something from the fridge, Cole quietly got up and slipped out. Behind him he heard PW say something that made Starlyn toot again, and though he had no reason to think it had anything at all to do with him, Cole cringed.

From his bedroom window he looked down on Mason, slowly pacing the front lawn and smoking a cigarette.

Cole sat on his bed and leafed through his drawing pad, which was filled with sketches of Starlyn. They all looked different now. Not everyone would be able to tell, but he could tell. She was not the same anymore. His brand-new portrait was out of date.

At the end of that long day he lies on his stomach, seeing Mason's dark hands on Starlyn's white skirt and the bright smile of underpants, thinking what a wild thing it must be to have someone rubbing and squeezing your cheeks like that, fingers digging into your crack, like he owns you. He crushes a pillow between his thighs and he kneads it, kneads it, seeing the hands, being the hands, and feeling them, all at the same time.

An hour earlier, in the kitchen again but this time alone, he'd found himself standing by the chair Starlyn had been sitting on in her scrap of a dress, and almost without thinking, he'd bent down and sniffed the quilted chair pad handmade by Tracy.

He'd have thought any smell would have faded by now. But there it was. Neither as good as he'd heard nor as bad as he'd heard. Wet sand at the beach.

After the unbearable tension has been relieved, he feels soiled and vaguely mournful, he feels a little sorry for himself and a little disappointed, too—he feels the way he always feels when he masturbates. He is tired, but when he tries to sleep the teasing image of white underpants is still there, like the grin of the Cheshire cat.

PART THREE

PART THREE

It was their secret, and Cole respected secrets. He would not tell anyone what he had seen. Only he wanted to know more himself. For example, he wanted to know if what he had seen was the first time Mason and Starlyn had ever made out. He thought probably yes, but this was mainly because of the number of times in recent weeks he'd heard Mason mention the fact that on her birthday Starlyn would become Sweet Little Sixteen.

And now, of course, she was sixteen. But she was still a girl, and Mason was not a boy. He was seven years older than Starlyn, and Cole knew most people would say it wasn't right for a man to touch a girl like that, even if she let him. Even if she begged him. And the idea of this particular man and girl together was somehow particularly shocking. Her perfect face, his disfigured one. Her perfect skin, his snakeheads and skulls. Her shining blond hair, his shaved scalp. Her whiteness under his grease-monkey hands.

But she must have liked that, Cole thought. The eye-patch scar, the crusty palms and black nails. You'd think a girl would be turned off by those things—

And what about her boyfriend in Louisville?

Mason didn't have a girlfriend, as far as Cole knew, and people were always teasing him about still being single. Everyone knew that, before his conversion, he'd sown his share of wild oats and, as he confessed, had not always been respectful of ladies.

"Maybe that's why the Lord put all that on hold for me. When the time's right, I expect he'll introduce me to the one meant for me. I know the next step for me is to take a wife, but I'm leaving it all in his hands." Meanwhile he lived with his mother. Lucinda Boyle, who'd raised Mason all on her own, was still in her forties but might as well have been an old woman. She was one of those people who, a year after getting over the flu, had developed symptoms of parkinsonism. She almost never left the house.

Cole wondered what was going to happen next. Did Mason believe that, even though she was so young, Starlyn was the one God intended for him? And did that mean they'd be getting married one day? But if that was the case, he thought, they wouldn't have to keep their love a secret. Whatever the story was, he knew he shouldn't be spending so much time thinking about it. It was none of his business. His mother used to say when it came to people's love lives you should always look the other way. And: Never be the kind of boy who talks about what he did with a girl. Nice boys don't kiss and tell.

Here the taste of cherry burst on Cole's tongue, and he remembered: passing the cough drop from mouth to mouth— like kissing and not kissing and more than kissing all at the same time. And afterward, strangely enough, they'd gone on as before. Not girlfriend and boyfriend, not even friends, just ordinary classmates again—as if the accidental collision in the closet had never occurred. But he hadn't talked about it. He'd never told anyone what he'd done in the dark with Jade.

Jade Korsky. Whose hair was like a poodle's if poodles had been red. Who always had to sit in the front because she was both nearsighted and incapable of holding on to a pair of glasses for more than a week. First girl he ever kissed—and he'd forgotten all about her. How sad was that?

That had been sixth grade. In seventh grade, a boy named Royce had told him about an eighth-grader named Sage, a tall girl with hair like licorice twists and a faceful of piercings. A nympho, Royce said, and when Cole asked him what that meant he'd laughed and said, "It means you don't got to pay her or nothing, dude. You just hook up and get your rocks off." But Cole would have been terrified of hooking up with a girl he didn't even know. Until Royce told him, he had no idea, either, what a chicken head was. He could not see how any girl could become famous for that. Enough boys had confirmed what Royce had said about Sage for Cole to think it could be true, but he could not imagine ever finding out for himself.

And now he could not imagine himself in Mason's place. He could not imagine himself touching Starlyn the way he'd seen Mason touching her—like he owned her. But lately all that—kissing, touching, having sex (whatever that was *really* like)—had begun to take up more and more space in Cole's head. It was another one of his "ideas" (he didn't know what else to call them): you could never grow up, let alone be a hero, without the help of a girl. And say it didn't happen. Say you couldn't find a girl who would help you. Well, then, you'd be hopeless. Whatever else you might do in your life would be meaningless; there'd be no point in growing up at all.

He remembered how, in the period right after he got over the flu, it was as if he'd aged backward. Night terrors. Bedwetting. Fear of the dark, fear of being kidnapped or lost—all his little-boy horrors had come back to him. He was smaller then, too, he'd lost so much weight, and it seemed to him his voice was higher—maybe the flu could do that, too. Later, studying himself in the mirror, he was dismayed at the scrawniness of his arms and legs, the thinness of his waist, and his sharply protruding ribs and shoulder blades. His butt looked like a baby's. He had skin like a girl's: too pink and too pale. Even at its biggest the Yearning Worm did not reach the six inches he knew was the absolute minimum requirement. And who would ever want to kiss a mouth ringed with acne?

But he had gained back all the weight he'd lost plus a few new pounds, and he was a good two inches taller. His voice wasn't exactly deep, but it had a certain resonance now, a huskiness at times, like when he had sinusitis. And he was shaving every other day. He knew he could barely be called a teen, let alone a man—even a man as young as Mason was obviously way different from him. But you couldn't call him a child anymore. He was not a child. He had caught up. He had moved on. And now that he was almost there, fourteen felt even older than he'd thought it would feel.

It was all set. Early on the morning of Cole's birthday, he and PW were going on a three-day camping trip. Not to the Bible camp some kids from Salvation City went to every summer and where Cole, too, would probably go later that year, but to a site in the Kentucky hills where PW used to go when he was a boy.

Ever since he'd been promised this trip, Cole had been looking forward to it. There'd been days when he could think of little else. He was still looking forward to it, but he wasn't jumping up and down inside like a little kid anymore. In fact, he was embarrassed to remember how overexcited he'd been. He couldn't say exactly why things had changed, but it saddened him to have to admit that the trip had lost some of its magic. He was afraid PW might figure this out and be saddened, too.

If it ever came out that he'd seen Starlyn and Mason making out and kept quiet about it, Cole was sure PW would understand. What he wasn't so sure about was the way he'd caught PW looking at him the day of the party. It mortified him to think PW could have read his thoughts then. How many times had PW already told him, "If there's anything you want to talk about, anything to do with girls, any feelings or urges or questions you might have, you just let me know. I believe you'll always find me open to that kind of chat." But Cole had always shied away from that kind of chat. He didn't want PW to know how he felt about Starlyn. He wanted him to look the other way. Now he worried that sometime while they were away PW himself might bring up the subject.

Sex had been a topic in Bible class ("Good Sex Is Clean, Not Seen, and Never Mean"), and Mason had explained that, in this particular case, Jesus' example was not meant to be followed. A man cleaving to a wife and the two of them creating a family— that's what the Lord wanted to see. ("Cleaving," though he knew what it meant, bewildered Cole and gave him a physically uncomfortable feeling.)

Cole was thankful sex was not one of the subjects he had to tackle with Tracy—though, since the day of the radio show, his feelings toward Tracy had changed. Whenever Cole thought back to that awful day, the most awful part was remembering what he'd done to her. A knee to the chest had to be a very hard thing for a woman to forgive, he thought. He'd been told that, for a woman, being hit in the chest was like a guy being hit in the balls. Not that he'd meant to hit her there—he hadn't meant to hit her anywhere! On the other hand, he *had* been trying to push her away, so you couldn't say it was purely accidental, either. Like the time his father threw his phone at the living room wall. He hadn't meant to break the phone, or to mess up the wall. But, like Cole's mother said: "It doesn't matter what you fucking meant, it's what you fucking did."

"I won't lie and say it didn't hurt," Tracy said. "But you know, any time I feel any kind of physical pain I think about our Lord's three hours on the cross."

Even weeks later, remembering her full and instant for-giveness could bring a lump to Cole's throat. He had always wished he could like Tracy more than he did. He'd still have given anything not to have to sit through lessons with her. ("What I don't know about geography could fill all the tea kettles in China.") But to see her with different eyes—to feel a new affection and respect for her—was blessing enough.

"What's wrong? You forget something?"

"Nope."

"Then why do you keep looking back at the house? Didn't we go over the checklist? You homesick already?"

PW was teasing. They had already had this conversation. The words hadn't come easily to Cole, but he'd wanted it clear: he wouldn't have any problem with Tracy coming along.

In fact, it was her not coming along that had become the problem. Wouldn't it hurt her feelings to be left out?

"You kidding? She's probably happy as a clam to get us two lugs out of the house a couple days. Besides, she's no camping fan. The great outdoors is definitely not that woman's thing."

But Cole had seen photos of Tracy in the great outdoors. She'd looked pretty happy to him.

"Yeah, well, maybe once upon a time."

Was it Cole's imagination or was PW annoyed with him? The suspicion alone hurt his stomach.

"But don't take my word for it, Cole. Ask her yourself."

"Sleep on the ground? Wake up with the birdies? Snakes and bats and creepy-crawlies everywhere? Yuck!" It was true she'd gone camping many times in the past and enjoyed it. But now: "I guess I'm getting soft in my old age."

It was something, Cole thought, the way adults could almost always find ways of not telling the truth without actually lying.

So why couldn't they all go on a different trip, then? It was his mother's voice he heard asking this, and he thought how it wouldn't have happened back then. He couldn't recall ever going on any trip with just his father—a thought that was immediately overshadowed by a more significant one: he was starting to think of PW and Tracy as his parents.

This was another subject he was afraid might come up sometime in the next three days.

"We're not going to push you, son," PW had said. "We just want you to promise you'll devote some serious time to thinking and praying on it." And Cole had promised, but in fact he'd been mostly avoiding thinking and praying on whether or not to be adopted.

It felt good to be wanted—and PW and Tracy had a way of making him feel like the most wanted boy in the world. In most ways they were easier to live with than his parents had been. They were certainly a lot happier than his parents had been. He had heard them quarrel a few times, but he had never heard them curse each other, and he could not imagine Tracy walking out on PW. He knew how happy he would make them both if he agreed to be adopted. And why shouldn't he make them happy? They loved him, they were kind to him, and what could there be to stand in the way? It wasn't like anyone else wanted him.

And if he could have agreed to be adopted without having to see his parents' horrified and wounded faces, then probably Cole would have done so.

There had been a time in his childhood when he used to pretend quite a lot that his parents were not his real parents. And sometimes then, when he was out in public, he would see a particularly cool-looking couple—a couple who looked like they never fought and never worried about money—and he would spin out fantastic reasons why they, his true parents, had had to give him up. ("It would've been wrong to expose a child to the dangers of our lives as secret agents.") It was never a question of their not having wanted him but rather of their having been forced to make the supreme sacrifice.

When he looked back now it seemed to Cole he had played this game for years, and he writhed to recall those scenarios in which his long-lost mom and dad whisked him off to their private island or rodeo ranch or traveling circus or spaceship.

And he remembered how, when he was still in the hospital,

he had convinced himself that once he was well Dr. Hassan was going to adopt him—a fantasy that had *not* conjured up his parents' scandalized faces. On the contrary, Cole was sure his parents would have approved of his being adopted by someone like Dr. Hassan.

But if dead was dead—if they were truly *nowhere* and *nothing* now—how could his parents be horrified at anything? How could they approve or disapprove of any decision he made? How could he hurt their feelings?

This was why he avoided thinking about adoption. It was too hard, too painful and bewildering. Sometimes it made him want to scream or break something; other times it just made him cry.

Up in the dark, and even though she wasn't coming along Tracy was up with them, fixing peanut butter and grape jelly sandwiches and filling the cooler with iced tea while Cole and PW loaded the minivan with their gear.

Now that the day was finally here, all Cole's excitement had bubbled up again, and in that hushed hour before sunrise it was as if something epic was about to unfold. Once again, as on that day years ago when his parents came to pick him up from summer camp, he was overwhelmed by the terrible power of happiness, how it threatened to crush you, or to suck all the air out of your lungs, and his hands shook as he helped PW pile firewood into the van.

It was spring, but all that week had been hot as July and even at dawn the air felt like something sprayed on your skin.

"Now, don't you all get eat by a bear," Tracy warned.

PW said black bear—the only kind of bear to be found where they were going—didn't eat people. And as long as you didn't rile them they wouldn't attack. Even so, Tracy said, she'd sleep better knowing PW had his gun.

The gun had taken Cole by surprise. Not one of the hunting rifles from the gun cabinet in the den but a 9 millimeter Cole had never seen before, and which he figured was kept somewhere in PW and Tracy's bedroom. But how close would the bear have to be—

"It's not for bear, son."

"It's not?"

"No. Now, don't you worry, I'm just playing it safe. I wish it were otherwise, but the truth is, the scariest thing out there goes on two legs, not four."

The rifles in the den hadn't been used in years. It was one of Cole's favorite stories. PW and some buddies had been out tracking a whitetail when one of them was accidentally hit by another hunter. PW had been standing close by when it happened.

"Saw his cheek explode, got splashed with his blood, even thought for a couple heartbeats I'd been hit myself. Well, poor Carter survived, but I wasn't much of a happy hunter for a while after that. 'Course it didn't help seeing him all the time with his face so messed up. He had a bunch of operations, but I never did see much improvement. He still made Mason look like a beauty queen. I don't like to say, but his wife up and left him. After that he stopped going to church and started talking crazy. He was going to *finish the job*. Anyone could tell he meant business. That's when I promised the Lord I'd give up hunting for good if he'd do a work in Carter's heart."

"And that's what happened?"

"Carter met a girl—much prettier than his wife, I don't mind saying. He married this girl, Shane, had three kids with her, worked his tail off making a nice life for them all. Then the flu got him. And where he is now it don't matter what his face looks like. His life is one pure joy."

Hunting was second only to church in Salvation City. ("There's a reason the Indians thought of heaven as the Happy Hunting Ground," said Boots.) All the boys and more than half the girls Cole knew did some kind of hunting, and there were kids his age who'd been doing it for years. Clem had killed his first turkey at seven and his first deer at nine. There was no shortage of people eager to train Cole to hunt any time he was ready. But the idea did not sit well with the animal lover in him. He'd gone fishing just once and even that had been too much for him, his stomach mimicking the convulsions of the hooked fish.

Tracy was no hunter but she knew how to shoot, as she knew how to load a rifle and how to take it apart and clean it, too.

"My daddy always said that's how you prevent accidents. Not by keeping young'uns away from guns but by teaching them how they work."

And what was it with people who were scared of keeping guns in their homes? For her it was just the opposite. "I could never sleep in an unarmed house, especially after what happened with the flu," she said. "And when you think about what might be coming, well, what are you going to do, just sit there defenseless?"

Defenseless was how she looked to Cole that morning as

he and PW drove away. Smaller and smaller through the van's rear window, in her short hot-pink bathrobe with white pom-poms at the belt ends, waving two-handed like a child.

The sun popped into view behind her just as she vanished from sight.

PW liked to drive fast. Once they got to the highway they would zoom up to eighty or ninety and maintain that speed most of the way. He turned on the stereo and they listened to Veronica playing their new song, "So Angel." He kept the volume high, the way he did only when he was driving alone or when it was just the two of them. Cole thought Veronica was an awesome band and that "So Angel" was their best song yet.

The music was too loud for them to talk, but he and PW glanced at each other from time to time, grinning. Veronica was one of PW's favorite bands, too.

Already they were having fun.

Next on the mix was "O Lonesome O Lord," a bluegrass song about a man who'd lost his wife to the flu. Sung by Earl E. Early, in that famous wailin'-failin' voice that gave everyone goose bumps. "O Lonesome O Lord" was a super hit, but there were lots of people, like Tracy, who couldn't listen to it because it made them too sad.

"Man, this dude got a voice," said PW, raising his own voice above the music, and sounding—as Cole had rarely heard him—envious. It was the part about the man forcing himself to dance alone so he'll remember the steps and be able to dance with his wife when he gets to heaven.

Cole's eyes filled with tears. It wasn't because of the singer, though. It had nothing to do with the song. Today was his birthday. Happy birthday! But the truth was, as the day had approached, Cole hadn't expected it to be happy. The only thing he could remember about his last birthday—passed in the hospital and totally ignored—was thinking that he would never be happy again.

One of the reasons people love to speed is for the illusion that they are escaping something, and though he wasn't behind the wheel, that is how Cole felt now: as if he'd left some trouble behind. There was a vibe coming off PW that suggested he was feeling something like this, too. He steered with his left hand—his left palm, mostly—his right hand tapping his thigh to the song. Cole always studied the way people drove, losing himself in the dream of how he'd one day handle a car. This was how it should be, he thought: fast, but smooth and laid back. His mother, as she'd liked to boast, had been an excellent driver. But for some reason, his athletically graceful father had been a klutz at the wheel, the cause of several minor accidents, each of which had made him a more nervous and therefore worse driver. He drove squeezing the wheel with both hands, shoulders hiked to his ears, checking around so constantly in every direction he made Cole think of a bobble-head.

Cole had to laugh. *Bobble-head!* Just the word was hilarious.

The laugh came out a giggle, and he clapped a hand over his mouth in embarrassment.

"You know, son," said PW, pitching his voice low like he was about to say something stern. "Most people *cry* when they hear this song." They both cracked up then, and as their laughter died down a new feeling swept over Cole, one that almost made his eyes well again.

If only they could keep going. If only they could keep driving, just the two of them, it didn't really matter where. Out west. To California. Or down to Mexico. Or to New York City. Or all those places. Images fanned before him like a hand of cards: The two of them riding horses, riding choppers, riding big waves. The two of them piloting and co-piloting a small jet plane, eating steaks under a giant chandelier. There'd be daring adventures, heroics, and so forth wherever they roamed. It would get so that before they even arrived in a place, people would know their names.

It was crazy—where did he *get* his crazy ideas—and it made him feel selfish and guilty. No place for Tracy in any of his grand plans. But it wasn't the first time Cole had felt the urge to run. Now that he was completely healthy again, he often felt restless, bored, as if he was stuck somewhere, waiting for something to happen or for some special knowledge to come to him. Bible study, lessons with Tracy, church, the games he played with the other children—it was not enough. He wanted more. And there were times when he felt as if there was a force holding him back. Some force was sitting on top of him, squelching and trapping him and preventing him from growing into who he was supposed to be. Like a colossal spider, it pressed its boulder of a body down while its legs caged him in. He would have to be Samson to break free.

If only they could keep going. It wasn't like he was asking them to run away from God. God would be with them if they wanted him there. He remembered how he had missed Chicago after he moved to Little Leap. But if they never turned back, he did not think he would miss Salvation City.

If there was anything he yearned to talk about with PW it was this. But he did not know how.

ON THE WAY, they stopped at the place where PW's great-grandparents were buried. Cole had been expecting a real cemetery, but this was just a cluster of a dozen or so weed-choked graves on a rise off one of the mountain roads.

It wasn't a real family plot, either. "Though everyone here was kin to some degree or other." PW had brought a trash bag for all the litter he knew they would find. Beer and soda cans, mostly; he gathered them up without a word. But Cole was surprised to see so much litter in that lonely spot. There weren't even any houses nearby. The closest thing to a house they'd seen had been miles back: a horseshoe of weather-beaten mobile homes sharing a clearing with several vehicles in various stages of being gutted. Rust city. A swaybacked horse tethered to a post, head hanging low to the ground, and some equally forlorn-looking dogs staring mutely at the van as it passed, as if they didn't have the strength to bark.

Some of the gravestones were sticking out of the ground at such odd angles it was easy to believe someone had tried toppling them. PW's great-grandfather's slab had a long crack running down it, and Cole pictured a night of pounding rain and a zigzag of lightning striking.

Jasper Carson McBell was only forty-four when he died, but that was not unusual for a man who'd worked in the mines from the time he was a teen.

"That's what men did for a living here, generation after generation," PW said. "Only my daddy broke with tradition. He always loved where he was born, but he didn't want to end up in the mines. Besides, those jobs were melting away like snowflakes in June and there wasn't much of anything to replace them. He roamed around a bit till he settled in Lexington. His main job was supervising deliveries for a big furniture outlet, but he had good carpentry skills, too, so he did some of that to earn extra. He liked doing that kind of work more anyway. But I know for a fact he never did feel at home in the city. He might even have gone back if it hadn't been so hard to find work. Also, Mama was no country girl, and it would've been hard for an outsider like her to fit in. But my daddy went back to the mountains every chance he got. And once we kids come along we went, too, and those were the times we were happiest as a family, especially in summer.

"I remember it'd be suppertime and we'd all be outside, either at my grandparents' or some other kinfolks'. Or it might be a church supper that night. And there'd be games, like sack races or darts, and there'd be singing and banjo playing, and the sun'd be going down behind the mountains, and of course there'd be good eatin'—though I remember one time there was this dish that gave me the heebie-jeebies: a whole hog's head on a platter of white bread slices.

"My granny was a great cook, though. She didn't need a pile of money to put cuisine on the table. All she needed was some fish from the creek or a chicken or a couple squirrels and what she gathered from the earth. She taught my mama to cook the food my daddy loved.

"Right before he passed, he couldn't swallow, but he kept ordering Mama to cook his favorite dishes. She'd stand at the stove with tears dripping into the pot, and when she brought him the food all he could do was smell it and maybe hold a bite in his mouth before spitting it out.

"Mama couldn't stand it. She said it felt like she was torturing him. But I think it must've been a good thing. That smell and that little-bitty taste did the trick, so he could feel like he was back in the mountains that he loved again.

"Once you had a taste, you never forgot Granny's chicken and dumplings, and her biscuits and gravy were even better than that. Hey, we got any more of them sandwiches left? I'm making myself hungry, talking like this."

It was the most Cole had heard PW say about his family at any one time. In general, neither he nor Tracy talked much about the past. It made Cole wonder if maybe sometime during this trip PW would end up talking about Delphina. Cole couldn't ask about Delphina, because when he'd asked about her before, PW had said, "If I tell you the story now, do you promise never to bring it up again?"

He couldn't ask Tracy about Delphina, either, though he once overheard her tell Adele: "That girl come a hairpin close to assassinating Wyatt." Which turned out to mean she had waved a gun at him.

PW had kept the story short. They had met when he was in community college, studying business administration and working part-time in her father's stable. They had eloped right after his graduation. They had fought a lot. She had been untrue. But she was the one who walked out. PW had tried to stop her. This was where the gun came in. Wresting it away from her had somehow involved dislocating her shoulder and cracking a bone or two.

An accident, but she told the police—and later the world— a different story.

PW was so distraught over what he'd done he almost turned the gun on himself.

("Lord forgive me, Adele," Tracy said, "but if I'd been around then there wouldn't have been one bone in that girl's body left *un*cracked.")

Cole has heard it said that one of the worst things that can happen to a man is for him to love a woman more than he loves God. This, of all things, appeared to have happened to Pastor Wyatt.

"I'm not saying she was a bad person. She was in many ways the sweetest woman I've ever known. She was spoiled, was all. Her mama and daddy had spoiled her but good. They were kind of fancy, her folks—horse breeders—and they had just the one child. That child didn't get her way, she'd about lose her mind. She had a wicked temper, and enough tears in her to float Noah's ark. But the man is the head of the woman. Wife goes wrong, you look first to the husband. Where'd *he* go wrong?

"I was an arrogant man. Make that *fool*—arrogant fool. I thought I could handle everything myself. I was too blinded by my pride to pray—not that I was much into praying back then. And the longer I was with Delphina, the further I fell from the Lord."

Cole had expected the story to end with something bad happening to Delphina. He thought maybe she was dead, and that's why it was so hard for PW to talk about her. In fact, she had married again. But her second marriage hadn't lasted, either, and now she was with someone else, a horse breeder like her father. Flip Boody, a man known for his high-rolling style, whose private life sometimes made the news. It was old news but evergreen scandal that he'd abandoned his wife and that he and his girlfriend were living in sin. She was worse than dead, Delphina.

Though his every attempt to reach her over the years had been met with silence or rage, PW continued to feel responsible for Delphina. If she was lost, he was at least partly to blame. "Just 'cause now I got a marriage that's a success doesn't mean I'm absolved of that failure."

Delphina gone, PW had plunged headlong into darkness. He had started drinking in that way that has only one purpose and, unchecked, only one likely outcome.

Cole was fascinated by the idea of PW madly in love with an apocalyptic girl. He'd never seen Delphina, not even a picture of her, and no one had ever described her to him. But that she was apocalyptic he had no doubt.

Cole didn't know why all of a sudden he was thinking so much about Delphina. Maybe because Tracy wasn't there. Maybe because of Mason and Starlyn. Before the trip was over, Cole would find himself several times on the verge of spilling the beans about them. (Later, he'd be appalled to think how close he'd come to tattling.)

PW referred to the days after Delphina left him as a time when he *wandered in the desert.*

A desert that was, however, anything but dry.

"Many were the nights I could not find my way home."

179

Passed out in the street, he got rolled more than once. All the while, he kept trying to get back with Delphina. He called it love, she called it stalking. "The law was with her." Served with a restraining order, PW chose to leave town.

"I had this idea about starting over in Louisville."

But in Louisville he only drank more.

One morning he woke up to find himself lying next to a Dumpster in the back lot of the Red Star Bar-B-Q.

"My wallet, my watch, my cell, my keys, my jacket, my belt, and my two shoes—they were all gone. I got up and was staggering around, hoping maybe at least my shoes were somewhere in the vicinity, when I noticed this skinny dude in a hoodie and diddy rags leaning against the Dumpster. He was smoking a cigarette and watching me.

"I was never a mean drunk. But the morning after? Dude, look out. So I cussed him in my best French, you know, and I asked him what he wanted. And he told me he knew where I could find what I was looking for. Is that right? I said, real sarcastic. But he just flicked his cigarette away and jerked his head, like, follow me. I thought maybe he really did know where some of my stuff was, so I went along, and I didn't know whether to laugh or punch his lights out when all he did was lead me over to the other side of that Dumpster. Then I saw there was this other dude lying on the ground, and the one thing I could say for sure about him was that he didn't have my stuff. He didn't have anything except for one piece of clothing, a pair of filthy old hospital p.j. bottoms about three sizes too big, and a smell on him so ripe I come this close to hurling.

"This was the middle of winter. I was shivering to death

myself with no jacket, and I didn't know how he could stand it half naked like that. I didn't see any bottles around, but I knew he was a drunk like me, or a meth head or some other kind of junkie. His eyes were open, but I might as well have been invisible. Lying next to him was this pile of bones he must've got from the Dumpster, and they were all picked clean. He was nothing but the sorriest sack of bones himself, and I didn't know why I was supposed to be looking at him.

"I wheeled on the first guy and started to cuss him again. And he points a finger at me and he goes, 'Tonight you lost your coat and your shoes. Tonight you lost some money and some of your other possessions.'

"I felt my scalp tighten up. I was thinking, How'd he know all that? Then he points at the dude on the ground and he goes, 'This man is your brother. Won't you help him? You lost your coat but you still have a shirt. Won't you give him that shirt of yours? Can't you see he needs it more than you do? You have a home to go to. But this man has no home. Take him with you, invite him into your house, and let him wash himself. Feed him a good meal, give him some clean clothes and a bed for the night. And if he needs to talk, listen to his story.'

"That's when I had to sit down. Next thing I know I'm crying. I'm hiding my face in my hands, bawling my eyes out, like I hadn't done since I was maybe five. I don't know how to describe what my soul was going through. All I can say is it was the worst feeling I ever had in my life, the fullest measure of misery and shame I believe it is possible for one human being to experience. It was like seeing myself clear for what I was: a sick, selfish, cowardly sinner, a man without hope, without peace of mind, without any joy in his twisted heart.

"It seemed like I cried for a couple days, and with every tear I was cleansing something foul and perverted out of me. And when I was able to pick my head up again, I saw that the stranger who'd spoken to me was gone. And I knew he was the Lord. The man on the ground was gone, too. And I knew he was one of the angels of the Lord. All that was still there was the pile of bones, and when I saw them I felt the hairs all over my body rise. I knew whose bones those were. And I looked up and saw that I was wrong, it wasn't morning at all. The sky was dark, even though it'd been light before. It was still the middle of the night.

"Many folks pray for a sign from the Lord. I hadn't done that but the Lord sent me one anyway. I knew that I had been called to be a fisher of men. After that it all came—I won't say easy, because the Lord's work is never easy—but it came natural. I was just obeying Isaiah: 'Raise your voice up like a trumpet! Tell the people they have sinned!' And I was following Paul, bringing the Good News straight to the people by teaching in public, testifying repentance toward God and faith toward our Lord Jesus Christ."

Of course, he was not the only street preacher in Louisville.

"But it seemed like most of the time folks would just walk on by without paying those preachers any mind at all. With me it was different. People would slow down and stop. I started to draw crowds. I got them to listen."

At the same time, he started working as a volunteer at a rescue mission.

"And that's where I really preached my heart out. These were the poorest folks in town, the hungry and the homeless and the really hurting. Lots of them were addicted to one substance or another. Some had done time and didn't have much hope of ever finding any employment. Helping them with practical needs was the easy part. But I also had to make them believe that no matter how much trouble they had, they were not forsaken, that it's the lost sheep that are God's most beloved, and that they were the blessed of the blessed."

At the mission he got to know several pastors, one of whom invited him to preach at the Church of Hope and Joy, a nondenominational congregation of about sixty people. He accepted, and a year later the number of church members had nearly doubled. Hope and Joy moved to a bigger space, Pastor Wyatt was given more worship services, and the congregation kept growing.

Among the parishioners was a very pretty young woman suffering from cancer, who always sat with her family down in front. By this time, Pastor Wyatt was well on his way to becoming a church leader and a popular Louisville figure. ("First time I ever saw WyWy was on the hospital TV," Tracy was fond of recalling.)

Though pleased with his success—a kind of success that had never entered his mind before—Pastor Wyatt was not without doubts.

"I didn't know why, but I just wasn't as fulfilled as I'd been preaching in the open."

The unsettling feeling that he was being watched, that some-one somewhere was mocking him, that some kind of trap was being laid for him—what could it mean?

"I started worrying I was basking too much in all the attention. It wasn't that I was losing my faith, but there was a line there that I felt was getting blurry. Was I in it for God or for my own ego?"

Mysteriously enough, the more doubtful he became, the more effective was his evangelizing.

"If the purpose was to win souls for the Lord, there's no denying that was being accomplished."

So why did he have the nagging sense that the Lord wasn't happy with him?

Meanwhile, Delphina had filed for divorce.

"Again, I was stupid. I thought I could handle my problems all by my lonesome. I should have sought advice from church elders, I should have been more open with my flock. I only saw the truth later on: I was too proud. I'd put out the welcome mat for the devil, and sure enough the old boy showed up."

One night he found himself in his car, speeding toward Lexington.

"I guess maybe I was thinking now that I was some kind of big dude Delphina would have to change her mind about me, to heck with that old restraining order."

In this case, being drunk turned out to be lucky. Well before he reached Delphina's door, he jumped the car like a horse over a guardrail and plunged down an embankment. The car was wrecked but, as sometimes miraculously happens—and even though he wore no seat belt—PW walked away.

"Like they say, drunks don't break, they bend. The real crazy thing was I didn't feel grateful."

He might not have been physically hurt, but the accident had jarred something loose in him; he fell into a gloom that would not lift.

"I was mad, too—hopping mad at the Lord. I felt like he'd set me up somehow."

He spent a month in the university hospital psych rehab ward, where his side of shouting matches with God shook the padded walls of the Quiet Room.

When he was himself again, PW went back to preaching. The people kept coming; he'd lost none of his gift. But he longed for a change. He was his father's son. He was tired of cities. It wasn't of the big time that he dreamed. A simple life was what he believed God had always intended for him. He felt this even more strongly after his year's mission service in Kenya.

And so, when the pastor of a small church in a small town in southern Indiana was called home, Pastor Wyatt did not have to think long before accepting the offer to replace him.

It would not do, however, to begin his new life alone. He was now legally single again, and as a friend and frequent dinner guest of Ronnie and Priscilla Wegner, he couldn't help being aware that their lovely younger daughter had a crush on him.

There was something almost saintly about young Tracy Wegner.

"I looked into her eyes and saw the innocence of a child and the might of a lion."

Tracy would have followed him anywhere, but how nice that it was only across the river, not too far from family and friends. The wedding was a low-key affair—the bride had not yet fully recovered from her illness—and three weeks later they moved into their new home.

Of course they both wanted children, but neither was in any big hurry. There was Tracy's health to consider, and also they wanted time to get to know each other. The better they knew each other, the more they loved each other. Tracy's cancer was cured. They were researching adoption programs when the flu broke out.

❦

IT WAS THAT TIME OF YEAR when going between sun and shade can feel like a change of season. They kept peeling off their jackets and shrugging back into them. Their first hike, they were caught in a brief but heavy shower. When the sun reappeared it was brighter than it had been before, and the sky held not an arc but a kind of rainbow-colored cloud that was like stained glass. Within seconds it had vanished.

Already much of the woods was dense with green and there were clouds of insects so thick in places if you took a deep breath you'd start coughing.

Once when they were resting, lying in the sun by a creek they might have been swimming in if the water hadn't been still winter-cold, Cole thought how upset his mother would have been that he wasn't wearing sunscreen. And what would she have said to PW driving without a seat belt?

It was the middle of the week, and they did not meet many other campers. These days people were wary about going too far into the woods at any time. The plague *before* the flu had been a ravaged economy, enough already to swell the population of survivalists, and as the disease spread, many people had tried to escape infection by fleeing into the bush. Not all of them had returned. Now places like the Kentucky hills were said to be hiding large numbers of people who believed that either the end of the world or, at the very least, new and hor-rible disasters were on the way. They were said to be mostly men and to include many ex-cons, waiting it out in their bunkers and caves, loaded shotguns on their laps.

But PW scoffed at stories like this, calling them way exag-gerated.

"I'll protect you, son," he said, grinning. And Cole wasn't afraid. In fact, it only excited him when they came across cer-tain signs: a mattress airing in the fork of a tree, a broken rock-ing chair, trash well beyond the usual backpacker's litter, like an economy-sized box of laundry detergent. It was Cole who happened to spy, well camouflaged though it was, a fantastical-looking structure, like part of a wooden boat growing out of a hillside. He wanted to climb up and investigate, but PW held him back, and not till they'd left it far behind did he say any-thing to Cole about the eyes that had been watching them from the surrounding brush.

Now and then Cole startled at the sound of gunfire, but according to PW the shooting was always much farther away than Cole thought it was. "You'd know that if you'd been raised around guns like the rest of us." The memory flashed of Mason asking, "If Jesus'd had an AK-47, would he have mowed down the soldiers before they could crucify him?" and Clem responding no. "Without the Crucifixion, mankind couldn't be saved. And the whole reason God sent Jesus in the first place was to save us."

Cole had known this was the answer, too. But it had al-ways troubled him that the Crucifixion hadn't been Jesus' idea, that it was his father's idea, though his father wasn't the one who had to go through it.

Cole was surprised that they weren't doing any Bible study on this trip. They had brought pocket Bibles with them, but they would never open them. Of course, they prayed first thing in the morning and before they ate and again before they went to sleep. But, except to comment each time they came upon another great view that a person had to be insane not to believe in the Creation, PW appeared to be giving religion a break.

And once they'd reached the camping site, PW appeared also to have lost interest in reminiscing. No more stories about his family. (And not a word about Delphina, ever.) Some of the trails they hiked were steep enough to make conversation impossible anyway, and PW set a fast pace, with Cole sometimes having to struggle to keep up. Cole was amazed at how fit PW was, especially since he almost never got any exercise. In spite of his size he moved with a lightness that made it easy for Cole to pretend they were two braves walking Indian file.

Even when they rested or sat by their fire at night, they tended not to say much. The silence didn't bother Cole. You missed a lot if you talked in the woods, he recalled his camp counselor saying. He liked not having to talk, not having to listen to anything but the birds and the tramp of boots, the snap of twigs underfoot (what was it about that sound that made it so satisfying?). Hearing a waterfall long—surprisingly long—before you saw it.

The tune to "O Lonesome O Lord" kept coming into his head, and once, at the exact moment this was happening, PW started whistling the very same bars. Ha! Two people didn't have to be talking to be on the same wavelength.

But it struck Cole that, away from home—or at least here in Kentucky—PW was a different person. Not just quiet but often so absorbed in his own thoughts he might have forgotten anyone else was there. The trip didn't seem to be so much about Cole's birthday anymore, which was fine with Cole. For one thing, it made him less worried that the dreaded subjects of sex and adoption were going to be mentioned. And the thought that PW could relax and be himself around him made Cole glad—even proud.

He thought about how, on the road down, he'd started wishing the two of them could run away together. And there had been other days when he'd wished that everyone around them would go away so that he could have PW all to himself. When he was younger, he'd felt that way at different times about each of his parents: why couldn't the one disappear and leave him alone with the other? And there'd been times when he'd wished they would both disappear. But his wish to be an orphan had always meant fun and excitement, great adventures in which he was the star, the darling of fascinating and admiring people. Never once had he pictured himself miserable, cast blindly among the shrieking, reeking, starving, heartless kids of Here Be Hope.

It occurred to Cole that, because of where they were, PW might be thinking about a time when his own parents were still alive and he was still a boy. It was always hard for Cole to imagine any grown-up as a child, except maybe Tracy. Then another wish came to him, the wish to have known PW—or at least to have known what he was like—when *he* was fourteen.

A reptile child, he'd called himself. Meaning what?

The nights were cold. After hiking all day they were both ready to bed down as soon as the first stars appeared. They lay side by side in their small dome tent. But long after PW had fallen asleep, Cole was still awake, his thoughts in tumultuous motion like the dance of the insects drawn to their campfire.

Alone, he could have—would have—rolled onto his stomach and massaged the tension away. But the fear that PW would wake and catch him in the act kept Cole lying as if at attention, rigid and filled with shame.

"It wouldn't be the worst thing," PW had told him, "if a person could masturbate once in a blue moon. But if you don't fight it every time, it turns into a habit. That's when it becomes a distraction from the Lord, and also more likely to lead to worse sin."

Whenever he'd start to drift off, some change in PW's breathing or posture would jerk Cole back to full consciousness. Once, he was shocked to realize he'd been thinking about his mother and PW together.

He knew it was wrong to have impure thoughts about Starlyn. He knew that dwelling on what he'd seen in the upstairs hallway was inviting sin. What could be said, then, about imagining his mother and PW in Starlyn and Mason's place? Probably there didn't exist a word bad enough to describe the kind of person who'd do such a thing. Add to this the guilt of betrayal—for he knew he could be accused of this, too: betraying his father, betraying Tracy.

Yet even as self-loathing clotted his throat, the idea stayed with him. His mother would have found at least a hundred things wrong with PW. The way he smiled all the time would have got on her nerves. The way he said things like "good eatin'." A Jesus freak. A preacher with a manicure and a handgun—his mother would have made so much fun of him!

But in Cole's fantasy Pastor Wyatt swept Serena Vining off her feet. And she would have done what Tracy had not been able to do: make him forget Delphina.

The man dropped to the earth like a bobcat that had been watching them approach. They barely had time to take him in—straightening up from the crouch in which he'd landed, dressed head to toe in cammies, his cap and dark beard and mirror shades hiding most of his face—when two other men entered the scene from behind trees, one stage left and one stage right, like actors at the same cue. Same costume.

Each of the men was over six feet tall, slightly hunch-backed, and rail thin. Brothers? The first people Cole and PW had run into who were toting rifles instead of backpacks.

The one who'd dropped from the tree had a broad fleshy nose that reminded Cole of one type of mushroom he'd noticed sprouting in the woods. Cole was fascinated to see himself reflected so clearly in the man's shades. It was like watching a video on a phone screen. PW was in the video, too, standing close behind him. They were both breathing a little hard from walking upslope.

The man spat an oyster onto the dirt between them, and when Cole jumped he knocked into PW, who placed a hand on his shoulder.

"Y-you b-boys lost?"

Besides the stutter, the man had a voice like a congested toddler. Growing up, he must have got laughed at every time he opened his mouth. Laugh at him today and he'd b-blow your b-brains out.

Before they could answer, one of the other men, who'd taken his cap off to reveal blond hair so dirty it was almost brunet, said, "You're a good ways off the main trail."

"I know that, sir," said PW. It was his preacher's voice: loud and firm. "There's a knob up yonder overlooking a couple caves. We thought we might see some bear."

"B-bear?" The first man shook his head. "Nossir. Y'all won't see no bear."

"No?"

"Like I said."

"They still sleepin'," threw in the blond, though he must have known this was false. He scratched his head vigorously before replacing his cap. "Law says you can't hunt them anyhow."

Cole didn't understand what had made the man say that. The only gun they had was the pistol PW had brought along. At night he slept with it near his head. The rest of the time it was in his right jacket pocket.

A movement in the sky drew Cole's eye upward. Red-tailed hawk, gliding. He was waiting for PW to explain that they weren't on a hunting trip, but PW said nothing. Now the stutterer was looking up at the hawk, so Cole couldn't see PW's reflection anymore. But the hand on his shoulder had grown heavy as a saddle.

That morning there were only wisps of clouds, the kind people called God's whiskers or angel hair. But suddenly it became much brighter, as if a cloud that had been covering the sun had moved on. In that light every tiny thing jumped out, leaf or pebble or acorn—every separate pine needle—as if under a magnifying glass.

Cole was having trouble breathing. For also magnified and microscopically clear was the fact that although he didn't know these men and had done nothing to hurt them, that didn't mean they would not hurt him. Such things didn't happen only in movies. Murder didn't happen only when there was a good reason for it to happen. Or any reason at all.

The blond pulled his cap off to scratch some more, and Cole wondered if he had cooties.

"They always warn folks should stick to the main trail." Without raising his voice the man managed to sound terrifying. A bitter taste flooded Cole's mouth. Not like this, he was thinking. To be terminated, for nothing, by strangers, by total fucking creeps. It must not be allowed to happen. And in the midst of his fear he had time to be amazed that he had ever thought it would be cool to die. "I was you," said the man, "I'd turn 'round now and head back. This ain't nowhere to be after dark."

As if dusk weren't ten hours off.

No one spoke for a few beats. Cole fought a vision of himself throwing his arms around PW's neck and screaming like a girl. He braced himself for the shoot-out. Saw PW in one smooth movement whipping out his gun and knocking him out of harm's way.

A squirrel watching from a maple dashed along a branch for a closer view, one paw curled toward its chest in a fretful gesture. Somewhere a window flew open and Cole saw his mother leaning out and making the same gesture. Probably only he could hear when PW finally sighed. The heavy hand lifted. Fingertips brushed Cole's nape. "Let's go, son."

Over his shoulder, PW said what he always said when they met up with strangers: "Have a blessed day." But there was no trace of warmth.

"You take care, mister." It was the third man, speaking now for the first time, and as they headed downslope he continued to call after them, in a mysteriously agitated voice. "You take care of that boy of yours." He sounded like a person trying to hold back laughter. "Don't you let nothin' bad happen to him, hear? Hey, mister! Take good care of your boy!" Then another voice snapped: "Goddamn it, leave it, Wayne." And the laughter burst.

The laughter faded, leaving just the sound of their footsteps, quick and sliding on the downward path. PW stayed in the lead, saying nothing. Cole noticed he kept his hand in his jacket pocket. A log lay across the path. As he stepped over it, Cole saw, sprouting from the bark, one of those fleshy brown mushrooms he'd flashed on before, and he heel-stomped it.

The first time he looked back, Cole could see nothing except for trees and brush. But farther on, after a sharp curve, he looked back again and he saw them. They had climbed up onto an outcrop, where they stood in a row, facing downhill. Cole caught just a glimpse of them before another curve in the path made them vanish again. Because of the angle of the light, the three men had appeared as silhouettes against the sky. Their faces were indistinguishable, but whoever was in the middle had his rifle propped horizontally across his shoulders. The echo of Calvary sent a shock through Cole. But later, when he was working on a comic strip about the whole event, he'd wonder if his eyes had played a trick on him, or if he'd somehow imagined this part entirely. PW, who'd kept his own eyes straight ahead and never once looked back, could not confirm it.

They came to where a huge dead tree lay alongside the path, a spot at which they'd stopped before, to rest on the way up. PW sat down on the hollow trunk, letting out a short blast of air as if he'd been swimming underwater. He reached for Cole, pulling him down beside him. "Well, well," he said. "How do you like them apples?"

Now that he wasn't afraid anymore, Cole was bursting with questions. "Were those guys real soldiers?"

"Maybe one time."

"You think they live up there?"

"Could be."

"Do you think they were brothers?"

"I think they were queers."

Cole knew that PW didn't really think this. He'd just wanted to say something really bad about the men. He had heard PW use the word *queer* like this before, though when he preached he always said "homosexual." ("There is no such thing as a saved homosexual.") He never said "gay." Instead of "gay marriage" or "same-sex marriage" he said "unnatural union." Sometimes, when he was repeating something some man whom he disliked had said, he'd use a falsetto voice.

Suddenly, an unwelcome picture of PW at around his own age rose to Cole's mind: a boy on a bicycle, almost running another boy down. *Outta my way, fag-boy!*

Was that the kind of kid he had been?

A reptile child.

These thoughts knotted Cole's stomach. They made him feel guilty and disloyal. Realizing that PW was staring sideways at him, he said, "Why did they make us turn around?"

"Don't know, exactly. Maybe they got something back there they didn't want us to see. Used to be moonshine stills you'd stumble on. Then it was marijuana crops. Now it's meth labs. Or maybe it's already on to something new."

"Why didn't you tell them you were a preacher?"

"Wasn't sure how they f-felt about p-preachers."

Cole didn't understand what there was about what had just happened to put PW in such a good humor.

"Do you think they're believers?"

"Do believers usually take the Lord's name in vain?"

Cole hesitated before his next question. "Didn't you want to try and save them?"

PW laughed so loud Cole was sure it could be heard as far as gunshots would have been.

"What, you think it's like some kind of magic formula I carry around? You can't convert the pagan without the power of the Holy Spirit. I was praying hard up there, and looks to me like Jesus heard. But the Spirit never took hold."

But before they started walking again, PW did offer a prayer for the men: "Father, may they come to find you and know you and choose life."

Later that day, they drove home. By then the encounter with the three men—which PW pointed out had lasted probably all of five minutes—no longer felt like such a big deal. Cole would have been glad to forget what now seemed to him a cowardly overreaction on his part.

They stopped for dinner at a Dairy Queen. The sun was low but still bright, so they ate their burgers and fries at a picnic table outside.

"By the way," said PW, "what happened this morning? With the Three Stooges back there? No reason Tracy's got to know any of that."

Just then a minibus driven by a man in a black baseball cap pulled up and about a dozen boys jumped out. The boys were all somewhere between the ages of eight and fifteen, and everything about them, from their sloppy clothes to the aggressive way they fought to be the first to reach the restaurant door, announced that they were orphans. As they passed the picnic table their eyes burned into Cole, this creature they could have ripped to pieces out of envy: a boy with a father.

When they were on the road again, PW said, "You seemed to take to the woods, Cole. Did my heart good to see it. And if you don't want to learn to hunt doesn't mean I can't teach you how to track. Nothing like getting close to an animal in its natural habitat. My daddy said he once got close enough to touch the tail of a fox. Sorry we didn't see any bear. But black bear's on the rise around here. We go back, chances are good we'll see one sometime. And you can forget what them old boys said. Bear are all up and about this time of year. Except maybe the really lazy ones."

Cole nodded. He definitely wanted to go back sometime, but he was thinking he didn't want to go into the woods again unless he, too, had a gun. First he'd have to learn how to use one, of course. Tracy would be pleased, but he'd have to be careful not to let on what had brought about his decision. It struck Cole that he was looking forward to seeing Tracy when they got home, which meant that, though he might not have known it, he must have missed her.

He said, "Do you think they knew you had a gun?"

"Yeah, they probably figured. Like they figured it wasn't something they had to worry about, neither." He laughed, and again Cole wondered what it was about those men that kept tickling PW's funny bone.

"Are you going to tell the police?"

"Tell who? Tell what? Did you see a crime being committed?"

"I meant, like, if there really was a meth lab or something."

"You see a meth lab or something?"

"No, but you said—"

"Hold on, Cole. Whatever I said, here's what I think. I think the best thing is for us to forget all about those dudes. Nothing happened, no one got hurt. And if there's a lesson in all this, it's that sometimes the right thing to do in a bad situation is to walk away from it. Not to worry about who's a bully and who's a coward, just beat a retreat. But the police. Well. I don't like the police. Might as well say it: I don't like the law. My daddy used to say, Too much law ruined this country. Jesus taught there are things that belong to Caesar and things that belong to God. But when you look at the big picture—the laws, the courts, the tax collectors, and all the rest—seems to me way too much is going to Caesar and not enough to the Lord. Sometimes I think if it was up to me, I'd rather let the bad guys go than condemn them to one of Caesar's prisons—especially after what happened with the flu."

Cole knew he was talking about the men's maximum-security prison about fifty miles north of Salvation City where he sometimes preached, and where he had brought many inmates to Christ.

"Imagine being locked up with dead bodies and no way to escape. If everyone was too sick or scared to stay and do their job, they should have let the men out. At least give them a fighting chance! I was there when they finally unlocked those gates, and it was like going back in history. I felt like one of those GIs that liberated the concentration camps. Stacks of corpses and a handful of walking skeletons, alive but half out of their minds. Same thing happened all over. You tell me, where was Caesar then?"

Where was God? Cole was thinking—but his eyes were closing. He didn't want to talk anymore. He hadn't slept well either night in the tent, and he was exhausted. His muscles burned from trudging so many miles. His limbs felt rubbery. His head lolled. He wasn't sure if he was dreaming or if he actually heard PW's phone ring.

He woke to find the blond man driving the van and the other two making out in the back.

He woke to find the van surrounded. The man in the black baseball cap and the orphans were trying to tip it.

He woke when the van hit a familiar little dip in the road that came just after the last turnoff.

It was dark out now. Light rain was falling. But why were they stopping? Why was PW sitting there with his head on the steering wheel? "Did we run out of gas?"

Slowly PW raised his head, and Cole could tell that he'd been praying.

"Hey, son." His eyes were strange—glassy, like a drunk's, or like someone who's just had a scare. "Tracy called while you were asleep. We got a surprise waiting at home."

"What surprise?" He was thinking it must be something to do with his birthday. But there'd already been a special dinner and presents and cake the day before they left to go camping. Maybe it was a present someone had dropped off late. But Cole was too tired to feel much excitement.

"You'll see in a minute," said PW, starting to drive again. "Nothing bad, don't worry. I just want you to be prepared."

A bat squeak of warning pierced Cole's fatigue.

A strange car was parked outside the house.

"Tell you what," said PW. "Let's not mess with unloading tonight. We can do it in the morning."

"In here, y'all!"

They followed Tracy's voice to the living room. She was sitting on the couch, but Cole didn't see her. All he saw was the ghost at her side. For the second time that day Cole felt the weight of PW's heavy hand on his shoulder. Then the room tipped. Cole shut his eyes. When he opened them again, his mother was still there.

PART FOUR

My sister and I were never into dressing alike. Actually, we thought that was kind of tacky. If anything, we wanted people to forget we were twins."

"Oh, isn't that interesting? And here I always thought it'd be double the fun to be a twin. Didn't you, Wyatt?"

"Never really thought about it. More coffee, ladies?"

"None for me, thanks. Look, I don't mean to be impatient, but do you think Cole will be up soon? I'm pretty worried about him after last night, and we need to move along."

"You don't have to worry about me."

Everyone stared at Cole as he entered the kitchen. Tracy started to get up but he gestured her down, saying, "All I want's orange juice, and I can get it myself." He poured himself a glass from the container on the table, but instead of sitting down with the three of them, he crossed the room and leaned against the counter. He wished they would all stop looking at him. As they did not, he faked a yawn.

"How'd you sleep, son?" asked PW. Cole saw Addy wince at the word *son*.

"Fine. I'm telling you, really, I'm fine." Not even trying to keep the irritation out of his voice.

There was more than irritation in Addy's voice. "Would it be too much to ask if I could speak with my nephew alone now?"

"'Course not," said PW. "Why don't you two use the den?"

Cordial words but the same cold-metal tone he'd used to wish the Three Stooges a blessed day. The hostility in the room was unmistakable. But at least this morning everyone was being civil.

"You sure you don't want some breakfast first?" asked Tracy. Cole studied the birdfeeder hanging outside the window above the sink and shook his head. He drained his glass and placed it in the dishwasher. When he turned around again, he saw that Tracy was crying. PW had put his arm around her, but his eyes were fixed on Cole as he followed Addy out of the room.

In the den, Addy recoiled at the sight of the rifles and Cole smiled in spite of himself.

"I guess this is gun country, isn't it. You have no idea how insane Europeans think the whole American gun culture is."

She sounded like his mother—they had the same voice—and the way she sat with her arms crossed and her hands resting on opposite shoulders recalled his mother as well. (For a while, when he was younger, he'd thought his mother did that so he wouldn't stare at her breasts.) But it was almost inconceivable to him now that he could ever mistake his aunt for his mother. Even looking at old photographs, he'd always been able to tell them apart.

The instant he sat down he wanted to bolt. He wasn't ready to talk to Addy. He hadn't even washed his face or brushed his teeth yet. And he never skipped breakfast. He needed to eat something. He needed to eat breakfast and then he needed to go back up to his room and do some thinking. He could feel himself getting queasy at the memory of last night. How everyone had fussed over him, insisting he lie down on the couch with a pillow under his head and another one under his feet, and how he had lain there for the next hour, like a rictus, listening to the two sides shout at each other.

Addy had accused PW and Tracy of kidnapping. She would not listen when they tried to explain how they thought she had passed. "It's true that I was very sick. But the only way you could have thought I was dead was if you made it up."

"Let's call it a mix-up," PW said evenly. "It's not like there weren't plenty of them. I don't know how bad it was where you were, but here it was total chaos. At the orphanage they couldn't tell us hardly anything about Cole. They said he'd been so sick he'd developed some kind of amnesia. They told us filling in the gaps could take months, maybe even years. There were way too many cases like his and not enough people for the job. They even managed to lose—"

"You must think I'm a complete idiot," Addy said. "As you can see, hard as you made it for me, I did manage to find *you*. I don't care what kind of story you told Cole. The fact is, you had an obligation to do everything possible to track down his family. Instead—admit it—you took advantage of the chaos to do whatever the hell you wanted. You had no right—"

"You act like we tried to hide the boy!" said Tracy. "It's not like we changed our identities or fled the country with him, for goodness' sake. We've always been right here. How can you call it kidnapping when the state placed him with us?"

"Oh please. Don't tell me you didn't do everything you could to cut him off from his past. Including pretending I was fucking dead!"

"This is a Christian household," Tracy said, enunciating each syllable. "I will thank you not to use Satan's language under our roof."

Addy started to laugh. She laughed merrily, as if genuinely amused by Tracy's words. Tracy looked ready to burst into tears.

"Pardon me, ma'am," said PW. "But there's something you're not getting here. First of all, from what we could tell, you've always been more of a stranger than any kind of family to Cole. But in any case, my wife and I had no obligation to go looking for you, none at all. That was for the government to do. And you're right, they don't seem to have done a very good job. Can't say as I'm much surprised, though. But it wasn't our responsibility. Our responsibility was to give Cole a good Christian home, and now that you're here you can see for yourself that is exactly what we've done. Did I try hard to find you? No, ma'am, I did not. What I did was *pray* hard. I prayed to the Lord and asked for his guidance. And I want you to know, I am right with the Lord on this. My wife and I are both right with the Lord."

Addy looked at him as if he'd just admitted he and his wife were cannibals. "You people are un-fucking-believable."

"You sure got a mouth on you, don't you, lady."

Cole held his breath. He had never seen PW look at anyone with hatred before. For a moment, he was afraid PW might slap Addy. If he did, Addy would go for his eyes. If she did, Tracy would rip Addy's throat out.

Cole sat up. "I have to go to bed now."

In the silence that followed, shame condensed in the room like a fog. Then PW said, "I think we could all use some time to chill. Why don't we call it a night. We can talk again in the morning."

Addy was whipping her head this way and that with an expression of mixed outrage and helplessness. PW and Tracy exchanged a look. Then Tracy cleared her throat and said, "Miss Abrams, at this late hour it only makes sense you spend the night. Please say you'll be our guest. Spare room's all made up." In spite of everything, her voice was sincerely hospitable. And though Addy looked as if she'd been offered a straw pallet with bedbugs, she gave a weary nod. She had been traveling for days, flying from Berlin to New York and then to Chicago, where, after spending the night with a friend, she had borrowed the friend's car and driven to Salvation City, beating Cole and PW by about two hours.

"I didn't give any warning because I was afraid to," she told Cole. "How could I be sure they wouldn't run off with you or send you away somewhere? Once I found out they were fundamentalists, I knew I had to be extra careful. To people like them I'm the enemy. An atheist expatriate Jew—what rights do I have? These fanatics will use religion to justify anything—especially the ones who believe in the imminent rapture. You do understand, don't you? That's what these monsters were counting on? The Messiah was supposed to show up before I did."

Addy told the story of her own bout with the flu. It had struck while she was away from home on a business trip. She had ended up in a hospital in Geneva. Almost the last thing she remembered before getting sick was that Cole's father had died. "It was one of the last things your mother and I ever talked about. I knew that you were getting sick, too, and that she was going between your bedside and the clinic at the college where she was helping out. But she never said anything about being sick herself."

When she was well enough, Addy had tried but was unable to reach her sister by any means. "I thought the worst, of course. I knew that the flu had hit its peak then in the Midwest."

The first official information she was able to obtain about the Vinings in Little Leap was partly wrong. "They told me that *all three of you* had died." It had not occurred to her that this might be a mistake. "Everyone said you couldn't trust anything you were told. There was way too much confusion everywhere, accurate records couldn't possibly be kept, and lots of mistakes were being made. In your case, things were even more complicated, I guess, because the hospital where you were treated had shut down. But since I hadn't heard anything from you or from anyone else about you, I didn't even think to question it. It's like everything played right into these damn liars' hands." *(Think of all the things that had to happen in order for you to end up here with us.)*

It gave Cole a funny feeling to learn that the hospital that had helped him survive had not itself survived the pandemic. He thought about Dr. Hassan and Nurse Asparagus. What had happened to them?

"As soon as the doctor said I could travel, I got myself back to Berlin. It took quite a while, though, before I could function again. I knew I had a responsibility to take care of your mom's affairs, but I didn't know where to begin. By then I knew your house had been looted—the computers and the other valuable stuff were taken first, and over time the place had been pretty much picked clean. Your parents were never the most practical people in the world, and they hadn't exactly done the best planning. I had a copy of your mom's will but no power of attorney. I didn't have access to her accounts, let alone to your father's. I didn't have any of her passwords. It was all extremely complicated. I had to hire a lawyer, of course, and he said to begin with, we should try to get hold of the death certificates. He was the one who discovered that you'd actually survived. He told me all the financial business was going to take a long time, and I'd have to be patient. But it turned out there was a database with photographs of missing children, state by state, and Cole Vining of Little Leap, Indiana, was on it."

When Cole saw the photo himself, he would barely recognize that pinched, mournful-looking child, unmistakably about to start crying. He remembered the day it had been taken, by the kindly chubby lady who'd reminded him of his bear, Tickle, and who'd asked him all those questions about religion.

Addy did not believe PW's story about the mysteriously missing cardboard box. No one she'd talked to at the orphanage had remembered anything about Cole's things being lost. "And if you believe that box just disappeared," she said, "you might as well believe in the rapture."

She took out a cigarette. "I'm sure this is a smoke-free house, but I don't give a damn."

Had she always been a smoker? Cole tried to remember but found he could not.

Next to the computer on PW's desk was a canister filled with pens and pencils. Addy dumped them out so that she could use the canister as an ashtray. At the same time, she noticed the screensaver: an image of the cross against an ocean sunrise, a changing selection of quotes from the New Testament written across the rosy sky. *Believe in the Lord Jesus and you will be saved—you and your family (Acts 16:31).* Cole watched her recoil again as she had at the rifles.

"Okay," she said, lighting up. "This whole nightmare is finally over. Here's the plan."

The smell of the smoke made his heart race. Ages ago he had stood on the freezing porch of the house in Little Leap, high as a kite off a few puffs of a Marlboro. The memory was so distracting Cole didn't hear what Addy said next. Then he caught the word *passport*.

"I'm not sure how long that will take. We'll stay in Chicago with my friend Lara. You'll like Lara. We met a few years ago at a translation conference. Lara Trachtman. She translates English and German into Russian." Addy leaned toward him with an avid expression. "You're going to love Berlin, Cole. Where, let me just say, what happened to you here would never have been allowed to happen. But compared to Germany, the U.S. might as well be in the Third World, especially if we're talking about health care. Why did every other advanced country get through the pandemic better than the U.S.? Maybe you don't feel it so much here in the sticks, but out there people are still really suffering. I guess you know what's been going on in the big cities."

He shook his head. No one in Salvation City ever talked about what was going on in the big cities.

"Oh. Well, maybe you don't want to know. But trust me, it's a horror show."

Cole remembered his mother and Addy arguing about New York, Addy insisting New York was finished, his mother insisting it was still the greatest city in the world. He remembered something PW had said, the one time they'd ever talked about Addy. "Seems funny to me, a Jewish person deciding to go live in Germany." But Addy herself used to say Germany was probably the safest place in the world today for a Jewish person to be.

"And it's so weird to see everyone here still shaking hands," she said. "That is so primitive!" Cole figured this meant everyone in Germany did the elbow bump, but it turned out they preferred the Hindu gesture of *namaste*.

His silence was making her nervous. She paused to look at the collection of framed photographs arranged on PW's desk. "I'll say this for him: he's incredibly good-looking. Here" (pointing to a wedding photo) "he actually looks a lot like Brando."

Cole wasn't sure he knew who Brando was.

"And who's the cute girl whose photos are all over the house?"

"Tracy's niece."

"And her name is—?"

He stammered when he said it, and Addy gave him an alert, knowing look. "Do I detect a smidgen of romantic interest, my blushing young man?"

He tried to shrug it off, but, to his confusion, what began as embarrassment flared into rage.

Addy saw her mistake and pretended to ask her next question idly. "What do you suppose those two are doing right now?"

He knew exactly what they were doing. They were praying. But he said nothing, and after a while Addy sighed and said, "Cole, I can see that you're upset. I think—I guess I didn't think about all the aspects of the situation. But I see now. You have a life here. These people are your friends." And when he still did not respond, she snapped her fingers in his face as if to wake him out of hypnosis. "Oh, enough now, Cole. Please. Say something, damn you."

"Can I have a cigarette?"

"What?"

"Hey, no worries. I was just asking."

"Very funny. But no. Of course not."

What a relief it was to laugh. But immediately they both fell somber again. Cole took a deep breath and said, "You don't have to do this, Addy. Like, really. I appreciate what you're trying to do for me and all, but you don't have to take me in."

"'Take you in'? Don't be absurd, Cole. I would've turned the world upside down to find you."

"I know, but—"

"But what?"

"It's just that, it's not the right thing."

"What do you mean?"

"It doesn't feel right to me."

"*What* doesn't feel right?"

"Going away."

"You mean, you think you belong here? With those two? I can't believe that."

"Look, it's not like you think, Addy. They're not monsters. They just want to bring everyone to Jesus, and they want Jesus to be part of everything they do. And they don't think you're the enemy, either. Only the devil is the enemy. They want everyone to be saved. Not just Christians, but Jewish people, and Muslim people, too. They pray for everyone. I'll bet they're praying for you right now."

"Oh my god." For the third time that morning, Cole saw Addy recoil. "They've brainwashed you."

Cole said nothing. He did not know how to explain. It wasn't that he knew exactly what he wanted or what he believed or where he belonged—he was as confused and torn about these things as he had ever been. But he knew he wasn't ready to pack up and leave today and go live with his aunt. He knew he didn't want to be adopted by her. (He didn't want to be adopted by anyone, was the conclusion he'd come to last night.) And he didn't believe she really wanted him, either. He hadn't forgotten what he'd been told.

"You don't want me tying you down, Addy. I know you never wanted kids."

He felt guilty, seeing her struggle. When she was able to speak again, she said, "Whether I wanted to have kids or not has nothing to do with this, Cole. Of course I want you! And what about your parents? We both know they'd be very, very unhappy about your being here, don't we? It's not just *that*" (gesturing at the screensaver) "or *that*" (the gun cabinet). "I sat with that woman—"

"Tracy."

"—for a couple of hours yesterday, and I almost fell off my chair when she told me she's been homeschooling you. A person like that could never pass herself off as a teacher in any other civilized country. In fact, homeschooling is illegal in

Germany. And let me tell you something, Cole. There are Christians everywhere, but it's only here that you have this craze for keeping kids out of school and trying to ban whatever's not in the Bible. I know you're too smart to believe there were dinosaurs on Noah's ark, but what kind of education can you be getting from people who do believe that?"

She kept trying to look him in the eye, but he kept his head down. He wondered if PW had unpacked the van all by himself that morning. He wondered if PW's shins ached as much as his own did today.

Addy's voice softened. "If you tell me they're not monsters, okay, I accept that. You wouldn't care about them if they hadn't been good to you. But I don't trust them. I don't trust a preacher who lies when it's convenient for him. Besides, I've checked this guy out. It's not like he's a real ordained minister or has a degree in divinity or anything like that." (Cole didn't see how, if you didn't believe in religion at all, these things could make any difference.) "As for those two praying for me, well, if they are, I know what they're praying for. They're praying the scales will fall from my eyes and I'll start believing the same incredibly dumb things they do. But it's not going to happen, Cole, not any more than this rapture thing is going to happen. Do you understand what I'm saying?"

"Please don't get upset."

"I'm sorry, I can't help it. It's not that I'm upset with *you*, Cole. I know none of this is your fault. It's just that, whenever I thought about this moment, I never pictured it happening like this. I guess I wouldn't let myself think you might not want to come with me."

Had he ever seen Addy cry before? He didn't think so. But

nothing she could have done at that moment could have evoked his mother more powerfully. *(Why did we come here? We never should have come!)* He sat there as he had done so often with his mother, anguished with guilt but unable to comfort her. And it struck him what it would be like living with Addy, seeing his mother and hearing her voice every day. They had the same smile, the same laugh, the same way of crying.

He would have cried himself then if Addy hadn't quickly pulled herself together.

"You know what I think?" she said, sitting up very straight. "I think we need to talk about something else. I think *you* should talk for a while."

"Me? About what?"

"About you. About your life, your friends—whatever you want."

She had to keep prodding him, and though his heart wasn't in it, he tried. She asked a lot of questions, listened intently to every word he said, asked more questions, and after half an hour announced that she wanted to see his room. Cole balked. It was a pigsty, he said. But that was an exaggeration (Tracy tidied his room often), and when Addy insisted, he gave in and led her upstairs.

He both wanted and didn't want to show her his drawings. He felt her stiffen at the biblical ones, but he could tell she was being truthful when she said she admired them.

"I had no idea you were such a gifted draftsman."

"It's fun," he said. "Someday I want to publish a book."

She was more interested, though, in the many drawings of Starlyn. "I don't suppose your wanting to stay here could have anything to do with her?"

It was like a light slap. "No. Who said that?" But even as he denied it he saw how it might be true. At which his face burned, and a drowning sensation engulfed him.

Back downstairs, they found Tracy alone in the kitchen. PW was at the church, she said, and she was going outside to do some gardening. They'd find the ham salad sandwiches she'd made them for lunch in the fridge.

"But if that won't do, Miss Abrams, please just help yourself. Let's see. Chips in the bread box, fig bars in the cookie jar. And that coffee in the pot is fresh."

Tracy was smiling, but her eyes and nose were red, and her voice was the voice of a small child trying not to be scared.

Just a few months ago it had felt very strange to Cole to pray before a meal; now it felt strange not to pray.

They were both too hungry not to eat, but they did so slowly, tentatively, like convalescents, or people breaking a fast. Addy finished her sandwich first and, ignoring the fresh coffee, made herself tea.

"It really is very peaceful and sheltered here," she said as she carried her cup to the table. Cole wasn't sure whether she meant the town or the house or maybe just the kitchen. He didn't think he had to respond, though. He was feeling calmer now, partly because Addy herself was calmer but also because he knew she'd soon be gone.

He expected her to light another cigarette after lunch, but she didn't. He wondered if the ashes in the desk canister had been discovered yet, and wished he'd thought to dump them.

Cole was right, Addy was leaving, but she still had some things to say. It was as if she had done a lot of thinking in the short time since her outburst.

"Before I got here yesterday, the picture I had of you was very different. In my mind, you were still just this little boy. But in fact you've changed more than I could've imagined. You've grown up so much, Cole, you're like a young man now—so handsome and so serious!—and I know I can't just pick you up and carry you off in my arms. And I understand that maybe I was in too big a rush. I didn't handle this whole situation very delicately, and I'm sorry about that. But we need to move on.

"I've decided the best thing for me to do is to leave you here for now, go back to Lara's, and give you some time to think. But that means really think for yourself, not just accept what everyone around here believes or tries to tell you. And I want you to remember that my leaving doesn't mean I'm giving up. I still want you to come away with me, but I need you to want it, too, and right now I can see that you don't.

"I'm going, but before I go, you and I have to agree on some things. First, you have to promise me we'll be in touch. I need to know that, no matter what happens, you won't disappear, you won't go anywhere without letting me know, you won't let anyone talk you into breaking off contact with me. Second, I want you to promise to think about your education. I want you to think about whether the way you're being taught here is any preparation for getting into a good college, and what this could mean for your future. You should know that, once your parents' affairs are straightened out, you'll have some money coming to you, certainly enough to pay for college.

"Another thing I need you to promise—and this is the absolutely most important thing—is that you won't let anyone turn you against your parents. Don't let anyone try to tell you they didn't love you, because they always loved you very, very much. Don't believe anyone who tries to tell you that because they didn't believe in God, they're now in hell. Because that's a lie, Cole, a sick and terrible lie. And if there really is a God and some kind of afterworld, a place we'll all meet again, trust me, your mom and dad are there and deserve to be there as much as anyone else. And I don't want you ever, ever to forget how brave your mother was. The last thing she did in her life was to help other people. I'm very proud of her for that, and you should be proud of her, too."

He thought it would be such a relief when she was gone, and that he'd be glad. But after she drove away he went to his room and he cried for a good long time.

HE SAT ON THE STAIRS, listening to Tracy. She was in the kitchen, cooking dinner and talking on the phone to her sister.

"Don't that beat all? And I tell you, Taffy, you could train every tot in Indiana on that potty-mouth of hers. And right in front of the boy, too. But I could tell he was used to it. Can you imagine having to send him back to live with folks like that? Well, yes, yes, it could! That's why I say, you got to start praying, we got to get everyone praying right away. You know, Wyatt himself spent a good four hours on his knees today. He's upset now Cole will think he's a liar. But I talked to the boy myself a little while ago, and I explained. We prayed night and day on this matter, we prayed and we fasted, and the Lord's message was clear. And Cole was doing just peachy before that witch flew in on her broom. Now Wy's afraid she's gonna make some kind of scandal, you know, with her wild accusations and such. Says she's probably got a whole mess of lawyers and self-called child experts on the case. I always knew this day might come, but I just about throw up if I even think about Cole leaving this house. Far as Wyatt's concerned, that's his son. And you know Cole being here has been such a help in keeping him steady, too. Full moon don't affect him like it sometimes can. Drink don't tempt him. I have talked to Cole, and I think he gets it. I told him Wyatt loves him more than he loves hisself. I told him how sometimes a person can seem like a he-man on the outside but inside they're really like a child, and he looked at me like he knew what I was talking about. That boy is *sharp*.

"I know what Satan is up to. But Jesus created us a family here, and he can't mean for Cole to be snatched away just to be corrupted and lost all over again. How can that be? Imagine, a woman like that. Mouth like that. Even a roach'd think twice before crawling in there.

"That's right. That's what I keep telling myself. We just got to hang on a little longer. And you know, Taff, the whole time the boys were gone I had that feeling I was telling you about. That whirlpool-stomach feeling? Like something's about to happen? Something big? Now I got it all the time.

"Ouch! Darn near chopped my own finger off. Hey, listen, that's Jesus telling me to quit gabbing and focus on my task. Wyatt should be home any minute and he's gonna need my full attention. What? Of course! Starlyn's welcome any day of the week and twice on Sunday, you know that. We're blessed she seems to like it here more and more. But I don't want you to be jealous about that, you hear?"

MEMORY DREAMS. Dr. Hassan had told Cole that they might happen. People with amnesia sometimes dream of things they actually experienced but can't remember at all, not even after being told about them. "And then sometimes, perhaps triggered by the dreams, the waking memory of those events comes back to them."

He is back in Little Leap, he is crawling through the house on his hands and knees when he discovers his mother in the bathroom, pitched over the toilet bowl. At first he thinks she is being sick, as he himself keeps being sick. Then he sees that she is drinking greedily, scooping up water from the bowl with both hands.

His mother is leaving the house. She is wearing her winter coat and her blue bandanna. She warns him to lock the door and not to let anyone in. "Even if they tell you Jesus sent them."

He is in the kitchen, trimming the mold from the last slice of raisin bread. The raisins are like bits of gravel.

He is standing outside his parents' room. Through the half-closed door he sees someone sprawled across the bed. Really, all he can see is a pair of bare legs. A woman, not his mother, the legs are too dark to be his mother's, the legs are black. He steps back, not wanting to intrude, not wanting to disturb this person, this mystery guest, he cannot imagine who she is—they do not know any black women in Little Leap—and he cannot imagine why she has been put here, in his parents' room, instead of in the guest room down the hall.

The way she lies there makes him think she's asleep, but it is daylight (the only time he'd be able to see since the power went out), and she is not still, she is restless, her legs keep moving, moving, as if she was dreaming of climbing stairs, and she is talking to herself, a muttering singsong that spooks him.

A single thought is being hammered like a nail to the inside of his skull: something must be done. But the thought that should follow—what it is that must be done—doesn't come, and will not ever come, there is just the hammering, harder and harder, the nail being driven in deeper and deeper, until there is only pain, unimaginable pain.

He didn't let them in. They broke in. He hears them banging and shouting. He hears them coughing and gagging, sees the scurrying beams of their flashlights before they tumble pell-mell into the room.

It's okay, you're safe now, they say. But they look as if they were seeing a ghost.

A woman's trembling fingers caress his cheek. "Poor little thing."

He says, "Are you from Jesus?" and everyone smiles.

He dreams. He remembers.

Now an old story comes back to him, a story his mother liked to tell—and one he liked to hear—about a man who saved a younger man from being run over by a subway train. A seizure had sent the younger man sprawling onto the tracks. The other man had only seconds to decide what to do. He jumped onto the tracks and lay down, protecting the convulsing man with his own body. The train rolled just inches above his hunched back.

Once, the story came up when his parents were having some friends over for dinner. The others laughed when his mother confessed that she thought about the Subway Superman all the time. He was the person she most wanted to be.

"Don't laugh, it's true. I'd rather pass a test like that than win the lottery. Maybe it's because I'm the kind of person who's afraid of everything and can't imagine ever doing such a thing myself. But just think, with something like that on your résumé, you could be at peace with yourself. It wouldn't matter what mistakes you'd made, or whatever stupid, shameful, petty things you might've done. Anytime you started to be down on yourself, you could look back to the day you proved to the world you were a good human being. How could you ever hate yourself again? Plus, everyone would have to treat you with respect, no one could say they were better than you.

"And think about his kids." (The man's two little girls had been with him that day.) "How lucky for them to know this about their father. Anyway, if it was me, even if I never accomplished another thing in life, I'd die happy. I'd have given my son a reason to be proud for the rest of his life."

Her voice had wobbled a bit as she finished, and Cole's father addressed the table in a stage whisper: "I think my wife's had a little too much wine." And though his mother laughed along with everyone else, Cole knew that later, after the guests were gone, his parents would fight.

"But hold on," one of the guests said then. "I know what

you're saying, Serena, but I'm not so sure a single incident like that would change a person's whole life. My guess is people who do heroic things still have the same problems and negative feelings about themselves as they had before."

"Yeah," said someone else. "And for some people, like soldiers and firemen, it's a job, something they do all the time—"

"But that's different," Cole's mother said, her voice rising. "This was just an ordinary guy. It wasn't his job to run toward danger, and there were other people on the platform that day who did nothing. It's a whole other level of sacrifice, in my book. Remember that pilot who landed the plane in the Hudson? That was admirable, of course. But I wouldn't call him a true hero like this other man. I mean, the pilot acted to save himself, too. He wasn't risking his life for a stranger."

"This might sound weird," said a third guest, Cole's mother's friend Shireen (the only other woman at the table). "But I'm thinking about what you said about the kids. I can imagine being one of his daughters, or his wife, say, and actually *resenting* what he did. Like, you're right, look at the risk he took. Didn't he stop to think what it would mean to those girls if he were crushed before their eyes? I'll bet his wife thought of that. I mean, he made a choice, and if he'd gotten killed saving that guy his family might have ended up hating him. Like, how could you put a total stranger ahead of *us*? I think it would be perfectly natural for them to feel some kind of anger."

Addy was right, thought Cole. His mother *had* been brave. But at the time he hadn't been proud of her. He'd been angry and frustrated and hurt. Even though she never left him alone for more than an hour or two, and even though during that time he'd usually just sleep—still, he hated her for going. He only had to tell her if he wanted her to stay, she kept saying, but he didn't *want* to have to tell her, he wanted her to *know* how he felt *without* being told and then *just do what he wanted*. He was deathly ill, but his stubborn streak was thriving. He didn't care how bad things were at the clinic. He didn't care about the other sick people, he cared only about himself. Once when he was alone he woke up dying of thirst. His mother had left a full pitcher of ice water by his bed, but when he went to lift it his arm was too weak and he sprained his wrist, spilling the water all over himself. He had lain there howling in rage and pain and thirst, and he had cursed her over and over. Miles across town she must have heard, for there she was, running up the stairs, taking him into her arms and rocking him, begging forgiveness and promising him he'd be all right. He remembered how hot her body was because her fever had started. And he would blame her for that, too. If she hadn't insisted on volunteering at the clinic, maybe she wouldn't have got sick and died.

He hadn't understood before how much he was still holding all this against her. He'd been told that this was a natural response, but it was hard not to feel ashamed. Whenever he looked back now he hated the boy he had been, especially the way he had treated his parents. In almost every memory he appeared selfish, spiteful, mean. He saw how difficult he had made it for them to love him. He had been heartless and unfair. And then he would think that he had no right to miss them, no right to feel sorry for himself. He who had wished so many times that he were an orphan. Who had cursed his mother over and over. He had not honored his father and mother. He had not loved them enough. They had died at the moment when he was feeling most alienated from them, when he had barely been speaking to them. It was a terrible punishment—like the kind visited upon one of the many bad sons in the Bible stories he was coming to know so well.

In this way, though, he had always understood his mother: he wanted to be the Subway Superman, too.

Later the night of the dinner party, while his parents had fought ("You humiliated me!" "You humiliated yourself!"), he'd logged on to YouTube and watched a video about the man, whose name was Wesley Autrey—the first of many views. Cole had even used Wesley Autrey's story to create one of his first comic strips. But like everything else that had once belonged to him, it had somehow been lost. In fact, he'd forgotten all about it.

Not just Wesley Autrey's story but other true-life stories of heroism obsessed him.

In Iowa, a group of Boy Scouts is caught in a tornado. Though injured and in severe pain, one boy struggles to pull his scout mates from under the rubble. Why couldn't something like that happen to *him*? For there seemed no end of such stories on the Net, and the population of heroes his own age was surprisingly large. Here a boy rescued not one but *two* people from drowning. There a boy helped his mother to give birth. In his neighborhood in Chicago there'd been a boy called Major who'd stopped a whole gang of kids from torturing a dog. The dog, scarred and lame from its ordeal, dragged everywhere behind Major like a broken tail.

A few days after her visit to Salvation City, Addy e-mailed Cole some pictures. One of them showed the light-colored six-story building where she had her apartment in Berlin, in a neighborhood called Prenzlauer Berg. It was the only picture in the group Cole hadn't seen before. Most of the others were copies of photos his mother had sent to Addy over the years. There were some baby pictures, including one taken by his father immediately after Cole was born, and there were several school pictures. In some of the photos he was by himself and in others he was with friends or parents or grandparents. There was a picture of him with Sadie when she was a puppy, another of him and his dad at a Cubs game. In the most recent photo, he and his parents were standing outside their building in Chicago. It was snowing. It was their last Christmas together and Addy was visiting; that would have been Addy behind the camera. There were also pictures of his parents without him (more of his mother than of his father), some taken years before Cole was born. It was a picture of his mother when she was a little girl (same eyes, much curlier hair) that brought him the greatest emotion.

It wasn't until he saw these photographs that Cole understood his fear was real: he was starting to forget what his parents had looked like. Recently he had tried drawing them from memory but had given up in frustration. He was thrilled to have the photos now—for one thing, he could use them for drawings—though every time he looked at them he suffered fresh pain. He would never see his parents alive again. There had been no mistake—they would not rise from the dead as he and Addy had done. But something had changed. Disturbing as Addy's visit had been, it seemed to have quieted some storm in him. It was as if in some way she had given his parents back to him. At least, they felt closer than they had before. He was still their son. They were gone, but they were still his parents. He did not need any others.

He did not care so much about the photographs of himself. He didn't like looking at pictures of himself, and he'd always hated having his picture taken. He could not recall a time in his life when he hadn't thought there was something (either big or *ginormous*, depending on his age) about his looks that was wrong. In fact, he was surprised anew each time he recalled how Addy had described him: *like a young man now, so handsome and so serious.*

Alone in his room, he stared bravely and hopefully at the young man in the full-length mirror hanging inside his closet door. So handsome and so serious. Yes, maybe. Sometimes he thought he could see it, too.

PART FIVE

It began as a small thing: a red round mark on the right shoulder blade, as if a hot dime had been pressed there.

"It's nothing," said PW. "It just itches." He asked Tracy to dab the spot with some calamine lotion. But the next day the itch was worse, and all up and down his spine he had tingling and pricking sensations, which soon turned into what he said felt like a bad sunburn across his back. He had a fever, too, and a mild headache. He took some aspirin and went to bed. "I'll be fine in the morning. You know me." Never sick a day in his life.

And maybe if he'd been able to sleep that night—maybe then he would have felt better in the morning. But the "sunburn" kept him up. And now there was a red stripe down his back ("Long as it ain't yellow!"), like the mark of a whip.

Tracy wanted him to see the doctor, but PW said he wasn't about to make a big deal out of what was probably just a simple case of hives. "Maybe I've developed some kind of allergy." After all, the person without some kind of allergy these days was the exception.

Tracy said hives didn't give a person headache and fever. "I think it's some kind of nerve thing," she said.

"Your wife was right," said the doctor. "I wish you'd come in sooner."

Nine days after the first symptom, painful oozing blisters covered much of PW's torso, front and back. Had he come in right away, an antiviral drug might have helped. As it was, not much besides rest and painkiller could be prescribed.

The rash should clear up in another three to four weeks, the doctor said. "But I've got to warn you it could be a rough ride. Things might get worse before they get better." *Much* worse, he should have said.

Cole had never heard of shingles before. It was frightening to see PW so helpless in its clutches. He couldn't help thinking about his father in his last anguished days, though no one had said anything about PW being in danger of dying. The pain was so bad ("It's like someone across the room is throwing knives at my back") that he could not give his sermons. Some days he could not even leave his room. At its worst, it turned him into a raving stranger.

"What is it now? Just what is it you're trying to tell me, Lord?"

Cole and Tracy huddled together downstairs, listening to the commotion overhead. Shouts and roars accompanied by much fist banging and foot stamping and now and then the crash of some object hurled across the room.

"Just why are you making my life so hard? Just tell me, how'd I screw up this time?"

But even as she wept Tracy assured Cole that PW would be all right. "The Lord never sends anyone more suffering than they can bear."

Not that that was going to stop her from blaming the suffering on Addy. An almighty coincidence, was it not, that PW, who was never sick, should have become so very sick at this particular time?

Cole had kept his promise to Addy to stay in touch. It was from her that he learned that another name for shingles was "the devil's whip."

WHEN BOOTS HEARD Cole was learning how to shoot, he blessed him with a Remington .22 from his own collection.

The first time Starlyn saw Cole with the rifle, she said, "Now you're complete." Said it lightly, like something that had just popped into her head. But Cole pretended it was her way of saying she liked him better now. Certainly these days she was nicer to him. But that niceness appeared to be part of a larger change taking place in Starlyn that summer. She was still apocalyptic, but it was as if some restless, ornery part of her had gone into hibernation.

Earlier, when she was in a mood, you'd know it by the way she flounced in and out of rooms and acted as if she didn't always hear what was said to her. Now she was more likely to lapse into something like a trance. Cole had observed her staring at the same page of a magazine for almost an hour. When something on TV made everyone else laugh, she startled, proving she hadn't really been watching.

Maybe it was about turning sixteen—no denying she acted more like a grown-up than when he'd first met her. More likely it was about Mason, the burden of her secret love. Or maybe it had something to do with being a rapture child (though Cole still wasn't quite sure what made her—or any other kid for that matter—one of those; and sixteen was old for a rapture child).

Whatever it was, he couldn't help preferring this new Starlyn, who was not only nicer but even prettier in her new soft dreaminess. Not that he'd lost all fear of her, but most of his feelings for her were tender ones, including something he wouldn't have expected to feel and which he thought she might find insulting. *He* found it baffling: what reason could there be for him to feel sorry for her?

Yes, he'd caught her crying while listening to her iPod—but what girl didn't cry at "O Lonesome O Lord"? Cheerfulness was beneath apocalyptic girls, but no one would have called Starlyn unhappy. Nothing came easier to her than making friends. And this summer there was an exciting new face: Amberly, who was twenty and newlywed and who'd just moved to town from Evansville. Amberly wasn't apocalyptic, but she had dramatic dark eyes and the grace and perfect posture of a ballerina. Starlyn was flattered that a twenty-year-old married woman would want to hang out with her. They saw each other almost every day. It occurred to Cole that at least some of the time Starlyn was supposed to be with Amberly she might actually be with Mason. But no one shared that suspicion as far as he knew.

At first he figured it was because of Mason that Starlyn was spending so much time visiting Salvation City—why else? But then he thought it could be Amberly, and later he learned of another factor. Starlyn's mother, divorced already a few years from Starlyn's stepfather (her real father had run off before she was born), had just started dating a certain man. There'd been other men since the divorce, but "This one's a keeper" (Tracy). Cole sensed a problem, though, something about which everyone was tight-lipped, at least around him.

Lovebirds need a little privacy, he was told. But Cole thought maybe Starlyn and this man, Judd, didn't like each other. Starlyn herself never spoke of Judd. But once Cole made the mistake of mentioning him, and Starlyn turned so sharply on her heel that her hair, which she happened to be wearing braided that day, smacked him in the mouth like a cable. The sting lasted a remarkably long time, and whenever Cole was tempted (and he was tempted a lot) to ask Starlyn whatever happened to that boyfriend of hers in Louisville, he felt it again.

Starlyn didn't talk about that boyfriend anymore, but she didn't talk about Mason, either, and for all Cole knew there was nothing to talk about. Say it was just one kiss, just that one time, just playing around, no biggie. No secret love. No *love* at all.

But Mason, too, was a different person these days. In Bible study he often had trouble sitting still, instead bouncing around the room or pacing the floor like someone expecting major news or an important visitor any minute. He mixed up names and faces as he hadn't done before. He mixed up Cole and Clem, for example, who, though they usually sat next to each other, looked nothing alike.

Riding his bike downtown one day, Cole saw Mason walking along, and though he waved and even called out, Mason ignored him.

Once again, as when they'd first met, Cole found Mason scary-looking. The same tense, starving-wolf look as the three men on the mountain. A wolf with one supersharp, blood-shot, ever-shifting eye.

Cole wasn't the only one to notice a change in Mason.

"It's like he's shook up somewhere deep" (Tracy). Probably for the same reason as her own whirlpool-stomach feeling. It wasn't just the two of them, either. It was another epidemic: more and more people feverish with the notion of living on the cusp of Something Big.

Partly it was the weather—though the era of extreme weather was old by now, and if the floods and droughts and violent storms that struck season after season really were a sign of the end, no one could say what the Lord meant by dragging it out. Once again that year, spring had brought a record number of tornado outbreaks and enough rainfall to cause flooding throughout the Midwest. Now it was heat waves. Late July was especially bad, and nowhere worse than in Chicago.

It's been over a hundred for five days straight, and I've never felt humidity like this before. The anxiety level is pretty high, too, because everyone knows the city doesn't have the resources to cope with an emergency.

With this message Addy sent Cole links to articles about the connection between extreme weather and global warming.

"Whatever you call it, and you can call it global warming or climate change or anything you want," said PW, "it's still the hand of God. Meaning it is part of his plan. And the only way we can understand any of it, or where God is going with it, is by praying and pondering Scripture and praying some more."

Many Christians had grown up believing that the Gospel age would end in their lifetime. Many had taken it for granted that, when the pandemic struck, the final days had arrived. But as weeks and then months went by, people began craving a sign. Was it wrong to pray for a clearer idea of how much longer the world had to exist? There were a lot of pastors who differed from Pastor Wyatt about righteous Christian behavior in this regard. They believed time was so short that people should drop everything else and focus all their efforts on preparing for Christ's return.

"And a little child shall lead them."

"If you do not change and become like little children, you shall not enter the kingdom of heaven."

On this point Scripture was clear. It was the small fry on earth who'd be the big fish in heaven. *Look to the child for the way.* It was because of this that rapture children were now more sought after than ever, and though child preachers were nothing new, congregations could not get enough of them.

Earlier that summer, during a service at a church in Denver, a three-year-old named Dewdrop had toddled down the aisle, cutting the minister off in midsentence by tugging at his trouser cuff. When the minister asked her what she wanted, she said, "I want to preach." Struck (as Reverend Gates later explained) by the authority in her tone and the meaningful way she locked eyes with him, he lifted her up to the mike.

And in a voice that managed to be at once like honey and a clap of thunder, she said, "Obey the Commandments. Love and forgive. Pray to the Lord, who is near." Like a tsunami, was how members of the congregation described the wave of emotion that swept through the church. Many broke into loud weeping, flinging their heads back or their arms into the air. Others hurled themselves to their knees in the aisles, crying out to be saved. All was caught on camera, and soon more than a million people around the world had sent messages to Dewdrop asking her to pray for them.

There wasn't really much of the child anymore about Clem Harley, who most people probably would have taken for older than his age of thirteen. He often seemed (people said) like a man in a boy's body (the way Pastor Wyatt often seemed like a boy in a man's body). With Pastor Wyatt too sick to do his duty, the Church of Salvation City's boy preacher was called to step in. But those who'd seen videos of Dewdrop or of other famous baby preachers couldn't get too excited about Clem. He had a crackly voice and a droning inflection, the complete opposite of Pastor Wyatt. And unlike Pastor Wyatt, Brother Clem never smiled.

Not that Clem wasn't a prodigy. But knowing the Bible backward and forward as he appeared to do just made him seem even less childlike. No one complained, of course; no one would have wanted to hurt his feelings. Though his feelings must have been hurt anyway when people nodded off, as at least some did every sermon.

It was now common practice to ask if any children in the congregation had received a word to share with their fellow worshippers. Pastor Wyatt had started doing this at every service, but so far (in spite of some whispering and sharp elbowing here and there) no child had stepped forward. Each time, the disappointment in the air seemed to grow a little thicker. Then Pastor Wyatt would chide his flock for lack of faith and for the sin of impatience, quoting from Lamentations, "The Lord is good to those who wait for him," and from the book of James, "Be patient, then, my brothers and sisters, until the coming of the Lord."

And, according to Clem, "If they hadn't been so darned impatient, Adam and Eve would still be in Paradise."

"I KNOW ABOUT YOU AND MASON."

Had he actually said it? Starlyn's face left no doubt that he had. And instantly Cole was sorry. And he was even more amazed: where had he got the nerve?

They were alone in the house. An hour ago, someone had called to say that one of Boots's grandsons, Jeptha, a leader in the Christian Zionist Defense League, had been killed by rocket fire in the Holy Land. Tracy and PW had gone to be with the Ludwig family.

Starlyn was using the computer in the kitchen while Cole waited his turn. He wondered if there'd be a message from Addy. He hadn't heard from her in a few days, which was unusual, but he figured it was because of the heat wave. The last time they'd spoken, Chicago was having power outages and Addy was in full-frontal freak. She had called from her cell, warning that it was almost out of power and they might get cut off.

"Yesterday it hit a hundred and seven. When there's a blackout all Lara and I can do is lie on the bare floor with wet paper towels stuck to our skin. Hello? Last night you could smell fire and hear sirens and gunshots and alarms going off—it was like a war zone. Hello? You still there? In the bad neighborhoods people are afraid to go out no matter how hot it gets. Some people have died because they were too scared to leave their windows open and their apartments turned into ovens. They say it's like—hello? They say it's like the flu all over again, with hospitals shutting their doors and the morgue running out of—hello? I feel like if I have to stay here much longer I'll lose my mind. I'm going to—" End of call.

Cole hadn't heard from Addy since, but he thought he knew what she'd been about to say. She'd been about to say that she was coming to Salvation City, where it was several degrees cooler and where so far they'd had only one little brownout and of course no arson or looting at all.

Before the heat wave began Cole and Addy had talked about another visit and how maybe this time, instead of her coming to him, he'd go to her in Chicago. Not that PW and Tracy were down with this plan, and Cole himself had mixed feelings about seeing Addy again so soon. But the idea of being back in Chicago was irresistible, something he'd started to dream about even before Addy came. And so he was disappointed to think that now the trip might not happen.

But then, this was becoming a season of disappointments. What with Addy dropping like a bomb into their lives, and the deadly weather, and PW's shingles attack, there hadn't been any more camping trips, either.

But even if he never made it back to the woods, Cole was

happy with his Remington and with his decision to learn how to shoot—though shooting turned out to be much harder than he'd been led to think it was. (Tracy's idea that a person who could draw well could probably shoot well, too, proved to be nonsense.) He discovered he was anything but a natural marksman, though he did at least a tiny bit better with a rifle than with a pistol. Not that he found it all that much fun, either. Firing at soda cans and plastic jugs and Satan's silhouette was no big thrill to him, and he was still not keen on the idea of hunting. Funny, he almost got more satisfaction from cleaning the rifle than from firing it. The series of snaps and click-clacks made by disassembling and reassembling the parts, the smells of the solvent and gun oil—these gave him real pleasure (oddly enough, since he couldn't recall ever getting pleasure from cleaning anything else before). But he discovered it was true what he'd been told, that he'd feel better, "more comfortable in your skin" (Boots), once he knew how to handle a gun. No denying. And when he saw on the news the gangs wilding in Chicago, he wondered how someone as defenseless as Addy could protect herself. He felt afraid for Addy and for whoever this Lara was, and he felt inexplicably guilty, too. As if protecting them was somehow *his* responsibility.

Bad a shot as he might yet be, were anyone to break into the house right then and dare touch a hair on Starlyn's head, Cole swore he would not flinch; his aim would be true.

And yet it was he who had put those tears in her eyes. How messed up was that?

"All yours," she'd said, getting up from the computer and starting to leave the room.

241

Maybe that was it. Maybe it was desperately wanting to keep her there that had made him blurt out those words. Which certainly had kept her there.

Or maybe he just couldn't stand the suspense anymore.

Was she or wasn't she sneaking out to see Mason? Were they kissing, et cetera? How far had they gone? These questions would not leave Cole alone. He knew that Starlyn had made a commitment to God to remain pure until her wedding day, and that she belonged to her church's virgin club. But everyone knew that teenagers who made this commitment weren't always able to keep it, and that when this happened, though you were judged to have fallen, you weren't punished; you were forgiven.

If he told her what he already knew, maybe she'd tell him more?

For sure he'd never have been so bold as to speak if she hadn't started being nicer to him. But that summer it had seemed to him they were even becoming friends. Not that she ever completely lost her air of detachment and superiority or gave him reason to believe he could be anyone seriously important to her. But when she wasn't off with Amberly or some other BF, she seemed happy enough to hang out with him, playing cards or video games. Or she would sit and let him sketch her head or her hands. (He was really dying to draw her feet, but even when she was barefoot he was too shy to ask.) She said she thought he was mad talented and even offered to collaborate with him on a comic: "Your art and my words."

Up till now she'd shown little interest in his art and no curiosity at all about his past. But one day she surprised Cole

242

by asking about his parents and what being in an orphanage was really like. Another day she wanted to hear what it was like to have almost died from the flu. These were, of course, the top three subjects Cole was least eager to talk about. But that didn't mean he wasn't grateful to be asked. He was grateful for any attention from Starlyn. And she had listened when he told his stories, and he could tell she was moved, as he was moved when she said she was sure his parents had been good people.

She said she knew—sort of—what it might be like to lose a parent because she had no father herself. "He's alive but I've never laid eyes on him."

Another new Starlyn thing that summer was how often she would say—usually out of the blue—how much her aunt and uncle loved Cole. "I don't think it's possible for two people to love a body more." It was hard for Cole not to suspect she had been put up to this. "I've been praying for God to do a work in your heart so you'll know this is where you belong."

But when he was honest with himself Cole knew the real reason he'd spoken up was to make himself look good. He wanted Starlyn to know. All summer he'd been dying to tell her, dying for her to know that he'd discovered her secret months ago and never said a word.

How could such loyalty fail to impress her?

How could it not bring the two of them closer?

And what on God's green earth did Cole want more than to be closer to Starlyn?

The thought that she would not always be there (in fact, her mother was coming to fetch her that weekend) made him deliriously sad.

As for Mason, Cole did not like him anymore. He did not trust Mason. He was only a molecule away from hating Mason Boyle.

"Please," she said thickly. "Please, don't."

Even if he'd stopped to think before shooting off his mouth, he'd never have predicted this. Don't *what?* As if he were about to get violent with her!

"Gosh, Starlyn, I was just saying. I won't tell anyone, if that's what you're thinking. I promise I'd never do that."

She dabbed a spilled tear with her fingertip (he *felt* this, as if she had literally grazed his heart). She hiccupped once and said, "Well, *th-that's* good to know." As she grabbed a tissue from a box on the kitchen counter and blew her nose, Cole delicately looked away. He thought she would leave the room then. Instead, she opened the cookie jar sitting on the counter and took out an Oreo.

He held his breath as he watched her eat the cookie, slowly and thoughtfully, as if she were consuming important information. The sound of her deliberate munching filled the room, and he felt that, too: her teeth, her tongue. Her wet eyelashes made him feel weak.

She was wearing her hair up today. Cole tried not to stare too obviously at her ears. (Sketching her once, he'd been struck by the thought that some ears, at least, really could be compared to seashells.)

She thumbed crumb dust from her lower lip and said, "I know you're a good boy, Cole."

Talking down to him: something she'd stopped doing recently, making it all the more humiliating for him to hear her do it now.

"Like, maybe you saw something or heard something you're too young to understand?"

Cole nodded, then blushed in confusion because of course he hadn't meant to agree with this.

"I'd never ask you to lie for me. But remember, a promise is sacred."

This time his nod was emphatic. He wanted nothing more than for her to understand that her secret was safe with him.

"If you were older," she said, "I could explain everything." Something withered in him. She was brushing him off, like the cookie crumbs. But at least she wasn't upset anymore. At least he hadn't blown everything and made an enemy of her.

She opened the cookie jar again and took out another Oreo. But this time, instead of eating it herself, she offered it to Cole. He didn't want it, he had no saliva in his mouth, the cookie tasted like grit, but he ate it anyway because he thought this was what she wanted. What a wonderful life that would be: day after day, doing nothing but what she wanted. "All I can tell you is, something awesome is going to happen."

She was smiling, her head tilted to one side, watching him as if she was seeing something curious about him, or something she hadn't noticed before. He thought she had never looked so soft. She had never looked so beautiful. *Something awesome is going to happen.* Something awesome was happening right now. She was standing just inches away from him. He thought he smelled peaches. He held the cookie mush in his mouth, unable to speak, unable to swallow.

She lifted her shoulders high and then dropped them again,

an exaggerated gesture, followed by an exaggerated sigh. "I was just thinking how much love for you there is in this house." She gazed upward, as if this love were something that could be seen, a pink cloud floating by . . . Cole pretended to see it, too. She said, "I feel so blessed that you're part of my family."

Touch me, his heart boomed. And to his astonishment she did. She put her arms around him, and because she was wearing her hair up today he was able to press his face right into the curve of her neck, where it fit like a puzzle piece. Not marble-cool like he'd always imagined, but very, very warm. She squirmed when she felt his lips move, and then, as if she'd heard a scream for help or smelled something burning, she broke free and fled the room.

Cole waited for gravity to pull him earthward again. He spat the half-chewed cookie into his palm and threw it into the trash. A tingling sensation low in his belly made him want to get behind a closed door as quickly as possible. But first he checked his e-mail.

Still no message from Addy.

THE MESSAGE WAS THERE the next morning. Addy was back in Berlin.

> I could not stay in that horrible place even one more day. It was bad enough the power kept failing, but then so many fire hydrants were being opened all over town we didn't have any water, and they were saying the heat might not break for another week. Lara left first. She

went to stay with some friends outside the city, and I was too scared to stay alone. I've never seen such chaos, not even when I had the flu. I was amazingly lucky to get on a flight. I had to pay a huge fee—a bribe is what it really was—but I couldn't lose this chance to get out while the airport was operating, as it hadn't been for days. I felt like I was escaping from some banana republic.

But she did not want Cole to think she had abandoned him.

Of course, I still want you to come live with me. That's not going to change. But in the end it's going to be up to you. If it comes to court, the judge will say you're old enough to decide for yourself who you want to live with.

If you want me to, I can always fly back to the States. But I've been thinking, how would you feel about making a little trip to Berlin, just to see what it's like?

He didn't answer right away. He was glad to know Addy was safe, but right now he couldn't think about her or about going anywhere. Starlyn was leaving tomorrow. He didn't know when he'd see her again. That was all Cole could think about.

THREE DAYS AFTER she'd driven to Salvation City to take her daughter home, Taffy called her sister Tracy. Her speech was so distorted she had to repeat herself twice before she could make herself understood.

That morning, she'd slept through the alarm (the lovebirds had been out two-stepping the night before) and was rushing to get ready to go to her job at the insurance office where she worked as a receptionist. She wondered about Starlyn, who was usually up before her. She hoped her daughter wasn't coming down with some bug.

When she was ready to leave the house, Taffy went to Starlyn's room and found her gone.

"Nothing else is missing. Not her backpack or iPod or even her wallet. No makeup or toiletries, far's I can tell, and none of her clothes. The things she was wearing yesterday, everything, including her flip-flops and her teensies, the angel locket you got her for her birthday, her scrunchy, her watch, her tears-of-Christ pendant, her purity bracelet—it's all there in a heap on the floor. And her cell's sitting on her dresser."

The shock had knocked Taffy flat. "When I come to, I was laying face down across her bed."

Later that same day, Lucinda Boyle, who was feeling too unsteady to leave her bed, called her next-door neighbor, Rutha Mae. She didn't mean to be any trouble, she said, but her son had left the house that morning to get a prescription for her muscle relaxant filled and he hadn't come back. She'd tried calling him but he wasn't answering. "Which, you know, ain't half like Mase." Who answered his phone even while leading Bible group.

Rutha Mae said she was sure there was a simple explanation, that if anything had happened to Mason they'd surely have heard by now, but she'd be right over anyhow so Lucinda didn't have to wait all by her lonesome. She'd bring some pineapple loaf cake, Rutha Mae said.

Minutes later, as she approached the house, Rutha Mae was surprised to see Mason's car parked in the garage. The garage door being open, Rutha Mae stepped inside, where she saw some clothes scattered on the floor.

"Everything he put on that morning," Rutha Mae reported later. "Plus his wallet and his keys and phone, and that silver stud he always wore in his ear? Everything but his tattoos! He must've been just about to get in the car."

COLE FOUND PW SITTING ALONE out on the back porch. The temperature had finally dropped, and the evening was humid but cool—too cool to be wearing nothing but a pair of baggy shorts. But that was how you'd usually find PW dressed these days.

The rash and the blisters that had itched him to such distraction were gone. But PW was not yet out from under the devil's whip. He could not bear the weight of even the lightest cloth against certain parts of his torso. A draft of air touching one of those spots was sometimes enough to make him hop up and down in pain.

Postherpetic neuralgia. Something to do with the nerves being confused and sending false messages to the brain. Occurring in about twenty percent of shingles cases, according to the doctor, and PW's case appeared to be unusually bad. The painkillers the doctor gave him weren't doing much good. Nor could the doctor say how long the condition would last. Maybe months, maybe years. He did not say maybe forever, but that grim possibility was understood.

The doctor was worried about PW's mental state. He wanted to put him on antidepressants. PW refused at first ("Rather put my faith in prayer"), and later, when he changed his mind, the antidepressants, like the prayer and the painkillers before them, would not do the trick.

One day worse than usual—the whip lashes raining down especially hard and thick—PW resorted to bourbon, whose medicinal effects he hadn't forgotten, and discovered that here was something that did help, if only a little, and only if he drank a lot.

"What is it, son? What's on your mind? Here, come sit closer to me."

Was it a sin to find the smell of whiskey on a person's breath so pleasant? (Cole's parents had drunk only beer and wine, both of which, like coffee, left smells he found gross.)

Not so pleasant was the way the whiskey messed with PW's speech and sometimes even made him drool. Also, Cole could not get used to him being half naked all the time. Something about those beefy shoulder pads, the tufts and whorls of black hair, and the Hershey's Kiss–like nipples hidden in there made Cole shy away from sitting *too* close on the wicker sofa.

"It's about Starlyn."

"Yeah?"

"I think Mason kidnapped her."

"Now, why on earth would you say a thing like that?"

A promise is sacred. Cole chose his words carefully.

"Because—because it doesn't make any sense. Why would just the two of them be raptured and nobody else?"

PW breathed a pungent sigh. "First of all, it hasn't even been one whole day yet. Second, Scripture tells us very little about the rapture, so we don't really know what to expect. No one knows the hour or day, not even the angels in heaven, according to Matthew. Only God the father knows. So maybe it was never intended for all believers to be taken away in exactly the same breath. We don't know. Like we don't know what's going to happen in the *next* breath, either."

Cole didn't understand how PW could be so calm. Others, he knew, were nowhere near calm. In fact, something very different from the joyful and triumphant celebration Cole had heard so often and so confidently foretold was now unfolding in Salvation City. To the stream of callers wanting to know such things as whether they should climb up on their roofs or keep their doors and windows open, whether they should eat normally or start fasting, whether it was okay to have sex, or safe to drive, and what should they do about the dog— whether there was any chance they'd actually missed the rapture and were now officially left behind, and how could such a thing have happened ("Weren't we *promised* we were saved?"), and how much time did they have before the tribulation began in earnest—to all these confused and shaken souls Pastor Wyatt responded alike: Be patient. Gather with your loved ones. Stay home. Wait. Pray.

Their own household had been turned upside down. Poor Tracy had already had enough to cope with in the weeks since Addy's arrival. Now her legs kept giving out from under her as if she'd been struck by a palsy. After she toppled downstairs, spraining her ankle and splitting open her eyebrow, PW had ordered her to bed. He made her swallow a handful of the painkillers the doctor had prescribed for him and which he knew had a sleep-inducing effect. She had slipped into oblivion babbling blessings and prayers, convinced that when she opened her eyes again she'd be resting on the clouds of 1 Thessalonians.

"I'll be the first to admit I am not sure what's happening," said PW. "But I'm also sure the Lord will let us know all we need to know in his own time. Have faith, and the mystery shall be revealed."

"But there's no mystery," said Cole. "There's an explanation."

"What? Two people naked as Adam and Eve and without a penny on 'em walk off into the yonder without anyone taking notice?"

"Mason—"

"Oh right, the Great Kidnapper. And how'd he get to Louisville without his car?"

"There are other ways!"

"Hunh!" PW lurched in his seat as if he'd been Tasered. "It's okay, son," he said quickly. "I'm all right." But he spoke through gritted teeth, and his face was milk white. "Don't look so scared." He tried to smile. "It hurts worse to see you scared."

Every time this happened—and it could happen several times a day—Cole felt not only scared but the worst kind of helpless. All he could do was sit and watch as PW struggled, breathing shallowly, skin sheened with sweat despite the cool air. Cole sometimes wondered why the bigger a person was, the bigger their pain could seem. The way a suffering whale was so much worse to imagine than a suffering mouse.

PW reached down to the floor next to the sofa and picked up a bottle Cole hadn't known was there. He took a few large sips and put the bottle back in its spot. Then he sagged back against the sofa cushion, a fist to his mouth, and bowed his head. Under his breath, but loud enough to be heard, he asked God to forgive his weakness.

If it was part of God's plan, then suffering was not an evil but a blessing. This was something PW often said when preaching about sickness and pain. Cole had also heard him say that he would not be suffering so severely now unless God was punishing him. "And it's for me to search my heart for what I've done to displease him." Cole thought he had a pretty good idea what that thing might be. But PW never wavered from his testimony that in everything regarding Cole he had done God's will.

There was no mistaking the Lord's voice, PW had told him. It was the morning after Addy's visit and they were sitting in the den. PW had one hand on Cole's shoulder and the other on the massive desk Bible. "When the Lord speaks to you, the words enter you in a special way. They become part of your flesh, and they never leave you."

The Lord had spoken. He had spoken clearly. And his words were *save the boy*.

Three times in one night he had woken PW with the same message. "And he wasn't taking no for an answer."

But why, oh why, Cole had to ask himself, didn't Jesus send a message to him and Addy, too? Wouldn't that have helped them all?

PW picked up the bottle again. It was past sunset now, and the dark was like some night animal rubbing its furred flanks up against the porch screens.

PW drank and drank. It was as if they could not start talking again until every drop was gone. Each time he took the bottle away from his lips he let out a heavy sigh, aromatizing the air with bourbon like room spray.

Just as Cole was beginning to think he'd been forgotten, PW reached over and punched him playfully on the shoulder.

"So let me get this straight. You're saying Mason somehow got himself to Louisville, sneaked into Starlyn's house, bopped her over the head like a caveman, and dragged her off by the hair?"

Cole refused even to smile.

"Mighty strange he waited till she was gone, don't you think? When just a couple days ago she was here? How'd you explain that?"

Cole said nothing. What was the point in explaining anything? Why couldn't PW see the truth? What was wrong with Tracy, and Starlyn's mother? What was wrong with them all? By the time they caught on (and Cole was beginning to fear this might never happen), Mason and Starlyn would be far away. In his mind, they were headed to Mexico and a life of drugs and sin.

PW spoke as if he'd been able to read Cole's thoughts. "Okay, then. That's the case, what we got to do is examine what happened and why it happened like it did. We got to ask ourselves just what is the Lord trying to make us *see* here. Now, it's possible he is *using* those two. Maybe he thought it was a good thing for us to go through a false alarm, just to show us how unready we really are. You see, God—"

"This has nothing to do with God," Cole said wearily.

"Shame on you, son. I know I've taught you better than that."

Cole was ready to cry. "Aren't you even worried about her?"

It was the laugh Cole swore he'd never forgive.

"Come on, now, Cole, you know your cousin can take care of herself."

His cousin! It was the first time he'd ever heard Starlyn called that.

PW reached for the whiskey again, forgetting there was none left. "Tell you who I *am* worried about, though. I'm worried about Jeptha's mama." He was talking about Boots's daughter-in-law, whose son had just been killed in Israel. "Losing your only son, that's got to be the worst kind of hurt. But I don't think I've ever seen anyone so torn up as that poor lady. Far's I know she's always had a powerful faith. But the other day it was like you could see it evaporating off her, like a mist. She would not be comforted. I'd try to get her to pray with me and she'd just give me this smile, this cold, twisted kind of smile. Like I tried to cheat her and she just got wise. Shook me up."

"She's only sixteen," Cole said, his heart breaking.

PW shrugged his big shoulders. "My granny had two babies already by that age. My mama had her first when she was barely seventeen."

"But aren't you going to call the police?"

"Dude, just what *is* it about you and the police? Didn't you and me already have this conversation?"

Cole wasn't sure if PW had raised his voice because he was angry or because he was drunk.

A promise is sacred. Cole made a quick decision and plunged ahead.

"I saw them. I saw Mason—I saw them kissing—that's how I know—"

To Cole's astonishment PW laughed again.

He *must* be drunk. How else could he laugh?

"Listen to me, son. You think you're the only one that's got eyes in his head? You really think I didn't know what was up with the two of them?"

Yes, he could see it now. That *had* been pretty stupid of him. He was seeing a lot, finally. No wonder he'd started to feel sorry for Starlyn.

"So you're mad at Mason. So you go and make wild accusations, talking a heap of nonsense about kidnapping—and why? I'll tell you why. Because you're jealous. *Because you think he stole your girl.* Isn't that what this is really about?" He punched Cole's shoulder again, less playfully this time. "Like you had any business sniffing after her."

"It wasn't like that," Cole said hoarsely. He was mortified that PW had used the word *sniffing.*

PW kept silent, as if to give Cole a chance to explain himself, and when that didn't happen he sighed and said, "Look. I don't mean to be harsh, but you got to understand this has nothing to do with you. We shouldn't even be discussing the matter, it's not fitting. I want you to promise you'll put it out of your mind and leave it to your elders to worry about, okay?"

Cole nodded mechanically.

"Good. Now, let's talk about something else. What do you hear lately from that aunt of yours?"

"I'm thinking about going to see her in Germany."

In fact, until that moment he had been thinking no such thing.

"What on earth are you talking about?"

Cole remembered that he had not yet passed on the news that his aunt was back in Berlin. He was about to explain when PW doubled over.

The attack this time was shorter but more vicious than the first. When it was over PW stood up, saying, "Let me go dry myself off."

Left alone, Cole tried—unsuccessfully—to pray. All his other emotions were now swamped by a new fear. What if PW never got better? What if he could never live a normal life again? What if he just drank and drank and drank?

Cole was distracted by the appearance of a moth that had come indoors and kept banging into one thing or another until finally it knocked itself onto its back. Fantastically large, almost the size of a sparrow, it lay quaking on the floor, filament legs kicking furiously. Then it went still—not dead, Cole figured, just wiped out from struggling. It could rest there all it wanted; no harm would come to it. He resisted the impulse to pick it up. He'd been told that touching a moth or a butterfly could hurt its wings and maybe even kill it.

This time, unlike a moment before, and without trying, he found himself praying. He prayed to God not to be too hard on Starlyn, and if it turned out she was never coming back he prayed that God might bring her, somehow, somewhere to safety. Amen.

PW returned wearing a clean white shirt, left unbuttoned, and carrying a fresh pint of bourbon. He tousled Cole's hair with his free hand as he sat back down on the sofa. He seemed to have forgotten what they'd been talking about before, and Cole did not remind him. They sat for a few moments without speaking. The second attack had so weakened PW that his arm shook just from the effort of bringing bottle to mouth.

"You know," he said, staring straight ahead as if he were addressing someone other than Cole beside him, "God put men at the head of women because we're the stronger sex. But it's my observation that when it comes to physical pain women can take more. Think of Tracy." Which Cole did very reluctantly, recalling the time he'd accidentally hit her in the chest. "People still talk about how brave she was when she had the cancer, and I can testify she was a real trouper when she got the flu. I just know she'd be able to deal with this neuralgia thing better than I can."

Cole said nothing. A cosmic sadness was seeping into him. He was afraid if he opened his mouth he would start wailing and not be able to stop. It was happening again, he thought. Everything was changing. The air felt supercharged, and there was a weight to every passing moment that said nothing would ever be the same. He saw how wrong he had been to believe he was no longer a child. He was a child, only a child, too young to know what to do. Everything was too hard and too complicated, and he was too young, he was too weak and powerless and dumb.

He wanted to be alone. He was tired and confused and filled with anxiety at not knowing what was going to happen next. Too much had happened already, and he wasn't able to put all his trust in God the way PW and Tracy and the others did. He would try, but it wouldn't work. It was like trying to stick a piece of paper to the wall with spit.

He wanted to be alone. He thought that if he was alone some idea would come to him. If he was in his room he could start to draw something, and that would make him feel calm and normal again. But then the thought of drawing—the thought of all the drawings he had done and the pleasure they had given him and the pride he'd felt at being praised for them—suddenly all this struck him as embarrassing, cause for shame. He thought of the comics he'd lavished so much of himself on, and he cringed. He'd made a fool of himself, he thought. Just like when he was on the radio. It would be a relief to destroy them, to burn every one of them. Then he could start all over again. This thought made his throat ache.

He wanted to be alone. But he could not leave PW. He had to wait until PW—already breathing heavily and listing at his side—was ready to pass out. Then Cole would help him get up the stairs and to bed.

THAT NIGHT HE RODE THE HORSE AGAIN.

A game—long forgotten—from the days when his mother used to tuck him in. *Time to ride the horse!* Scooping him up in her arms. Not into bed but onto the back of a horse he'd pretend to climb—*Now, off you go, pumpkin*—to ride through the night.

His mother's smell.

His bronco sheets.

That night he rode the horse again. A hero's horse, fast and thunderous as a train. Here and there along the path masked figures rushed at them. Hands reached up to grab and yank Cole to the ground. But the horse knew never to stop or slow down.

And he could never get lost, his mother said; the horse knew the way.

Morning: this was where she always promised to meet him.

He sat up, drying his eyes.

He had slept as usual with the blinds open. Outside the light was pale. The sky looked low and as fragile as eggshell, as if a rock hurled hard enough could smash it.

He glanced uneasily around the room, gripped by a vague pang of fear—but no, it was all right. He hadn't actually burned or destroyed anything, he remembered now. It was just a silly passing thought. Coming in last night and seeing the drawings lying around or taped to the walls, he'd felt sheepish about his vow to get rid of them. Most of them still made him cringe. They were childish, they belonged to yesterday, they should be put away in a box or a drawer somewhere. But there was no reason to destroy them. What if it turned out he never saw Starlyn again? Wouldn't he hate himself for not having kept those drawings of her?

His senses told him he was the only one in the house who was up. He got out of bed and dressed quickly.

Downstairs, he went first to the porch and collected the bottles. This morning the whiskey smell, though faint, made him queasy.

The moth! He searched, but it was gone.

He was waiting for the computer to boot up when he

heard someone coming up the back walk. He had no idea who it might be at this hour, or why he went cold, his heart hopping like a bird from rib to rib. When the bell rang, he stayed in his chair as if welded there, terrified and ashamed of his terror at the same time. He remembered a boy in their building back in Chicago who'd answered the door while his mom was in the shower and let in a man who then—

But this was Salvation City, where people kept guns in their homes but did not always lock their doors.

"Hey, didn't you hear me ring?"

Rather than lie Cole said simply, "Hey, dude, what's up?"

"I was supposed to come by and get some help with this sermon I been working on. I know it's way early."

"You ride your bike over?"

"Yeah. Actually, I been riding around since light."

"Why?"

"I don't know. Just checking things out. Lotta people didn't sleep last night, you know. They're way freaked out."

"What about your house?"

"I guess they're okay."

Like Cole, Clem was an only child. He lived with his mother and his grandmother in what had once been the town's little red schoolhouse. His great-grandparents had been pupils there. Clem's father had died in the Iraq war a few months before Clem was born. Clem kept his father's army medals in a special case on his bedroom wall. He kissed the case every night before he went to bed. The Harleys also had a flu orphan living with them, an eight-year-old retarded girl named Olettra who refused to leave the house, fighting like a wild animal if you tried to make her. Everyone thought this was

261

because she was too disabled to grasp the real reason her parents were no longer around and was scared that the monster that had got them could also get her.

Clem said, "I know some people are doing like PW said and staying home, but there's a pretty big crowd at the church. I figure he'll be going over there this morning. I don't know if he'll even have time for me."

Cole explained that PW was not up yet. Clem nodded thoughtfully and said, "That pain just won't let up on him, will it."

Cole told him about the two attacks of the night before. Clem listened, frowning. Then he said, "I don't know that drinking's such a good idea."

"But it really helps," said Cole.

"In the short run, maybe. In the long run, it may turn out to be worse than the disease."

It was this kind of thing that could make Clem seem older than he was. He often talked in this grown-up, authoritative way. Probably it had to do with the fact that his mother had never remarried and he'd always been the man of the house. A serious, level-headed, slow-if-ever-to-anger boy, precociously handy, and, like the father he never knew, a crack shot. Everyone admired him for the way he took care of his women. In general, he was more admired than liked, Cole thought. But he himself had always liked Clem, even though they didn't have much to say to each other.

He was tall for his age, but that was his only good feature. He was pear-shaped, his skin and hair were drab, he was prone to sties and chapped lips and cold sores. Huge, blocky hands and feet made him look clumsy, though he was not—just as a sharp nose and black-button eyes made him look inquisitive, which he also was not. (In turn, his lack of curiosity often made him seem less smart than he was.)

He had a habit, sometimes irritating to Cole, of hesitating before he said anything, as if English weren't his first language. Tracy, on the other hand, called it the mark of wisdom. ("He does like they say: Think before you speak.")

The boys in their church were like other boys, meaning obsessed with sex. They might not have been as gross as secular kids, but they told dirty jokes and used words like *boner* and *tits* and *hump* and *blow job*. They'd huddle about a girl they thought was hot and what they'd do to her, even though they'd all pledged to stay virgins until they got married. It pained a lot of them (and a lot of girls, too) to think that Christ could return too soon, meaning before they got their chance to have sex. Meanwhile they could dream, and, at least when there were no grown-ups around, they could talk. Most would rather talk about sex than just about anything else. Except Clem. Not that he'd criticize others for talking, or leave the room when they did. He'd just sit there with a blank look on his face, as if everyone else were speaking a foreign tongue, or as if whatever they were talking about did not, and would not ever, have anything to do with him. He didn't care—or at least he didn't appear to—that this had led some to say he was gay.

Cole found it a mystery that Clem wanted to preach even though he wasn't good at it. But though he knew he didn't have anything like PW's gift, Clem said he couldn't imagine any other life for himself.

"Ma tells how I used to talk about being a soldier or basketball star or some other thing, but I don't remember any of that. In my mind I was always going to be a preacher."

Also remarkable to Cole was that Clem had never seen Jesus or been spoken to by Jesus, not even in a dream. Jesus had never woken Clem in the night with a message for him or sent him any special sign. Not that this bothered Clem. The Lord shows himself to me every day, he said. He did not envy those who'd been granted signs and visions and face time. He did not feel lesser than any rapture child or baby preacher.

Though Cole couldn't help feeling there was something truly weird about Clem, something that didn't necessarily have to do with his calling, the two were usually at ease together. And now that he was over his embarrassment at not having answered the door, he was glad Clem had come. His presence warmed the kitchen like something in the oven.

"Are you hungry?" asked Cole, who'd just realized he was quite hungry himself. "Do you want some breakfast?"

"Actually, that sounds good. But why don't you let me get it? I could make us some French toast."

"Okay. I'll help in a minute." And as Clem took over the kitchen, setting out bread, milk, butter, and eggs, Cole typed a message to Addy.

The French toast was perfect: eggy and crusty and on the dark side, the way Cole liked it. Clem had microwaved some bacon, too, while Cole set the table. Mindful of those still sleeping upstairs, they moved quietly and kept their voices down, and in that hush, in the soft early light, they might have been performing some ritual.

They ate in silence, full attention on their food, hungry, growing boys first.

In his message to Addy, Cole had said, "I've been thinking over your idea about my coming to see you."

In fact, he had been thinking a lot about it, and the more he thought about it, the more appealing the idea became. He had always wanted to explore the world. Why not start with Berlin, Germany?

What he hadn't said to Addy was this: "I know you care about me, but I'm not the most important thing to you. I know that even if you never saw me again, you'd be okay."

Otherwise, he thought, she would not have left without him.

Not that he was going to hold this against her. "I'd like to make the trip as soon as possible."

Of course, PW wouldn't want him to go, even if it was just for a visit. Cole would have to explain—as he was going to have to explain about another decision he had just made: when summer was over, he did not want to go on studying with Tracy. Even if he had to commute all the way to a different town, even if he'd be the only kid in Salvation City not being homeschooled, he wanted to go back to regular school. He knew that Tracy and PW would blame Addy for this. But in fact: It was the day Taffy had come to pick up Starlyn. After they left, a forlorn Cole sat in front of the TV, clicking the remote until his attention was caught by images of some kids around his own age, maybe a little older. It turned out to be a news program about a special school in Washington, D.C.

Not a private school—the government paid the tuition—but not a school that just anybody could go to, either. You had to compete to get in, and ninety-eight percent of those who tried to get in were rejected. Those who were accepted studied subjects that were more advanced than what kids their age normally studied. The very top students took college courses.

The students, who came from all over the country, were shown in an auditorium at some kind of assembly. "You are looking at America's next generation of great leaders and discoverers and Nobel Prize winners," the TV reporter said.

Kids in classrooms or in the cafeteria or out on the school lawn discussed science and politics and even sports in a way Cole had never heard anyone his age talk before. Over his head. And he who had always hated school was smitten with envy. The reporter and all the other adults who appeared on the program were obviously in awe of these kids. The parents of one boy told the reporter that the school had saved their son's life. He'd been in a different school first, an ordinary school with ordinary students and teachers, and despite his extraordinary aptitude (among all those brainiacs, this kid might have been the brainiest of all), he had not done well. According to his parents, there'd been two reasons for this: their son had been bullied, and he'd been bored.

When Cole heard this he became flustered; he became enraged. He, too, had been bullied and bored. Forgetting all about the ferocious competition to get into the school, he failed to see why *he* hadn't been plucked out and sent to Washington to study with genius classmates and teachers who never bored them. Tears of self-pity stung his eyes. He bet none of *those* kids was an orphan. (He was wrong.) And what would it be like if he ever met any of them? He would not be like them. He would not know all the things they'd been taught; he would not be their equal. And how would they treat him? For sure, they would look down on him. They wouldn't bully him—they were above that, of course—but they would not befriend him, either. They would ignore him. Maybe even feel sorry for him. The one thing worse than bullying.

Cole had watched the program all the way to the end. He had turned the TV off then and sat for a long time, his soul in a stew. He felt cheated and humiliated and confused. Deeply, he believed he was more like those gifted kids than unlike them. His pride insisted on it: the future great leaders and discoverers and Nobel Prize winners—he belonged with them. A huge misunderstanding had been allowed to take place. Why hadn't anyone seen that just because he hated school didn't mean he was lazy and dumb? It was unfair; it was all a mistake. Somehow it must be corrected. If not, he would grow up to be something worse than an underachiever. He would grow up stupid, an ignoramus. He would have to hide himself away from the world or die of shame.

These were his thoughts, but they were not thoughts he would have been comfortable revealing to Clem. Nowhere in the program about the prestigious school had there been any mention of God or church or any kind of religious instruction. Clem would have no truck with such a place. He would have called it a school for fools.

But there were other things Cole could share with Clem, and to which Clem could speak better than most.

About that crowd gathering at the church—

"What do you think is going to happen next?" asked Cole. Pause.

"I think the more time passes, the more folks'll calm down."

Cole's heart beat faster. "So you're saying you don't believe it's the rapture."

Clem took even longer to answer this time. "I believe I know an elopement when I see one."

Cole could have kissed him. But his spirits sank when it became clear that Clem was no more concerned about Starlyn than PW was.

"Far as I'm concerned this is Mason's responsibility," said Clem. "He's done a bad thing, I admit, but it's not like it can't be fixed."

"Well, I think he's way evil," said Cole hotly.

Clem looked taken aback. "Evil? Mason?" He gazed sadly at Cole and shook his head. "That's not right, Cole."

"Then how could he pull a dirty trick like that?" Cole's voice cracked, but he was too angry to be embarrassed. He waited impatiently for Clem to respond.

"You know how it is. It's like, some people, they get religion and that's that. But other people, they get religion and after a while they lose it. Then they get it back, but then maybe they lose it again. It happens all the time, like falling off the wagon. And it's not just the weaklings and the hell-raisers who have to get born again and again. Lucky for us, our Lord is the Lord of many chances. If you fall—"

"But what about Starlyn?"

"Girls have always been hard for me to figure." The way Clem said this suggested any attempt at figuring them would be a waste of time. "I don't believe Mason would ever hurt her, though. I think he loves her. I guess love can make a dude do crazy things."

"Have you ever had a girlfriend, Clem?"

"Nope. You?"

"Not exactly," said Cole. He was thinking of Jade Korsky. But though it was he who'd steered them in this direction, he had no real desire to go there. "Where do you think they are now? Do you think they'll ever come back?"

"I don't know. But maybe if they do come back, there'll be three of them."

This outrageous thought had not yet occurred to Cole. He stood up and began clearing his dishes, making a lot of noise, as if the outrageous thought were a living creature that could be scared off this way.

Clem got up from the table, too. "Hey, I got an idea," he said. "Why don't I cook up some more French toast? Then we can keep it warm for when Tracy and PW get up."

He was already at the counter, cracking an egg into the bowl.

Cole was too agitated to sit down again. He opened the dishwasher and began unloading the clean dishes from the day before. The sun was slanting through the kitchen window now and birds were singing in loud, ecstatic bursts. Cole had heard it was supposed to turn hot again.

Cole didn't want to be angry with Clem. He wished that he could make him understand. He looked at Clem's tall pear-shaped back and found himself wondering what his mother would have thought of him. Lately this had been happening a lot: he'd be thinking about one thing or another and suddenly he'd start wondering what his mother or father would've thought about it. It was part of the spell that had begun to lift with Addy's arrival. He could remember his parents without horror, without feeling the need—the pain being too much for him—to shut them out. Now there were times when he wanted nothing more than to recall his old life. He would stare into the past and try to reconstruct things: The rooms of all the houses he had lived in. The last time he had seen his grandparents. The names and faces of every teacher and classmate he'd had since kindergarten.

It was like a game—it could be fun—but it felt like something more than just a game as well.

He even tried to recall bad things, like his parents fighting. Some T-shirt his dad had worn and that his mom said was juvenile . . . a slogan that rhymed . . .

Often as not he'd have to give up, frustrated. But there were times when he wanted to shout hurray.

Human Race, Get Out of My Face.

Of course! How could he have forgotten!

His mother would have liked Clem, he decided. Except for his religion, she probably would have liked him a lot.

"Clem," he said, laying the last spoon away in the drawer. "Are you saying it's not evil for Mason to run off and leave his mother all alone like that? I mean, she's so sick she can hardly get out of bed."

Clem raised his voice above the sizzling frying pan. "He probably told himself she'd be okay. He probably figured he could count on us. Nobody's ever on their own in Salvation City. Like, you weren't here, so you wouldn't know, but during the flu it wasn't like other places. There wasn't any fighting

over food or medicine, or stealing from sick or dead people—
none of that stuff. And Mason knows— Hey, sounds like we
woke someone up."

Either it was all the noise they'd carelessly started making
or the smell of the French toast, which Clem was now trans-
ferring from frying pan to platter. Someone could be heard
on the stairs. Someone was descending with thumping, exaggerated slowness, like an actor playing a zombie. Cole remembered that Tracy had sprained her ankle yesterday. They
waited, watching the doorway, and when she finally appeared
each of them involuntarily took a step back.

Maybe she was sleepwalking. She certainly didn't look fully
awake. Clearly, she had just rolled out of bed. Her face was
puffy and creased. Her wavy brown hair stuck out all over her
head like a fright wig. Yesterday, PW had cleaned the cut on
her eyebrow and put a Band-Aid on it. The Band-Aid was
now stained with blood, and there were smears of dried blood
on her forehead and cheek. The skin around the cut had
turned purplish, and her mouth—hanging open in a dumb-
struck expression—looked bruised and puffy, too.

She paused in the doorway, holding on to the wall, her
weight on one bare foot. The other foot she held poised, toe
daintily pointed, an Ace bandage binding the swollen ankle.

She was wearing her short hot-pink bathrobe with the
white pom-poms at the belt ends. At the moment the pom-
poms grazed the floor: she had slipped the robe on but had
neglected to belt it. The robe hung open, the weight of the
pom-poms pulling it open, dragging it half off her shoulders.

Maybe it was from hitting her head when she fell down
yesterday. Maybe it was all the pills PW had made her swallow.

Until she smiled at him Cole wasn't sure she even knew who he was. The sight of Clem clearly perplexed her. She stared at him as if she had never seen him before. And maybe this was not so strange, because in that moment Clem was utterly transformed. Cole himself might not have known him. A person thrown from a high window or a cliff might have looked as Clem looked now, his mouth an O, his black-button eyes ready to burst right off.

And the next instant he was gone.

Cole barely had time to take this in. It was as if a tornado had blown through the kitchen and whisked Clem out the back door—before the spatula he'd dropped to the floor had ceased clattering.

The commotion upset Tracy. She swayed precariously in the doorway, still balancing on one foot but looking as if she would not be able to hold herself upright much longer. The robe had slipped a little farther down her shoulders. Another move and it would be on the floor, and then she'd be totally naked.

He simply could not look away. And strangely, he did not feel guilty or ashamed—or rather, these feelings were there, but he had other feelings as well. More clamorous ones—ones he would have found hard to put into words—drowning out guilt and shame.

He said, "Tracy?" And again, "Tracy? You okay? Can you walk?"

She smiled at him without answering. She's going to fall, he thought, and as he stepped gingerly toward her, he flashed on PW's story about his father stealing so close to a fox he was tracking that he could touch it.

Cole noticed the scar. It must have been from the cancer surgery, he thought. He would have expected to find the scar ugly but he didn't, though somehow it made her seem even more naked and vulnerable. Her battered face, her limp, her lost and frightened air, made him think of a fallen angel.

She swayed, and when she swayed her breasts swayed. How was it he had thought big breasts were gross? They—*she* was apocalyptic.

He wanted to say something nice and reassuring to her, but when he tried to speak he could not. In the smell rising from her flesh he thought he caught whiffs of bourbon and vanilla. When he took hold of the robe to pull it back onto her shoulders, a thrill passed through him, making his hands shake. She looked at him and smiled again, but with the absent expression of someone not exactly sure why she was smiling. Her eyes were like PW's when he was at his drunkest. Would she be like him and remember nothing about any of this later? God, Cole hoped so.

When he picked up the ends of the belt, she let go of the wall and rested her palms on his shoulders. He had stopped breathing and his heart was wild. Gently he tightened the belt around her waist. There: she was decent.

She leaned her weight against him as he helped her hobble to a chair. Without her asking, he knew she must want water. He brought her a glass, which she gulped down noisily, water dribbling down her chin. He brought her another glass, which she also gulped down, and a third, which she drank more slowly.

The water seemed to clear her head. She sat up straight, belching softly. She glanced around the kitchen, her eyes lighting up at the sight of the French toast sitting on the platter on the counter. Cole remembered that in all the hysteria of the day before she hadn't eaten anything except breakfast.

He wet a dish towel at the sink, and as he wiped it over her face she closed her eyes and made a pleased, grateful-sounding gurgle deep in her throat, which made him turn red. When he stopped she kept her eyes closed for a moment and then blinked rapidly several times before popping them open. Wide-eyed, she looked like a girl. A pretty young girl. She looked like her niece, Starlyn.

"Good morning!" she said. Her gaze swept the room again and came once more to rest on the counter. "Do I see French toast?" She pointed excitedly. "Did you make that? Oh, what a peach!"

He had just set her breakfast in front of her when they heard a noise overhead.

"DaDa's up," Tracy said cheerfully. But Cole, familiar with PW's condition the morning after he'd drunk too much, felt a tremor of anxiety. He thought of the people waiting at the church.

He was glad he wasn't being forced to make conversation. With a hunger to match her thirst, Tracy was attacking her plate. (Though even in her befuddled state, she had not forgotten to give thanks.)

PW, on the other hand, would surely not want to eat first thing this morning. What he'd want was a whole lot of coffee.

As he was making the coffee, Cole started composing in his head another message to his aunt.

And later that morning, when he was alone—when Tracy was upstairs taking a bath and PW had dragged himself and his hammering head off to the church—Cole sat down to write Addy.

I can't explain everything now, it's too complicated. But things have gotten way crazy here and sadly I can't come visit.

Now that the sun was high the room was becoming stifling. The air reeked of maple syrup and bacon. Cole took a sip of coffee. He had decided to start drinking coffee just that morning. Before, he'd never liked the taste. Honestly, he still didn't like the taste, but everyone knew coffee was supposed to help you think. And he had so much thinking to do.

What I mean is I can't leave Salvation City right this minute. There's too much I have to take care of. I'll explain next time we talk. But one other thing. Do you think I could use some of that money you were telling me about now? I know it's supposed to be for college, but I want to get my own computer.

Yet one more decision he was going to have to explain to PW.

When he had sent his message to Addy, he went out and got on his bicycle. He was headed for the church, but once he started riding he decided to take the long way around, past the old railroad station, making a loop through downtown. It was hot but he wanted to be out for a while, and bike riding always soothed him.

After a mile the sweat poured down his face and gnats

swarmed him. There was no coolness in the shade of the large trees under which he passed, just a damper kind of heat. Only the faintest blue showed in the hazy sky. A dog on someone's porch began barking when it saw him, the noise like firecrackers going off in the calm street.

Downtown was mostly dead. He passed Hix's Hardware ("Not today, brother, I got work to do"). He passed the drugstore, the used furniture store, the barber shop, the yarn store, the pizzeria, and the gun shop. He made a right at the post office and rode past the bank and the thrift shop, in front of which a woman had just placed a sign: "Brand New Used Maternity Clothes." Beyond the thrift shop was a diner that had closed sometime before Cole moved to town. It had closed suddenly, and if you looked in the window you could see the tables still set for lunch, the dishes slowly filling up with dust. The car dealership at the end of the street had also gone out of business. A parallel Cole wheeled along in the glass.

The church was a plain beige building with brown roof and trim, the kind of place you'd expect to go for some mundane but useful thing, like lumber or tools or house paint. Cole knew it had once been an American Legion Post, and long before that, about a hundred years before, a meetinghouse had stood on this site, a white clapboard building that had been burned to the ground by the Ku Klux Klan after a Quaker pastor gave shelter to a black man—a hobo from Kentucky—accused of pocketing a nickel a white farmer had dropped on his way to town.

When he rode up to the church, Cole saw that no one was there. The parking lot was empty except for a few starlings pecking at the tufts of grass sprouting through cracks in the asphalt. Cole figured PW must have sent everyone straight home and then gone home himself (and most likely right back to bed). He must have just missed them. He figured Clem was probably right about people starting to calm down, and a feather of satisfaction tickled him when he thought how they must be starting to feel pretty foolish, too.

There was a cross mounted on the wall to the right of the church's main entrance. To the left, rising from a grassy circle on the pavement, was a pole bearing the American flag. There was not the slightest breeze to stir the flag, which was flying at half-staff. Cole had almost forgotten about Jeptha Ludwig. He'd never met Jeptha, but he knew his parents from church, not nearly as well, though, as he knew Jeptha's grandfather. He tried to think what he would say to Boots the next time he saw him.

"Whatever you say, don't say 'I'm sorry for your loss.'" That was his mother speaking. Those words had driven her mad after her parents had died. An expression people got from TV, she said. From cop shows. It had been said to Cole himself many times, and though it had never consoled him, it had always brought back his mother's disgust.

If he kept going on this road he would eventually reach the old schoolhouse where the Harleys lived. Cole thought of Clem. Poor Clem. He understood why Clem had run away like that this morning. He might be grown-up in a lot of ways, Cole thought, but he was still only thirteen. A year ago, maybe even less, Cole might have followed on his heels.

In his big hurry to leave, Clem had forgotten a notebook he had brought with him. Cole had found it where he'd left it, lying next to the computer. Inside were notes Clem had

made for the sermon he was working on. "2 B Xtn = 2 4gv."
The text was from Ephesians. "Be kind and tenderhearted
toward one another, and forgive one another as God through
Jesus Christ has forgiven you."

Yes, yes, he thought. He would forgive them.

He would forgive them all.

Except Mason.

Now that he was standing still, Cole felt the heat like a
hand pressing down on him. Even his elbows were perspiring.
He wavered, wondering if he should continue on to Clem's
and see how he was doing. But he wasn't really worried about
Clem. He couldn't worry about Clem—not when there were
so many other people to worry about.

Starlyn!

But he mustn't let himself think about Starlyn now, either.
It would be too much for him. It would leave no room for all
the other thinking that needed to be done. And when he
thought about all the people he knew who were in some kind
of trouble, he sighed and slumped over his handlebars. Who
could say when PW and Tracy would be all right again?

As he turned his bike toward home (yes, *home*, he thought:
they were not his parents but it was his home; he didn't have
any other), he felt the tension inside him ease. He was not
unhappy. In fact, he could not recall another time when the
future had looked so bright and full to him. He had made up
his mind, and he had no doubt that he would go to Berlin. He
did not know exactly when, but he was determined to get
there. He had no doubt, either, that he was going back to
school, and that one day he would go to college. What else was

he to make of that perfectly clear image of himself up ahead, wearing jeans and a leather jacket and the glasses he'd probably need by then (from all that studying), shaking up a lecture hall with his comments? (Girls would dawdle after class to ask would he mind clarifying some point he had made and he'd pretend not to know it was just an excuse to flirt with him.)

He did not believe the world was about to end, and he saw himself living a long time and going many places and doing many different things. "Your whole life ahead of you"—never more than just an expression before—now came to him with the ring of a blessing.

But it was not just to new places Cole wanted to travel. He felt a great longing to retrace his steps, to return to places he had already been, where so much had happened but which remained so dreamlike and murky in his head that he could not lay hold of them. Even if all he could do was stand in the street and look at it, he wanted to go back to the house in Little Leap, as he wanted to go back to Here Be Hope—just to see what it felt like to be there. He wanted to go to Chicago and find out for himself how much had changed since he had lived there and what had happened to everyone, even if what he found out was bad.

He knew that much of the world was dangerous, that America was far more dangerous now than when he was a little boy, but he wasn't afraid to go anywhere. He understood why Addy had left Chicago, but for the very reasons she had fled he wished he could be there. He thrilled at the idea of being somewhere truly dangerous, a place where anything might happen, a place mad full of action. A disaster area, a revolution, a war. What would it be like to be in a real war? What kind of soldier would he make? He might be a hero after all. If he could learn how to shoot.

He had decided his parents were right about life being too short, and the proof was this: no matter how long you lived you could never see the whole world. But when he thought about what lay ahead, all the adventures and discoveries waiting for him, he felt full to the brim with excitement.

He knew the things he wanted now he wanted badly enough that nothing would stop him. It was only for a little while longer that his place was here. He knew that he would stay, and then, when the time came, he would go away. He did not know if he would return.